ghost
< < < • > > > *radio*

ghost

< < • > > radio

Leopoldo Gout

*Illustrations by
the Fates Crew
and Leopoldo Gout*

WILLIAM MORROW
An Imprint of HarperCollins*Publishers*

A hardcover edition of this book was published in 2008 by William Morrow, an imprint of HarperCollins Publishers.

FIRST WILLIAM MORROW PAPERBACK EDITION PUBLISHED 2018.

Designed by Betty Lew

The Library of Congress has catalogued a previous edition as follows:

Gout, Leopoldo.
    Ghost radio : a novel / Leopoldo Gout. Illustrations by the Fates Crew and
    Leopoldo Gout. — 1st ed.
       p. cm.
    ISBN 978-0-06-124268-7
    1. Radio broadcasters—Fiction. 2. Radio talk shows—Fiction. I. Title.

PS3607.O895G47 2008
813'.6—dc22   2008008914

ISBN 978-0-06-285350-9 (pbk.)

23 24 25 26 27 LBC 8 7 6 5 4

To my extraordinary family—Caitlin, the most beautiful wife a man can have, y mis chiquitos: Inés Celestia and Leopoldo Valerio (you grew up ten years in a week and I love you). To my mother, Andrea Valeria, whose voice is loved by all radio waves, including the astrophysical powers that emit them. To all my big familia—my dad, Leon Garcia, Gwendollyn, Christianne, Everardo, Joseph, Robert, Eloise, Roman, Tula, Magaly, Alexis, Guillermo, Jane, Solveig, Jim, James, Sophia, Christina, Norbushka, Hubbaba—everyone else in this world and the other.

Phantoms are fingerprints of the soul.

—Anonymous, Babylon, 2500 B.C.

In the darkness, it moved, searching for something tactile.

Sensing the way, following its instincts. For instinct was almost all it had left.

Somewhere, sometime, some-*when* it had possessed identity. It had the characteristics and physicality that bound it to a world. But those were gone now. Now it was little more than an urge: a bundled collection of needs with the barest hint of form.

But the void around it possessed even less form.

It knew that somewhere within this void lay the thing it sought, and so it kept moving.

And as it moved, unfamiliar features inside it sprang to life. In a hidden fold of its being arose a thing called "language." With that came knowledge, and consciousness. Its journey deepened.

It passed through a cloud of something it could now call "sadness" and wept. It passed through "serenity" and its calm returned.

Something inside it prickled. What it sought was near. Moving toward it, pushing with all its might. The prickling increased, rushing through it like a torrent of needles.

It reveled in this sensation, for it signaled that the end of its journey was near.

And even as this thought formed, its journey *did* end. It had reached its destination. As it basked in this victory, a new word appeared: the name for this thing it had sought so desperately, so diligently, and for so long.

The word was . . . *radio*.

ghost
< < < • > > > *radio*

chapter 1

THE MAGIC BAND

Joaquin turned the dial on his ham radio, letting his fingers rub against the worn edge.

He was trolling the six-meter band. *The magic band*. Not transmitting, just listening. Looking for some conversation, a good "rag chew" as the hams called it, that might distract him, and help him forget his worries about the coming week.

It was called "the magic band" because of its unique ability, under the right circumstances, to transmit and receive messages over very long distances with short antennas and low power. For this reason, the band attracted a wide range of aficionados. From high school students looking to get the most out of a cheap rig, to the kind of techies who casually tossed around phrases like "sporadic E propagation" and "F2 layer refraction."

Tonight it didn't feel very magical. Pedestrian was more like it. The conversations were limp and surprisingly sparse.

But somewhere around 50.24 megahertz, just past some Morse-code warning of thunderstorms off the Catalina coast, he caught a burst of static that intrigued him.

Years ago, Gabriel had taught him about the majesty of white noise: the monoliths of structure hidden in the chaos.

And this burst was chunky with structure.

He cocked his head toward the speaker, taking it in. It came alive in his mind. He imagined hanging over it, watching it roil beneath him like an angry sea. Then the roiling sea solidified, becoming jagged rocks and mountains. And then it was just sound again. But with a purpose, accreting toward a common goal. Sound seeking personification.

The room receded as he leaned closer to the speaker.

The sound seemed to tease him: its lattices of structure briefly weaving together, only to slide apart seconds later. And what the static became, in those short moments of cohesion, sent shivers down his spine.

It was a voice.

It was very clearly a voice.

He tried to convince himself he was hearing bleed-over from another signal. But this wasn't mixed in with the static. It was a voice constructed *from* the static.

He caught several phonemes, and the click of a consonant or two; but he couldn't stitch them together. He couldn't make out words.

He leaned closer, concentrating.

Slowly, from the rise and fall in intonation, he realized he was hearing the same sentence repeated over and over again. But he still couldn't make out even a single syllable.

He bent even closer, his ear inches from the speaker.

His brow furrowed and his muscles tensed as he searched for the meaning. It was almost there. He felt it roll gradually toward him, like a slow-moving ball.

Almost . . .

There was nothing else in the world, just him and these sounds.

Almost . . .

Nothing but this struggle.

Almost . . .

The first word was on the brink of unveiling itself when he felt a presence in the room with him; something brushed his shoulder. He whipped around ready to strike, only to see the familiar, laughing face of his girlfriend, Alondra.

"I love this: the host of the 'scariest show on Mexican radio' is frightened by a tap on the shoulder."

"Very funny," Joaquin said, still somewhat shaken.

"You're a bit like a cartoon character when you're frightened."

"You're in 'tease mode' tonight, I see."

"A furry animal, I think. Cartoon rabbit maybe."

"And it's not over yet."

"No, a cartoon mouse! Big eyes, little whiskers twitching."

Joaquin forced a chuckle, and as his senses returned, he shot Alondra a sly grin.

"Bet you were one of those girls who got a bit weak-kneed over cartoon animals."

"Maybe," Alondra said, her eyes going wide and looking very much like a cartoon herself.

"Let's test the theory."

He pulled her close and looked deep into her big brown eyes.

"But you don't seem like a furry animal anymore."

"That's the thing about us furry animals. In the daytime we're all hijinks and songs, but at night we get serious. And I mean *very* serious."

"Now, that's a theory *I'd* like to test," Alondra said, pulling him toward the bedroom.

An hour and a half later, Joaquin lay on his side looking at Alondra's lean naked body beside him. It glistened with a thin layer of postcoital sweat. She snuggled close to him, looking into his eyes.

"You worried about the trip?"

"Not really."

"Your big play for 'crossover' appeal?"

"You know it's not about that."

"I know. Still in 'tease mode,' I guess."

Joaquin smiled and pulled her closer.

"Thinking about Gabriel?"

Joaquin nodded. He hadn't realized it until Alondra asked the question. But Gabriel had been in his thoughts a lot recently. Maybe it was the trip back to Texas; maybe it was just the time of year. Whatever the reason, Gabriel had felt especially close these last few days.

"Thought so. You had that look."

Joaquin decided not to ask her what she meant by that. He wasn't sure he wanted to know.

"Do you want to talk about it?"

Joaquin shook his head.

Of course, he really did want to talk about it. He wanted to talk about Gabriel and the voice on the radio tonight, and the countless other things that had been coursing through his mind since he first learned he'd be heading stateside. But he couldn't do it right now, maybe not ever.

"You know I'm always here for you. Anytime you want."

"I'd rather just try to get some sleep; emphasis on 'try.'"

Joaquin leaned over to shut off the light, still holding Alondra against his chest. As he lay back down, Alondra let out a contented sigh. Within minutes, her breathing deepened and he knew she was fast asleep.

Sleep didn't come as easily for Joaquin. His thoughts returned to the voice. He tried to convince himself it was some kind of illusion, brought on by anxiety about the week ahead. But he knew that wasn't the case. He knew this was the first sign that his trip would provide him an answer to the mystery that had plagued him for almost eighteen years.

As he drifted off to sleep, thoughts of the voice and the trip receded, and he found himself remembering a recent caller to his radio show.

chapter 2

CALL 2344, THURSDAY, 12:23 A.M.

I had to call you tonight. Well . . . I had to call someone . . . someone who might understand my story. Everyone thinks I'm crazy. But I'm not, I swear. Though I think if I don't find someone who believes me, I may truly go mad.

It all started when my marriage went on the skids.

You know how the closer you get to someone, the farther away they often seem? That's the way it was with my husband. He shut a door inside himself, and threw away the key. Every conversation became an argument. Every question, an accusation. Eventually, he even recoiled from my touch.

One night it got really bad. We said the kind of stuff you should never say to another human being. Evil stuff. Stuff that hurt right down to the bone.

I knew we couldn't go on this way. So I grabbed my children, Mateo and Josephina, and ran from the house. And I mean *ran*, pulling the children behind me like rag dolls. They screamed, they cried; but I just had to move, to feel the rush of wind against my face. Nothing had felt this good in months.

After a few blocks, my head cleared and the insanity of my actions kicked in. Where was I going? What would I do?

Before I could even begin to answer these questions, I saw a woman waving at us from down the block. It was Lorenza, a friend from my job. She rushed up to us, concerned.

I tried to explain what had happened. I don't think I made much sense. But she nodded compassionately, placed an arm

around my shoulder, and led me and the children back to her
house.

She put Josephina and Mateo to bed in her spare room,
fixed me a cup of tea, and I had a good long cry. She understood where I was coming from. She had a lousy marriage too.
And although I'd never met her husband, he sounded an awful
lot like mine: the same distance, the same coldness, the same . . .
well . . . everything.

After talking with Lorenza, I realized I couldn't go back. My
marriage had been over for years. It had just taken me a long time
to realize it. But I still had nowhere to go, and no way to get there.

Again, Lorenza came to the rescue.

She told me that her parents owned a small house on the outskirts of town. They rented it out to earn some extra income. But it
wasn't occupied at the time, and Lorenza told me that the children
and I could stay there as long as we wanted.

It wasn't much of a place, she said, but it would give us a roof
over our heads while I planned our next move.

She asked if I wanted to go. I nodded. The longer I stayed, the
greater the chance my husband might show up looking for me.

So we grabbed the children, bundled them into the car, and
drove off into the night.

We drove for hours. The house was not on the outskirts of town
at all, but in a sleepy desert community some two hundred miles
away. At that point I didn't care. The motion of the car relaxed me,
and the desert air smelled wonderful.

At around 2 A.M., Lorenza turned off the highway and onto a
gravel road. We continued on for about a mile, and then parked in
a clearing. I pulled the kids out of the car, and looked around. The
moon was almost full, and it illuminated everything around me. I
spotted a cactus or two, and the vague shape of distant mountains,
but no house.

I turned back to Lorenza, only to find that she and the car had vanished. Even the gravel road we'd been driving down only scant seconds before was nowhere to be seen.

Worst of all . . . my children were gone.

I called their names loudly, frantically, into the moonlit night. But the only response was the wind whipping across the desert, and the distant, plaintive call of a coyote.

Finally, not knowing what else to do, I started walking. I walked and I walked, each step more laborious than the last.

As dawn approached, I reached the highway. After several minutes, a car picked me up, and drove me to a nearby bus station. Once inside, I found a pay phone and called my husband.

I was shocked when Lorenza answered the phone. I asked her if Josephina and Mateo were all right. She told me they were, but was curious about why I wanted to know.

I told her that I had the right to know the whereabouts of my own children.

"Your children?" Lorenza said. "Josephina and Mateo are my children."

I can't remember what I said next. I screamed, I wept, I sounded like a madwoman.

Finally, Lorenza put a man on the phone. A man she called "her husband." I recognized the voice immediately. It was my husband.

He spoke to me calmly, sounding as distant as ever.

chapter 3

THE PAST ENCROACHES

"Get into the cab, we're going to miss our flight," Alondra said insistently.

Joaquin wanted to comply. The car was only inches away. He could be inside it in seconds. But he couldn't move.

It was the car: a 1990 Ford Taurus. Color: metallic green.

Fleetingly, he wondered why a taxi service would use such an old car. But this thought was quickly pushed aside by a crush of memories about a car just like this, and a trip so long ago.

He could smell the upholstery, see the back of his father's neck, and feel the ground bumping beneath him. The memory was so vivid it almost hurt. He could even remember how the volume knob felt on his beat-up Sony Walkman.

"Joaquin, c'mon!"

Joaquin took a deep breath and reached for the door handle.

chapter 4

1990 METALLIC GREEN FORD TAURUS

Joaquin stared out the car window, listening to a mix tape on his run-down Walkman. The sun, suspended in a bright cloudless sky, swept the highway with a harsh, blinding light. He found it hard to keep from blinking.

He maxed the volume.

Another sunny day, he thought, squinting at the passing vehicles through the insect graveyard on the windshield.

The sun had shone this way before. It would shine this way again. A forgettable day, an anonymous day.

But Joaquin welcomed this.

He wanted this day—this trip—to be over as soon as possible. He wanted to return to Mexico unaffected, unmarked. So much had gone right in the last few weeks: things that had never gone right for him before. Things that made a difference. Things that made him happy.

He prayed that nothing on this trip would change that.

A lot of fifteen-year-olds say prayers like this. They're rarely answered.

This one wouldn't be either.

Up to this point, the trip from Mexico City with his parents *had* been uneventful. Airport to airport with no delay. Through customs without a hitch. Their luggage among the first off the carousel. And there wasn't even a line at the car-rental place.

They grabbed a quick bite at a roadside steak joint, and then headed for downtown Houston and their hotel.

Joaquin hoped it would continue this way. Then his father opened his mouth.

"What do you say we take a tour through the skyline district before hitting the hotel, Joaquin? I really want you to see that Dubuffet."

Joaquin cringed. *Dad and his art lessons.* Why was it that adults always wanted to teach you boring stuff?

"Dad, I'm actually kinda tired," Joaquin said, hoping that would be enough.

It wasn't.

"This Dubuffet changed my life. You're gonna look at it."

Joaquin sighed, resigned to his fate.

At fifteen, the idea of a family trip felt ludicrous to him. His differences with his parents, more now than ever before, seemed as vast and impassable as the empty, silent reaches of outer space.

His father tried to nurture in him a taste for modern art, but Joaquin never paid much attention. He had his own ideas.

He flipped the tape and hit play. The mix of punk, metal, classic rock, and electronic music crushed reality—hurtling him into a world of aural bliss.

As Tangerine Dream's *Phaedra* came on, his father stopped the car in front of 1100 Louisiana Street. Joaquin looked up and saw Dubuffet's *Monument au Fantôme.*

Without a word, he got out of the car and walked up to the sculpture. Strange irregular shapes outlined in thick black lines, suggesting human and animal forms. Christopher Franke's Moog synthesizer caressed these irregular forms while the amber light of sunset gentled against the rough edges.

He was captivated by the sculpture. He moved into the center of the piece and sat cross-legged on the ground. He looked up, watching clouds roll overhead through Dubuffet's embracing forms.

As he unhurriedly slouched back to the car, he felt a strange sensation, as if he'd spied the corner of some immense, hidden object. It sent a tiny bat-squeak of recognition through his body. Had his father's lessons finally sunk in? If true, he wouldn't let on . . . ever.

"What do you think about Dubuffet?" asked his father.

"Like him. Already knew his work," mumbled Joaquin, and then he was silent.

Those were the last words Joaquin spoke till they arrived at the hotel. His parents were accustomed to these long silences. Joaquin often milked the silences, hoping they might read his teenage angst act as something more profound. Not today. He wasn't thinking about them. Something else occupied his thoughts.

Her name was Claudia Guerrero.

Considered the prettiest girl in school, she had filled his thoughts for months. Even before they started dating. They had intended to spend the weekend together . . . unsupervised. Every teenage boy's dream: a weekend, alone, with the hottest girl in school. But this trip had blown that out of the water.

He tried to convince his parents to let him stay. But they wouldn't budge.

"Your grandmother is very sick. Who knows how much more time she has?" his mother said.

Just the same, he didn't know how long his relationship with Claudia would last, and to lose that precious time was devastating—doubly so because Claudia's parents had kept her under close watch after finding a pile of Polaroids of a dick (Ernesto Meyer's, they later learned) in their daughter's mouth. It didn't help when she explained that all of her friends had pictures just like those.

Joaquin's argument did gain him something. His mother agreed to buy him an inexpensive electric guitar. The bribe worked. He stopped resisting the trip.

Immediately afterward, he regretted it. Why did he give in for so little? He should have insisted on a vintage '62 Stratocaster. Or at least a Fender.

At the hotel, while his parents were out, Joaquin called Claudia. She picked up on the second ring.

He immediately launched into a rant. He told her that he was fed up, that he hated the food and the hotel. There was nothing that disgusted him more than hospitals; he would have to spend the entire next day in one. When he tried to tell her about the Dubuffet sculpture, he couldn't find the right words to describe it, and ended up changing the subject. He was too embarrassed to tell her that he loved her or missed her, or that he wanted to touch her breasts, so he said good-bye with a cold ciao.

"Ciao"—excellent move, he thought.

The conversation frustrated him.

For a while, he lay in bed and watched TV. He wasn't enjoying it at all. He couldn't believe the caravan of imbeciles that paraded around, submitting to the most ridiculous stunts imaginable. He fell asleep numbly contemplating the decomposing wasteland of late-night television.

The next day, after a bland hotel breakfast, they got into the rented Ford and went to the hospital. Joaquin listened to the Dead Kennedys.

> *Efficiency and progress is ours once more*
> *Now that we have the Neutron bomb*
> *It's nice and quick and clean and gets things done.*

His parents listened to the radio. Some talk program. Under Biafra's growl, he heard a voice say: *You really should listen.* He rewound the tape and played it again. It wasn't there. Weird, he thought, must have been my imagination. But somewhere deep in his brain, nestled in the limbic system, a preternatural fear arose.

Danger was near.

chapter 5

1990 BLACK VOLVO MODEL 740

Gabriel stretched out in the backseat, but the minute sneakers met leather . . .

"If you lay down back there, take your sneakers off."

Gabriel moved his legs slightly, so his feet just dangled over the edge.

"Gabriel, I'm serious."

"Dad, they're not touching the leather."

"Gabriel."

With a grumpy sigh, Gabriel sat up.

Dad and his pristine leather seats, fuck him. What's with him and this car? Gabriel thought as he stared out the window. It was all so boring. Another day with his parents. Another drive in the "fantastic Swedish machine." Tedium.

This would have been a great day for jamming with his band or just hanging out in his room listening to records and smoking a little weed. But once again he was forced to endure the unbearable ritual of the drive.

It was just a pretext for taking a spin in his Dad's brand new Volvo Turbo. Fuck him. And fuck pristine leather. And fuck Swedish engineering too.

Gabriel was so sick of hearing this crap.

The only thing that excited Gabriel about his father's new car was the sound of its engine. He liked that. He imagined recording it in all different ways. How would it sound, he wondered, if he poured two pounds of sugar into the gas tank? What if it blew up, or was showered with a powerful acid? How would it sound then? Gabriel imagined amplifying and replaying, in slow motion, the sputter of gasoline as it combusted inside the pistons. Gabriel had no love of cars. Music and sound were his passions . . . his obsessions, they were what he knew best.

A penchant for sonic experimentation awakened in him when he discovered Hans Heusser and Albert Savinio, the Dadaist musicians of the early twentieth century, industrial bands from the eighties like Throbbing Gristle and Coil, and the synth-pop groups Art of Noise and OMD. After diving deep into numerous avant-garde bands and immersing himself in the entire musical spectrum, inch by inch he formed his own concept of what music should be. One of his first compositions was based on a Diana Ross record played backward.

Sound fascinated him, from the crackle of static electricity to the brutal, sordid, macabre, and raw qualities of *Einstürzende Neubauten*. He was also fascinated by playful compositions, elegant sound collages, and smart paraphrases of the Pixies, Bad Brains, and even the Carpenters. His taste was eclectic. He enjoyed Stravinsky and folkloric *jarocho* songs from Veracruz. He liked listening to pop, he loved the most demented virtuoso performances, and he could fall into a virtual trance surrounded by the loud and ferocious sound of prog-metal. He didn't have a favorite genre. He believed that styles should merge and fuse in order to produce something more vital. He knew that was what he wanted to do.

He had no doubt that he was meant to be a musician. The only reason he hadn't already quit school was that it was the best place to meet girls. Of course, there was the little detail that his parents would never, in a million years, allow that, even though they generally supported his musical adventures. Their support was no small matter; his acoustic arrangements were loud, incoherent cacophonies of incongruous sounds that would drive anybody crazy—and frequently did. They always encouraged his desire to be a musician, as long as he finished high school and got into the conservatory first. Likewise, if he continued with photography, he would have to take it seriously and probably go to art school. This, they said, would allow him time to give it careful consideration, to avoid making a decision he'd regret.

"Imagine what it would be like if you realized at forty that you chose the wrong profession. Just think about how hard it would be to change your direction at that stage," his father always said.

Gabriel knew he was right. The life of a musician could be difficult. Most ended up doing menial jobs just to put food on the table. On one occasion he had even answered his father by saying: "I don't plan on living that long."

Because of this offhand remark, Gabriel's parents sent him to a psychologist. Dr. Krauss. Right out of central casting, he was bald and bearded, with a stern mouth and soft, considerate eyes. By the second session Gabriel had the doctor snowed. He made Krauss believe that he had religious hallucinations, homosexual desires, parricidal instincts, and later, as he improved his routine, bulimia and attention deficit disorder.

Gabriel read psychiatry books to better craft his imaginary conditions. He studied Freud, quoting cases verbatim, leaving Dr. Krauss confused and frustrated. After six months he resigned from treatment. A final admission that Gabriel was immune to his methods and techniques.

To the untrained ear, Gabriel's music sounded chaotic, an auditory jumble. Yet a patient, educated ear heard form and structure. Gabriel had a natural aptitude for composition. He created strangely elaborate soundscapes: canons, fugues, exceptional paraphrases and interpretations of a variety of musical forms, both classical and popular. Of course, few people understood what he was trying to do. Since he didn't have any formal training, he could only write rudimentary music, which often didn't fully express what he intended.

But it didn't matter. He felt music. It was his language. He could say things with tone, note, and meter that he could never have done with words.

While Gabriel listened to the engine, his father fiddled with the car's numerous gadgets, turning handles, pushing buttons, changing the radio station. He switched quickly from classical music to an interview with an astronomer discussing radio telescopes, and then to "Sympathy for the Devil" by the Rolling Stones. He looked back at Gabriel:

"Do you want to hear the real masters?"

"Stop fooling around and focus on the road. I don't like the way that van is driving in front of us," said his mother. She had been very quiet up to now.

"Not crazy about the Stones," said Gabriel.

"What do you mean? The Stones started everything."

"Yeah," answered Gabriel without any interest.

"Okay, your loss," said his father, and he changed the station again.

Then Gabriel noticed the gray van that had worried his mother. It swerved wildly.

A deep voice came over the radio: *You really should listen . . .*

chapter 6

12:34 P.M.

A van skidded out of control . . . wheels lifting off concrete . . . flipping.

Joaquin saw a woman flailing inside the van, her eyes wide with horror. He thought he could smell the sparks flying off the vehicle as it scraped across the concrete. Then he heard a squeal, and turned to see a Volvo hurtling toward them.

"Gonna kill kill kill kill kill the poor: Tonight," Biafra howled in his ears.

His voice made everything seem like it was happening in slow motion. A strange apathy overcame him. He found himself studying the Volvo driver's face as it careened toward him. It was a pleasant face, only slightly marred by the rictus of fear. It looked familiar. Did he know this person? he wondered. No, he told himself, it must be some kind of "future memory" without really knowing what that meant.

In this expanded moment he thought about a lot of odd things. He realized the accident meant they wouldn't get to the hospital in time to visit his grandmother. This would delay them for hours. Bummer. Then he thought about telling this story to Claudia. She was deadly afraid of car accidents. She would be scared as he described it, then he could console her . . . console her with sex. It would work, he knew it.

Oh, right, he thought, I'm about to be in an accident. The notion seemed distant, remote. I could be disfigured. Would Claudia still love me? Would she still want me with a face full of scars?

Could she be that superficial? Maybe. Joaquin had no idea how she'd react. What if he injured his hands or fingers? How long would it be before he could stroke a female body, or his guitar? What if he never could? He hoped the accident wouldn't affect his mother's promise to buy him a guitar, even if it was just a cheap one. In *Guitar Player* magazine he'd seen an ad for a store in suburban Houston where they sold used Fenders at unbelievable prices. He'd written the address down on a piece of paper that he put in his pocket.

Maybe he'd at least get a Fender. Not the cheap Japanese job he'd almost settled on.

He'd forgotten about writing down that address.

Why had he forgotten?

The moment this thought crossed his mind, a sound like a thousand power chords filled his ears. Bits of twisted metal flew at him from every direction.

Oh, right, he remembered, I'm about to be in an accident.

What's happened to gravity? he wondered.

Everything went black.

chapter 7

12:51 P.M.

Gabriel opened his eyes. Through a chrysalis of jagged metal, he saw a woman in the distance, covering her face and repeating, "Shit, shit! My skin's burning, my skin's burning! Come quick, Roger, it burns!"

He wanted to see what was wrong. He turned.

Searing pain.

Blackness.

Fourteen minutes later, Joaquin awoke on a stretcher with an oxygen mask strapped over his face. He could only see rough shapes, and he heard voices, distant, garbled.

"Front seat . . . killed instantly . . . meat wagon . . ."

Another voice mixed with his, complaining:

"Can you imagine? What would you do if your boss said something like that?"

The first voice again, clearer:

"You did the right thing, but you got to think about how this is gonna affect your retirement. Pass me the scissors—thanks. There's nothing more we can do here. How long before the meat wagon arrives?"

He couldn't understand what they were talking about. It was as if they were referring to strangers. For a moment he thought he was hearing a medical show. He continued to listen.

"If we can't stop the hemorrhaging, this one's gonna code on us," said another voice farther away.

I don't like these shows, Gabriel thought. I'm going to change the channel.

"Where's the remote? Will someone pass the remote?"

He heard laughing and a joke about couch potatoes that he didn't understand. Then he sank back into the blackness.

Wonderful, welcoming blackness.

chapter 8

A VOICE AT THIRTY THOUSAND FEET

Blackness . . .

The lights flickered several times and then sprang back to life, filling the plane's cabin with a warm glow.

Joaquin glanced at Alondra. She was asleep. He brushed a strand of hair from her face, and she let out a peaceful sigh.

Sleeping, she looked like a different person: a calmer, more centered soul. Joaquin wished he could join her. But he always had difficulty with this, and on planes it was virtually impossible.

He picked up his book and tried to read, but his mind wandered and he found himself becoming intrigued by the sound of the engine. What had been a mere background hum revealed deeper and more specific characteristics.

He put down the book, cocked his head, and listened. Concentrating, he heard organic rhythms, almost like breathing, hidden within the blare. He looked around the cabin. The other passengers went about their business unaware: reading, chatting, drinking, and eating. Oblivious to the symphony surrounding them.

Joaquin looked away, drawn in by the sound. It pulled him away from the mundane concerns of the moment into a universe where layers of meaning rested in bizarre and unknown places. Where overlooked details of life become a secret code embodying hitherto unimaginable mysteries. Dragging him deeper into this world was the increasing feeling that there was sentience coiled within the engine noise.

He leaned his head against the window, pressing nearer to the vibrations. He hoped this closeness would not only allow him to hear more clearly, but bring him into communion with this awareness . . . make him part of it.

With his ear to the window, he did pick up new layers. The pulsating rhythm under the hum shifted from merely organic to distinctly human. It became the labored breath of a human being: a person gasping for air. A person trying to speak.

He mashed his ear harder against the window, and stilled his own breathing, willing himself to hear, willing the engine to speak.

A part of his brain told him this wasn't real, an aural illusion. But he quieted that voice and listened more intently.

All the extraneous noise fell away and only the strange labored breathing remained. Joaquin heard the rasping of dry, cracked lips. The suggestion of a tongue sliding across the roof of a mouth. He almost saw the mouth. A mouth flecked with blood, the victim of some trauma. An act of violence that made speaking all but impossible. He held his breath and sent out calming, soothing thoughts, hoping to ease the being who owned this injured mouth. Ease its mind and help it speak.

At first, he sent this request out as a feeling, just an amorphous suggestion. But his desire to hear more coalesced into words. Not spoken, but as real as if they had been. The sentence in his head began in a vague and rambling form:

"C'mon, please speak! I want to hear your voice. C'mon, c'mon!"

Then he pared it down, simplifying it into the essential request.

"C'mon, talk."

Then it just became:

"Talk."

He repeated the word over and over again in his head.

"Talk . . . talk . . . talk . . ."

He waited and listened. He heard the dry lips crack and the breath gasp in an elephantine struggle for speech.

"Talk . . . talk . . . talk . . ."

The gasps increased, a desperate attempt to fill lungs (which could not possibly exist) with air. Air so this hidden sentience could finally deliver its message to Joaquin. And he desperately wanted to know what that message was. He switched to a coaxing word:

"Yes . . . yes . . . yes . . ."

The gasping stopped. Joaquin's skin prickled as he waited for the first word. The seconds ticked by.

Tick . . . tick . . . tick . . .

The moment expanded. The cloud of "now" hovered around Joaquin, embracing him with its large maternal hands. Thoughts of destiny and the buried mists of his painful past rose slowly to the surface, as he waited for a word.

He closed his eyes willing himself deeper into the communion, deeper into this new world. Images flashed through his mind: faces contorted in pain, burned flesh, walls splashed with blood.

Still the being did not speak.

Joaquin felt his entire body tense, his eyelids jamming together, his hands clenching into fists.

The plane shook, knocking his head against the window. The lights flickered. He sat back, rubbing the side of his head. His link with the being, the sentience was gone.

The plane lurched again. Something skittered across the floor, knocking against his foot. He bent down and picked it up. It was an iPod. Through the headphones he could hear the words of a familiar song:

"Kill, kill the poor."

chapter 9

DEAD KENNEDYS IN AN AMBULANCE

Gabriel felt himself being lifted into an ambulance. Through bleary eyes he saw another stretcher rolling in alongside him. On it lay another boy about his age. He looked battered and bruised. His eyes flickered open and closed. The boy seemed to be struggling for consciousness.

Two paramedics got in and the ambulance took off, sirens wailing.

Gabriel stared at the boy. He wondered if he looked as bad. The paramedics were working around him, putting some kind of needle in his arm. But it all seemed far away, as did his pain. He felt like he had a broken leg, but it was information from outside, like a telegram he'd received from a far-off land.

The boy next to him began to hum as if his life depended upon it. Maybe it did.

Over the blare of the siren, Gabriel recognized the lines from "Kill the Poor" by the *Dead Kennedys*. That song had been running through his head lately. An odd coincidence, he thought. He started humming as well. The other boy caught on and this seemed to energize him. Then they sang together:

> *Jobless millions whisked away*
> *At last we have more room to play*
> *All systems go to kill the poor tonight*
> *Gonna Kill kill kill kill Kill the poor: Tonight*

Gabriel knew they weren't quite capturing the spirit or energy of the song, but he found this punk anthem comforting. It was as though the song had been created for this moment, for this purpose. A giddiness swept over him, a joy unlike anything he'd felt in his short life. Sure, it might be the painkillers pumping through his veins, but he didn't care. He embraced it.

The paramedics laughed at the strange display. But Gabriel kept singing. Perhaps he subconsciously understood the darkness of this day. Perhaps, somewhere deep in his unconscious he knew of the pain and grief that lay ahead.

But now it was just about this odd duet. It was about dreaming himself into some dingy punk club. Standing on the stage, screaming into the microphone, while he looked down at the roiling mosh pit below. Giving voice to the pain and cynicism of a generation of lost youth. The crowd shouted and cheered.

He was in that club, singing his heart out, until he finally lost consciousness.

chapter 10

ST. MICHAEL'S HOSPITAL

When Joaquin opened his eyes, he was prostrate in a bed. He knew he was in a hospital, and realized that intense pain had awakened him. There was someone in his room, she was dressed in white. He asked her about his father. Without even turning to look at him, the nurse answered as she left the room.

"Dead, just like your mother, both of them dead."

He didn't see her face. He tried to yell and call her back, but no sound came out. He couldn't move.

He spent the next few hours suffering, immobilized, in profound silence, surrounded by blank white walls, sweating, shivering, every bone in his body hurting. When the doctor on call finally arrived, Joaquin told him what the nurse had said. The surgeon, visibly upset, left the room without another word.

Joaquin heard raised voices in the hallway. Then deeper, more professional tones. Several moments later the doctor returned.

"I want to apologize on behalf of the hospital. This is not how we do things. I'm profoundly sorry," the doctor said."

That's okay," Joaquin said, not sure why he was so forgiving.

"If it's any consolation, they didn't suffer. In these types of collisions, death is usually instantaneous."

Joaquin found himself wondering why a painless, instantaneous death should be thought of as comforting. It terrified him.

"Son, you have some hard times ahead. You're going to have to be very strong."

< • >

Across the hall, in another white room, Gabriel opened his eyes. Almost before he was fully conscious, he was yelling. Yelling for someone to come. No one did. He found the call button and pressed it. Moments later, a nurse entered.

"My parents are dead, aren't they?"

"I wouldn't know that, I wouldn't know. You'll have to talk to the doctor."

"Are they dead?" he asked, raising his voice.

The nurse looked at him. The mixture of compassion and pity Gabriel saw in her eyes was all the answer he needed.

He sank down into the bed. The notion of tears crossed his mind. None fell.

Both boys were alone, wounded and scared. Their futures were suddenly completely unsure. Joaquin's only relative in Houston was his grandmother, who'd undergone surgery a few hours after the accident. No one knew about the deaths until after the operation was over. They were waiting for her to be out of danger before giving her the terrible news. None of Gabriel's relatives had been located yet.

Several days passed before Gabriel and Joaquin met. They were both in wheelchairs. The nurses who were pushing them down the hallway gave them a moment alone. Joaquin recognized Gabriel as the person from the ambulance without knowing exactly how, since they'd never actually seen each other, and spoke to him:

"You crashed into us, right?"

"I what?"

"You were in the Volvo that hit us."

"You were in the Ford? The nurses told me about you."

"Do you like the Dead Kennedys?" Joaquin asked a little anxiously, wanting to change the subject. He wasn't ready to talk about the accident yet.

"Yep. 'Kill, kill the poor,'" Gabriel intoned, his voice off-key.

Joaquin was relieved that Gabriel also remembered what had happened in the ambulance. This meant it hadn't all been a hallucination. He raised his hand as best he could to give him a high five. Gabriel stretched out his arm and touched his palm.

"It'd be nice to have some music in here," he said.

"There's a TV in the room they put me in, but I don't even get a stinkin' radio. I love music. I *need* music."

"You play an instrument?"

"Yeah. How'd you guess?"

"I can just tell."

"Guitar and synthesizer. But I don't know if I'll ever play again. I can't feel these fingers," he said, lifting his right hand.

"Maybe we'll be able to jam together sometime."

At this point, as Gabriel's nurse returned, both boys noticed her slim, athletic legs, which were barely veiled by a skirt that modestly covered her knees, and each suddenly got a hard-on. They realized that they had something else in common: a taste for women whose long legs were encased in uniforms.

"See you around," he said as he rolled away.

"I'll be here," Joaquin said, thinking that neither of them had even asked about the other's injuries, or mentioned his parents.

Joaquin had been dreading an encounter with the van's survivor, and he was surprised by what had just happened. He wasn't able to truly comprehend his parents' deaths until much later on; the famous stages of pain—denial, anger, bargaining, depression, and acceptance—were all jumbled together in his confused mind. In his darkest hours, he'd hated the driver of the other car and told himself he'd seek revenge against its survivor.

He imagined cutting the bastard's head off with a machete, and feeding it to the stray dogs of Tijuana.

But when he saw the focus of his hatred that first time, his anger melted away. He had no desire for revenge. He just saw another sad, wounded boy. A kindred soul. He looked forward to speaking to him again and even, perhaps someday, playing music together. Something good had to come out of this horrible catastrophe.

He sought the good on those dark and painful days. Days he spent silently crying in his room, avoiding the looks of compassion and pity in his roommates' eyes. And there were the whispers: "He lost both of his parents." "He'll never walk again." "They're sending him to an orphanage." Joaquin pretended not to hear, wishing for his music, something, anything to shut out their voices. But his prized Walkman, which he'd had for years, was lost, pulverized on the highway. So he lay there with only the TV for distraction, stoically bearing the soap operas, talk shows, and entertainment programs his roommates watched.

The days passed and he slowly healed.

chapter 11

HELICOPTER WISHES

"I hate hospitals," Joaquin said, tossing his suitcase on the bed.

"You mean hotels."

"Why? What did I say?"

"You said 'hospitals.'"

"Jeez," Joaquin said, shaking his head.

Alondra walked over to him, and rubbed his shoulders and the back of his neck.

"You've been in a mood since we landed. Is there anything you want to talk about?"

Joaquin pulled away, unzipped his suitcase, took out a manila folder, and leafed through the papers it contained. He couldn't find the paper he needed, and tossed the folder across the room in disgust.

He walked over to the window and drew back the curtains. The Dallas skyline spread out before him, glittering in the night sky. Whenever he thought of America, this was the image that sprang to mind, gleaming skyscrapers against a night sky. But looking at them now, he felt removed. He wasn't sure he wanted to be in America. Wasn't sure he could tolerate the shimmering newness of Dallas.

He'd expected this to be a sort of homecoming. The prodigal son returns to show he "made good" in the great wide world. But he didn't feel like a prodigal son. Not in the slightest. He felt like a child: a sad, lonely child crying in the night for his parents.

And Alondra wasn't helping. She thought he needed to share his feelings about Gabriel and those painful and glorious days so long ago. But talking wouldn't ease his feelings. It would only make them more intense.

And then there was this other thing. The strange being that sought communion with him. He'd sensed it back in Mexico. Sensed it at some deep and transcendent level. Back there he thought it held answers, answers to the deepest and greatest questions of his life. Now he wasn't so sure.

Perhaps it was a dark force, drawing him in. A spider perched on its web, waiting. Spiderwebs are seductive; he couldn't pull himself away even if it meant ruin, even if it meant death.

Some distance away, a helicopter was circling a skyscraper. Its lights flashed as it dipped and turned. A part of Joaquin wished he was inside that helicopter, flying through the Dallas night.

As he watched the helicopter he noticed something strange. The flashing lights didn't strobe; they pulsated. And it was a type of pulsation he was familiar with.

It was Morse code.

Almost unconsciously he translated the code, thinking it was probably a humorous whim on the part of the pilot. But halfway into his translation, he realized that wasn't the case.

He backed away from the window, gooseflesh rising on his arms and legs.

"Are you okay?"

He spun around, focusing on Alondra.

"This is going to be intense."

"What is?"

"Everything."

Alondra demanded that Joaquin explain. But he couldn't even formulate a sentence. Other words filled his head, the words from that helicopter's pulsating light.

He moved back toward the window, almost tiptoeing. He looked for the helicopter. It wasn't there. No, wait. There it was. And the light was still pulsating, repeating its ominous message.

He watched it carefully, making sure it said what he thought and wasn't a figment of his imagination. He was correct. And it was even more shocking, seeing it a second time.

"Joaquin, we'll be talking soon."

The casual, mundane nature of the message made it especially frightening, like a demon wearing a T-shirt.

Joaquin stared at the helicopter as the message repeated over and over again. Each time, he shivered.

Then the light flashed "break," and Joaquin steeled himself for another shock. But again he was met with banality:

"Good-bye and best wishes."

It sent this message only once. Then the light returned to its normal strobe, and the helicopter veered away, disappearing into a cloud.

chapter 12

A DARK HAPPINESS

It felt Joaquin's fear. And it liked it. It also liked the new words it was learning: airplane, engine, iPod, helicopter, and Morse code. It liked the taste of these words. They possessed a crisp tang, as did the first moment of communion with Joaquin, which it cherished.

Although it could not see Joaquin, it felt him. It felt his confusion and his seeking heart. These feelings gave it sustenance and purpose.

When it knew Joaquin had received its message, these sensations intensified. In its vast somewhere, it reeled and spun with joy. It knew in another time, another place, it had felt this revelry before. It had marveled at accomplishment. It had spun and leaped in another shape, another form. But it pushed away such concepts, and plunged itself into the moment.

As it felt Joaquin receiving the words again, it drank in his fear; gobbled up every morsel. And once again it whirled and whirled, marveling in its supreme majesty.

Abruptly, this jubilation stopped.

Joaquin was gone.

It was alone. Alone? This too was a new word. But this one tasted sour. After swallowing the word, it felt empty inside.

Emptiness.

Another distasteful word. This further emptied it. It became so hollow it couldn't move, so it drifted down into the dark valleys of its someplace.

It felt dissipated. It wanted to give up.

Then a power coiled deep inside sprang open. Filling it with energy.

It couldn't immediately identify this new energy, but it welcomed and embraced it.

As it careened around its world, it remembered Joaquin's fear and the lovely taste. It wanted more. It needed more. Now it knew that no matter what happened, no matter what, it would find that fear and devour it.

chapter 13

MINIBAR, MAXI-PROBLEM

Alondra shot out of the elevator and headed down the corridor in search of Watt's room. After several wrong turns, she found it and knocked on the door.

Watt answered wearing a hotel bathrobe and holding a cocktail in one hand and an open jar of macadamia nuts in the other.

"Hey, Alondra," he said, ushering her into the room. "Just hitting the minibar a bit."

"A bit?" she said with a chuckle.

There was a range of electronic gadgets strewn about the room. A Nagra tape recorder sat on the bed. A cornucopia of microphones erupted from a black plastic case. Some battery packs and chargers sat on the dresser. And on the floor lay a battered laptop connected to a variety of devices via a spiderweb of USB cables. Other than a black iPod, Alondra couldn't identify most of it.

"Could I get you something to drink?"

"What are you having?"

"Red Bull and vodka."

"Eww," Alondra said with a shiver of disgust.

"You should try one; it's really good."

"No, I think I'll pass. But the vodka sounds good. I'll have that. Ketel One if they have it."

Watt opened the minibar and scanned the shelves.

"Hmmm . . . Ketel One, Ketel One . . . ah, there it is!" he said, snatching a bottle. "Want anything with it?"

"Ice and . . . ah . . . tonic water?"

Watt grabbed a few cubes from the ice bucket, cracked open the bottles, poured with a bartender's flourish, and handed Alondra the finished product.

She accepted the drink, sat down on the edge of the bed, and took a sip. The cold vodka tasted crisp and clean, and she had an intense flash of a sauna she'd visited in Finland.

"So how's the man?" Watt asked cheerfully.

"That's kind of why I came down here."

"Really, something wrong?"

"I'm worried about him."

"What's the matter, he's got the jitters or something?"

"No, I mean *worried*."

"Not sure I get you."

Alondra sipped her way back to Finland, and took a long deep breath.

"Well," she said, searching for the right words. "It's like, um, God, it's like . . . um . . . shit . . . I don't . . ."

"C'mon, just spit it out. Jeez, I thought I was supposed to be the one with 'communication issues,'" he said, popping a nut into his mouth.

"Okay, I'll just say it."

Seconds passed, Alondra remained silent. She looked into Watt's expectant eyes. She'd always liked his eyes. Wide, blue, intense, and dotted with flecks of green. But as much as she liked them, she expected them to narrow in disbelief at what she had to say.

She just had to get it out. And so, after another quick trip to Finland, she did:

"I'm worried about his sanity," she said.

As she'd predicted, Watt's eyes narrowed, and he turned away.

"Oh, don't be ridiculous."

"I'm serious."

"Well, of course he's crazy. I mean we're all crazy. But he's not crazy, crazy."

"I'm not so sure."

Watt paced as he went on a long, rambling rant about everything he knew and felt about Joaquin. About insanity and how it works. About why Joaquin didn't fit the criteria, either constitutionally or pathologically. And on and on.

Alondra tried to listen. But the words became a background hum. She was too worried to accept what sounded like rationalization.

Finally, Watt stopped talking.

Alondra looked up. Watt must have sensed her desperation, because he grabbed her by the shoulders and, staring into her eyes, said: "He's fine. He really is. This is an intense time for him. Cut him a little slack."

Alondra looked away.

"Okay, okay," Watt said. "I'll tell you what. Tomorrow morning I'll have breakfast alone with him. I'll pay attention; I'll listen to him. I'll keep an open mind."

Alondra looked down at the bedspread. Its blue-and-green lattice pattern perfectly reflected the mix of complexity and order she currently sought in her life. Maybe Watt was right. Maybe there was nothing wrong. Maybe she was projecting her own fears and concerns about the show, and their life together, onto Joaquin. She really wasn't sure.

"Alondra, did you hear me?"

"You can't have breakfast with him tomorrow. He's doing an interview with *Newsweek* magazine," she said, her eyes still fixed on the blue-and-green bedspread.

chapter 14

THE INTERVIEW

Before entering the café, I called Alondra. She answered with a long, languid hello. She knew it was me again, trying to convince her to come to the interview.

"Alondra."

"What is it now?"

"I just wanted to be clear: I'd be happier if you were at the interview with me."

"And I told you I would if you have lunch with me and talk about what's going on."

"There's nothing going on with me. I'm just worried about the show."

"Even you don't believe that."

"Will you be there?"

Alondra hung up.

She was probably right. I should talk to her about what has been going on. But I know it scares her when I talk about these things. She always says:

"This is just crap from your show. Don't bring it home with you."

She was right. Partly. Hell, one of the reasons I created *Ghost Radio* was to convince myself that the strange experiences I'd had were nonsense. Of course, another part of me had launched the show to justify them.

And now I was minutes away from glossing over these salient facts, promoting the show as an entertaining bundle of "things that go bump in the night." I knew that was another reason Alondra wasn't eager to join me for this interview. She hated this crap. She wasn't interested in having to answer fatuous questions like "Isn't it difficult to work with your significant other?"

He couldn't imagine her revealing such intimacies to a stranger. She was already ambivalent about participating in *Ghost Radio*; it had taken a lot of coaxing for her to accept the role of cohost. She claimed it could affect her credibility as a researcher and professor. But I knew it wasn't that.

I humored her, arguing that the program would be a "hands-on" laboratory for her work on urban folklore. Yet I was certain that the reason she finally accepted had nothing to do with research. It was something deeper. She feared I'd lose myself in the show, and she wanted to be there to pull me back. She claimed to be a committed skeptic. But I often felt that deep down she believed, and it scared her. It made her mock everything paranormal or supernatural. She was a master of circular logic. How else could she hold down a serious academic job while continuing to edit provocative underground zines?

She used that slippery quality on the show. She had a knack for evading intense or uncomfortable situations, for speaking cogently but vaguely. She always bowed out gracefully without having to run or hide, but never drew attention to herself. I'm sure many saw this behavior as "cool" or "aloof." I had another word for it. That word was "fear."

Whatever her stated reasons, I was sure that this was the fundamental reason she hadn't joined me for the interview. She was afraid.

I entered the café lost in these thoughts. The reporter from *Newsweek* was there, waiting for me. He was easy to spot: his recorder sat on the table, and he was simultaneously talking on his cell phone, taking notes, reading e-mail on his laptop, and frenetically typing a text message into his BlackBerry. A pile of magazines and newspapers filled the only empty seat.

"Joaquin," I said, offering my hand.

The reporter shook it tensely, and made a mute grimace that might have meant "pleased to meet you," followed by a quick "give me a minute" hand raise. One by one, he terminated his communications. It was like watching an assembly-line robot. Then he cleared the chair and, finally, looked me in the eye.

"Sorry about all that. I'm supposed to do this interview with Nicole Kidman. And her people just 'got cute.'"

I saw through his attempt to develop a bond with me by letting me in on this little "confidence."

Again, I didn't see this interview with *Newsweek* as a personal triumph. I had no love of publicity. On the contrary, I didn't trust it at all. But I wanted people to listen to my show and this would help make that happen. As a consumer of popular culture, I appreciated that *Newsweek*'s interest meant that *Ghost Radio* had "made the jump." It had slipped out of the fringe and into the mainstream.

The reporter introduced himself as "Eric Prew," then immediately launched into comparisons between my program and the TV series *Ugly Betty*, a Colombian soap opera that had streaked its way, like lightning, into an American prime-time slot. I replied that comparing a soap opera to a program like mine purely on the basis of their Hispanic origin seemed simplistic to me. I stopped myself from adding that it seemed idiotic and borderline racist.

Should I have stopped? Maybe that tack would have worked.

Instead, I accepted the general amazement that these programs had garnered acceptance from a public that is not used to consuming foreign culture. I almost used the word "alien," but caught myself at the last second.

I spoke about how the program had started in Mexico, spawned with no expectations:

"It happened pretty much before I realized what was going on. The music program I was hosting started to revolve more and more around the death-themed readings and comments I made between songs, but things really took off when I started taking calls on the air. So many wanted to talk about the supernatural. And I let them. The program evolved. It grew and expanded, becoming something new and different."

(This wasn't entirely true. But it was the story I always told.)

I told Prew that my main influence, although I wasn't really aware of it at the time, was another radio show that I'd discovered and listened to compulsively while I was hospitalized in Houston after the accident that killed my parents.

"I loved its horror stories, which still fascinate and on occasion still terrify me, but I loved its format even more. It was thanks, in large part, to that program that I was able to begin to recover from the tragedy I'd endured."

"When was this?"

"Nineteen-ninety."

Prew nodded and made a note on his pad. I could read his scrawl even upside down. It said: "Research—Supernatural Radio Show, Houston, 1990." "But you said that your show's format happened almost accidentally; this story makes it seem more like a plan."

"You might think that, as the host, I guided the program. In fact, it was the program that guided me. Within a year we had an extremely loyal fan base . . . some obsessive . . . troublingly so."

Prew agreed that many of my listeners did seem fanatical. He compared them to groupies, and the followers of marginal religions. It wasn't the first time someone had pointed out that my audience acted like members of a cult. I nodded, accepting this; then silently waited for his next question.

"Can I get back to the original *Ghost Radio* again? The one you listened to in the hospital."

"Okay."

"Did you listen to this show by yourself? Or was it popular with the other patients?"

"Sometimes I listened alone. Sometimes with a friend," I said, trying to sound casual and vague.

"Was this friend Gabriel?"

I nodded. Shit, I had hoped the interview wouldn't go in this direction. But this guy had clearly done his homework.

"And this is the Gabriel who died during some kind of pirate radio broadcast?"

I blanched.

"Do we really need to talk about this?"

"You host a program about death and ghosts, and you had an experience in your life in which a good friend died during a radio broadcast. It seems related."

Prew was right, they were related. I owed almost everything to that catastrophe. I'm still marked by its scars . . . literally and figuratively. And I lost Gabriel. Gabriel . . . I still consider him my best friend despite the fact that he's no longer with us.

No longer with us.

Such an inapt term for Gabriel. No one could be more "with us" (or "with me" at least) than he is. It's been eighteen years since his death and I still feel him around me. That's not meant as a sappy cliché or a bit of tearful, cloying nostalgia. It is a pragmatic affirmation of his inescapable, daily presence.

"Don't you think it's important?" Prew asked, breaking my ruminations.

"I'd just prefer if it wasn't the focus of the interview."

"Well, I don't think it's going to be the focus. But I plan to include some facts about the event, and I'd like them to be as accurate as possible."

"It's a painful memory for me."

Prew wouldn't let it go.

"Okay, but remember, if I don't go over this with you, we'll be forced to present the facts based on our research. You'll have no input. Some of the people who told us this story may be biased. I'm giving you the opportunity to ensure that what we print accurately reflects your point of view."

I looked out the window; on the street a homeless man walked by screaming. I could hear his words through the glass and I felt like joining him. Instead, I turned back to Prew, and fixed him with a forceful stare.

"I think we've covered this," I said.

After several seconds, Prew nodded, took a breath, looked through his notes, and then, like the good reporter he was, tossed me a softball question.

"How do you explain your program's success?"

"We talk about stuff that interests a lot of people. I believe that modern society is deeply affected by technological progress. Technology is no longer a tool we use every day; it's inserted itself into the way we perceive reality, the way we see ourselves, the way we relate to our peers and our own memories. Our fears, aspirations, and fantasies are filtered through technology. I see my work as a way for the media to help people reestablish their bond with things that have nothing to do with science, like mythology, the unexplainable."

"I didn't realize you were a Luddite."

"I'm not. But I think there's more to life than Google, Facebook, and YouTube. There are other forms of communication. Deep forms. And people want to share their experiences," I said, knowing my tone had become sharp, but I couldn't shake my anger at Prew for bringing up Gabriel's death.

"But it's largely about death, isn't it?"

"Have you listened to my program, Mr. Prew?"

"Your fans have what might almost be termed a necrophilic obsession, an addiction to the macabre. What's your opinion about that?"

"What culture *isn't* fascinated by everything horrific and terrifying? I'm simply channeling the zeitgeist, giving a form to our subconscious fears. But I also give them hope: the ultimate hope. That death isn't an end. That there's something more."

"And you don't think that nourishing those fantasies is exploitive, even a form of emotional blackmail?"

"For over twenty thousand years, people have been telling ghost stories. We're not trying to blackmail, or bribe, or extort anyone. We're seeking communion, a way to get a handle on the inexplicable. Hell, I need this program as much as they do. I need these wild conversations. I don't presume to be able to unravel the mysteries of life and death, but I do believe that we can connect more intimately through a feeling as transcendent as terror."

"Isn't your interest in death just morbid, plain and simple?"

"Morbid?" I stopped myself from replying with an insult.

It wasn't the first time I'd heard this accusation, but I never got used to it. It always struck me as arrogant and offensive. What the hell did Prew know about my views on death?

"As I see it, morbidity is the urgent and uncontrollable need to see that which is forbidden—to peer into the repugnant. What we examine on *Ghost Radio* is rarely repugnant. It's often quite beautiful."

"But it's the stuff of horror movies."

"We don't exploit those emotions in the same way. I'm not out to scare people. The listeners and I frighten each other, and together we work through it. It's new every night. It's not some Hollywood formula that makes *Ghost Radio* work. It's just human communication . . . pure and simple."

Prew took notes as I continued:

"I don't like resorting to clichés, but we live in uncertain times. The wars and the catastrophes that have assailed the planet over the past few years threaten to trivialize our mortality, to desensitize us. But in my culture, we maintain a different relationship with death. We play with her. We write to her as if she were an old friend. We invite her in like a drunk who visits unannounced."

Prew seemed satisfied with the interview. But as he reached over to turn off the recorder, I stopped him with one final thought:

"Something as natural as walking consists of repeatedly setting the body momentarily off-kilter. Each time we shift our weight from one foot to the other, we lose our balance for a fraction of a second. We learn to walk by learning to displace ourselves without falling, by losing and recovering our balance almost simultaneously. In the same sense, one might say that we are in a constant balancing act between life and death."

"What made you tell me that?"

Joaquin smiled.

"Because you are about to get up and walk out of this café."

Prew chuckled.

Then, as if possessed by a cybernetic spirit, he reconnected himself to his various communication devices. As he turned on and consulted his technological extensions, recovering the information lost in his time with me, his face lit up, he squinted, and reality seemed to dissolve around him.

He gathered up his belongings and walked out of the room, losing and recovering his balance with each step.

The instant he left, I returned to one central fact: this interview would tell the story of Gabriel's death. A story I wanted to keep to myself. This was bad. This was very bad.

But what could I do? I couldn't stop the magazine from publishing it. It was true.

Then the obvious solution revealed itself. I'd steal *Newsweek*'s thunder. I'd beat them to the punch. I'd tell the story myself on the American premiere of *Ghost Radio*.

chapter 15

THE CONFESSION

There were only ten minutes left in the show. It was now or never. So I took a deep breath and began:

> *Listeners, I know we're new to each other. But I'm going to end this broadcast with a story. A very personal story. I hope it draws us closer together. I hope it makes you understand that you won't be mocked here on* Ghost Radio *no matter how wild your tale. Because I have wild stories as well.*

It felt good being in a studio again. Alondra seemed to be enjoying it as well, and Watt, well, he was in his usual loony self. Maybe this would be okay. The show had gone well. Most of the callers wanted to talk about politics. But I still felt good. I knew this final story would change things.

It was a nice to be calm after the unpredictability of the last few days, when I wasn't fully in control of my emotions or thoughts. Now I was in the place where I always felt in control. And doing what I loved: telling the truth in the dead of night:

> *When I was a kid, my friend Gabriel and I had a group called Los Deathmuertoz, a Latin rock, punk, experimental, progressive band. Maybe some of you still remember us. We had a following back then in the Houston area. Our music was strange, but I don't think it would be an exaggeration to say that it was also intoxicating. We used "found" noises that we had recorded. Sampled sounds from the most varied sources. Initially we only wanted to*

jam, to explore every possibility offered by our crude instruments and equipment. But beyond these experiments, our musical world was colored by tragedy. That was perfectly understandable. My parents, and Gabriel's as well, died in an automobile accident, the same accident. The car I was in crashed head-on into the car carrying Gabriel's family. Only he and I survived. After the accident and the time we spent in the hospital, our lives became increasingly intertwined. I went to live with my grandmother in Houston a few blocks away from Gabriel's aunt, who took him in for a while. We shared our time together in a strange limbo, a quasiabsence of authority.

We were both pretty wild, but Gabriel was always more daring. Nothing intimidated him. He was always eager to experiment with a new drug, make danger where there was none; get into all kinds of trouble. In short, he was a hellion. Every time we got toasted, he would disappear. Usually he didn't remember where he had been or what he had done, so he started documenting these sprees with Polaroids. The photos he would find in his pockets the following morning were placed in what he called his "Diary of Lost Days." I always wanted to keep up with him, but his escapades were so personal, at times I didn't feel welcome. Besides, Gabriel didn't care where he spent the night: in jail, in the bed of an elderly prostitute, in a wealthy person's swimming pool, or in the monkeys' cage at the zoo, it was all the same to him. I always went home to sleep.

Gabriel's aunt couldn't cope, so he took on a nomadic existence. He slept anywhere, my house, his other friends', a girlfriend's, a stranger's, even the occasional park bench. In time he became a squatter, living in abandoned buildings. I soon followed him; we shared the most bizarre dwellings.

As I spoke, Alondra and Watt grew more disconcerted and irritated. I could tell my decision to confess publicly clearly struck them as idiotic. If

I had told them what I was planning to do beforehand, things would have turned out the same. We would have argued, and in the end, they would have allowed me to do whatever I wanted. It was not their decision. To spring it on them, though, was insulting. I knew that. It implied that I didn't give a fuck about their opinion.

And, when it came to this, I didn't.

> *We devoted ourselves to our ambitions, two musicians on a mission. We thought of ourselves as a kind of fusion of Stravinsky and Dr. Frankenstein, making hybrid creations combining melodies and organic noise, like the amplified sound of a spider devouring an ant or a praying mantis as it ripped off its mate's head. We recorded everything we could imagine and took it further, mixing those sounds with the static from our homemade "radio telescope," an antenna we had built with old circuits that received and distorted radio signals. With a modest sequencer, we mixed these tracks into patterns and added guitars, percussion, synthesizers, and other instruments, not to mention a lot of other noisy junk. It was all part of our experiments. Later, we added computer programs, MIDI samplers, and vocoders to our sound repertoire.*

Alondra and Watt seemed to drift further away. I knew they wondered why I would unmake the character I'd created for *Ghost Radio*. They liked that creation. It worked. *He* worked. Explosive at times, composed at others, sometimes sinking into a hermetic reserve.

But whatever he was, he wasn't a confessor. He eschewed the maudlin world of the personal. *He* wasn't the star of the show. The callers were. He was a conduit. A welcoming voice. He lit the campfire and told the world to gather 'round.

I liked him too.

But tonight I had to set him aside.

This wasn't only about the *Newsweek* article. I realized that now. This was about truth. If I launched the American version of *Ghost Radio* with such a bold declaration of truth, maybe the show would become what I needed it to be. Maybe it would give me the answers I sought.

Alondra nervously applied Chap Stick to her full lips. I know she would have willingly given a liter of blood to escape, but she didn't dare abandon me, especially after her fervent requests to discuss this very subject.

> *We did a lot of crazy things, but we were genuine. At school, when we actually attended, people treated us as freaks. But when we made music, everybody's perception of us changed. It was encouraging to see surprise, fascination, or bewilderment on the faces of those who usually ignored or slighted us. We lost our virginity easily; we had plenty of opportunities with our growing crowd of groupies.*

Watt, enshrouded in the wires, handles, and buttons of his sound equipment, forced out a smile.

> *Our parents' deaths brought us together. Relationships that develop in situations like ours are so profound that they're difficult to explain. We created our own world, and offered the audience visions of it during our performances. They were like a musical Grand Guignol; onstage we presented our fantasies as well as our nightmares. This was before the concept of flash mobs, those instant crowds that gather using text messages to relay the time and place, but we used low-tech methods like flyers, the loudspeakers of a run-down ice-cream truck, or spectacular street signs inviting people to semispontaneous concerts and performances held in unique locations.*

I took a long drink of water. Alondra gazed at me with a mix of hostility and compassion. But Watt looked resigned as he cleaned his nails with a pocketknife.

> *At every concert or performance, we tried to outdo ourselves. We still listened with passion to the great noise groups and bands of the industrial era but thought, ingenuously, that our music was a step beyond what those legends had accomplished. We compulsively read William Blake, Aleister Crowley, and Eliphas Lévi. We were obsessed with all types of death rituals. During one period we wrote songs in honor of the deceased, chosen randomly from obituaries in foreign newspapers, our lyrics inspired by their stories. We often found profoundly poetic passages in those obituaries.*

The telephones were ringing. There was no way of knowing whether the callers wanted my head, if they had a generous comment or just a question, if they wanted to share similar experiences, or if they wanted to ridicule me. I ignored them.

> *Once, we connected our guitars and equipment to the school's loudspeaker, sparking a revolt of legendary proportions that ended in a fire and dozens of arrests. We played in public places, abandoned buildings, old churches, pretty much anywhere we could cause chaos and confusion. We were constantly in trouble and spent a lot of time running away, hiding, or under arrest, which only increased the number of our followers. We made CDs that we sold ourselves, and with the money, we bought more equipment and expanded our sound system. It felt like being on a train going at full speed. I guess anybody could have predicted that we were hurtling toward an abyss.*

A strange expression fell across Alondra's face, like a mother whose child is clumsy at soccer: an expression of humiliation and empathy that you never want to see on a loved one. But I couldn't stop. I was almost at the end.

One night we went to an abandoned radio station at a Mexican university, close to the border. We set up an improvised—and undoubtedly historically inaccurate—altar for Teoyaomqui, the Aztec god of dead warriors. We connected our equipment to the transmitter and managed to get our music on the air. Afterward, I learned that many, maybe even all, of our fans were listening with euphoria. Eleven minutes in, at exactly two in the morning, there was a sudden power surge. I'm not sure how it happened since there was never an investigation, but it's clear that our equipment caused a short circuit. It was raining that night and water was everywhere. We were more careless than usual and it appeared to outsiders that we had intentionally caused the disaster. Sometimes I wonder if Gabriel had wanted it to happen, consciously or unconsciously. I am sure of the time, because the digital clock at the studio, perhaps the most modern piece of equipment in the entire station, was blinking, flashing 2:00. The last thing I saw, before I flew eight yards in the air, was Gabriel.

In a deliberately anticlimactic tone of voice I recounted being saved by the paramedics and how Gabriel was already dead when he arrived at the hospital. I turned off the microphone and took a drink of water, wishing it were tequila, then I stood up and left the studio. Alondra and Watt didn't follow.

A few moments later, I heard Pink Floyd's "Shine On You Crazy Diamond" coming over the monitors. A DJ spouting nonsense on the air is bad, but dead air on a live program is unforgivable.

The studio door opened. Watt came out to join me.

"What the fuck did you just do? What are you going to do next, describe your masturbation fantasies? Talk about hemorrhoids? You're going to destroy us."

"I had to do it."

"Why?"

I gave him my car keys.

"Give these to Alondra. I'm going to walk back to the hotel."

And I left.

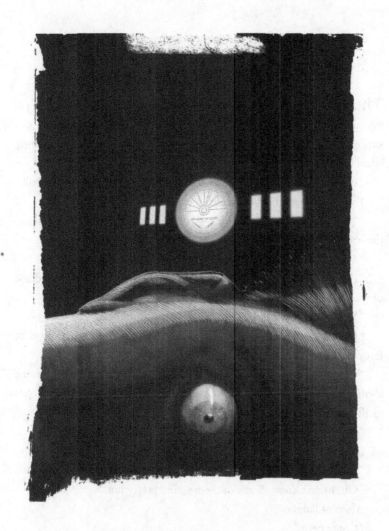

chapter 16

MY OTHER GIRLFRIEND

The walk left me feeling liberated and elated. There was a spring in my step as I unlocked the door and entered the hotel room. Alondra was sitting on the edge of the bed; she greeted me with a cold stare, remaining silent for a long time.

"I don't understand you," she finally said. "I don't understand you at all."

I told her about the *Newsweek* interview.

"That doesn't explain it. Not really. You said we could never refer to that story on the air."

"You're not mad at me," I said.

"I'm not?" she said, jumping to her feet and shooting me the maddest of mad girl faces.

"No, you're not. You're jealous."

"Jealous? Jealous!" she screamed, her face reaching a new level of ferocity.

"Relax and think about it for a second. You've wanted to talk to me about Gabriel for days. And look what I go and do? I talk to my 'other girlfriend' about him."

"The listeners," Alondra said, her anger fading.

I nodded.

"Pretty crazy, huh? Being jealous of a bunch of anonymous people."

"Oh, I don't know. Some of them sound pretty hot."

Alondra laughed.

"Come here."

Alondra walked over to me. I put my arms around her and pulled her close.

"You know what is crazy?" I said gently. "You thinking you could be second to anyone."

She melted in my arms, and together we collapsed onto the bed.

Even before we received the first ratings, we were picked up for an indefinite run. The station moved us into an expensive, though impersonal, condo, and ads for our show began appearing on billboards, in magazines, and on the sides of buses. For a time, everything looked bright and shiny and normal. But I knew it wouldn't last.

It didn't.

chapter 17

CALL 1288, 12:22 A.M.

SANDY'S MUSIC

"Is that me? Am I on?"

"Yes, caller, you're on the air."

"Oh God, I'm so nervous. I didn't know I'd be this nervous."

"What is your name, caller, and where are you from?"

"My name is Sandy, and I'm from Amarillo."

"All right, Sandy, where are you going to take us tonight?"

"I've never told anyone this, because I thought people would think I was crazy. But listening to your other callers . . . well . . . I just have to tell someone."

"That's what we're here for."

"Oh, I'm so nervous. Am I really on the air?"

"Just take a deep breath, Sandy, and tell us what happened."

"Okay . . . okay . . . well, this was when I was in high school. Some of us had gone to a party. Nothing wild, just kid stuff. But it had run pretty late. It must have been like one, maybe two in the morning by the time we were driving home.

"Now, there were four of us in the car. Me and my boyfriend, Jake; my best friend, Tawnie; and her boyfriend, Carson. The party was, like, in this weird part of town. None of us knew it very well. And on the way home we got lost.

"And not just lost. It was weird. We ended up in this big area with all these industrial buildings. You know, like warehouses or something. And it was like we couldn't get out. Or like the complex went on forever.

"No matter how long we drove, or which corner we turned, we still found ourselves driving down these empty streets, past these big empty

buildings. They looked weird, scary. Not like any buildings I've seen before. And it started to creep us out pretty quickly.

"Jake and Carson tried to make jokes about it. But I could hear in
their voices that they were scared. You know what I mean, what that
sounds like, especially with boys that age?"

"I do, Sandy. And then what happened?"

"I think Tawnie heard it first. Or maybe it was me? No, I think it was
definitely Tawnie. Because I clearly remember her saying, 'Sandy, do you
hear that?'

"Those words, the way she said them, I remember it like it happened
yesterday."

"What was it?"

"Well, I couldn't tell at first. But when I listened real close, I heard it
too."

"Sandy, what did you hear?"

"Well, you know the music an ice-cream truck plays? I don't mean
the song, but the way that music sounds. I don't know what it's called. But
you know what I'm talking about?"

"Uh-huh."

"Well, it was like that. But sad. I don't think I've ever heard such
sad music in all my life. It made me want to cry and scream at the same
time. It made me want to run and run and never look back. And Tawny
took it worse than me, she began to scream about how she wanted to get
out of the car, how she had to get out of the car.

"But that was crazy, where was she going to go? We were lost. We
didn't even know where we were. So we just sat there silent and frightened, driving and driving, with the music playing and Tawnie screaming
about wanting to get out of the car.

"I don't know how long this went on, but the sun was coming up
when we finally found our way out and got home. When I climbed into
bed, I heard that music again. Just briefly, for, like, ten . . . um . . . twenty
seconds. Like it was trying to reach me one last time. Like it was trying
to say good night."

"That's quite a story, Sandy."

"Wait, there's more."

"I'm coming up on a break, Sandy. You've got thirty seconds."

"Okay, I tried to find that part of town for years afterward, those warehouses or whatever, and I never could. It just wasn't there."

"Phantom industrial parks and the saddest music you've ever heard. This is *Ghost Radio* live with you till five. And if you want to join us, I'll give the numbers to call after this break."

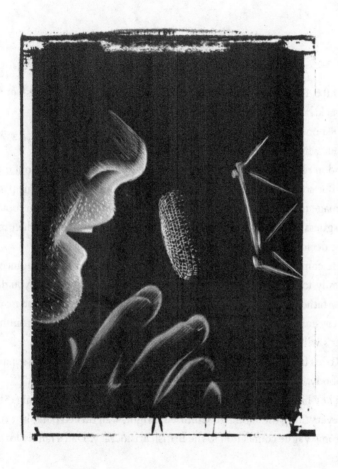

chapter 18

THE PRISON OF CONVENTIONS

I write these words in ink, in a composition book. No cross-outs. No backtracking.

Just one big vomit of truth.

But where do I start?

I don't like talking about myself. I don't even like thinking about myself. But sometimes you need to dig around in the garden of your past, rummage through the weeds and grubs—searching for that main root.

I guess the root of my life, and all its problems, sprouted when my father decided to marry my mother.

He came from a family ruled by social convention and appearances. A family for whom it was less important what you did than how you did it. My father hated this attitude. And, by marrying my mother, he made that crystal clear. He was ostracized by the family and erased from his father's will.

To his family, my mother would never be anything more than a squaw. A nobody. A nothing. Marrying such a woman "just wasn't done."

They had someone else in mind. Her name was Marlene Koenig. She was everything they wanted. Cultured, bright, well turned out. She even had some vague connection to the British aristocracy. Dad's family loved that!

She would make "a proper wife." Miss Koenig was keen on the idea too. Dad stood out among the parade of well-scrubbed suitors who frequented her parents' Fifth Avenue apartment: Those "Bradleys" and "Carltons" elicited little more from Miss Koenig than the occasional "nice" or "sweet." Dad was something different: a scientist with a bohemian edge. And both of these characteristics filled Miss Koenig with a demure debutante's version of lust.

Father seriously considered the match. Miss Koenig's knack for conversation would suit him well as he climbed academia's greasy pole. She also had the approval of the Spencer family of industrialists. He would need grants for his work. They could provide.

Did he love her? Not really. But he was a scientist and thought when it came to marriage, pragmatism might be a more rational guide than emotions.

So, as he left for a conference in Mexico, he believed he would return a week later and ask Miss Koenig to marry him.

He did not return for ten years.

He was chairing a panel on string theory at the National Autonomous University and my mother was in the audience. She'd gone there on a whim. It was raining. She missed her bus. You know the drill.

Despite the fact that she was no specialist, and, frankly, not even very interested in the subject, she torpedoed the panel of speakers with a series of incisive questions. By the end of the session, my father was both annoyed and intrigued. Who was this girl? Her simple common sense had shredded his presentation like one of the paper cutouts Mexicans make for the Day of the Dead. He caught up with her at the subway that evening and never left her side again.

Love at first sight, they say.

Whatever.

Miss Koenig married a banker and spent much of the next twenty years in and out of the Betty Ford Clinic.

My parents smile whenever they see her name in the headlines.

And so into this world of fairy-tale love I came, like the eel in a koi pond. I wasn't what my parents expected or wanted. Almost from birth, I fought their attempts to mold me into the perfect sunny expression of their love.

I was queen of the temper tantrum. Princess of "no." And mistress of rage.

My parents largely ignored my behavior. They turned inward, losing themselves in their idyllic romance. Their relationship actually was idyllic, powered by equal amounts of goodwill and affection. And passion too, I guess.

It's baffling, but I can attest to it. I was there for most of the soap opera.

My father may have sent his inheritance straight to hell, but my mother also made sacrifices, dropping out of med school to follow her crazy Irishman. He, meanwhile, complaining that his colleagues were unimaginative and incompetent, resigned from his professorship in quantum physics at Harvard. The two of them lived on their modest teachers' salaries in the Colonia Roma, a hip neighborhood in Mexico City, until my father finally decided to go back to the United States. He had some new ideas he wanted to bounce off his former colleagues, and more important, he needed financial backing, something that would be hard to find in Mexico for a problematic gringo who didn't know how to kiss university officials' asses and who virulently despised politicians and opportunists.

My mother tried to convince him to stay. She loved her city, life made more sense there than it ever would in an anonymous American suburb. But for once, my father wouldn't listen. He was convinced that it was time, not just for professional reasons, he explained, but also to deal with unfinished family business—and to express his opposition to U.S. interventionist policies in a way that "really mattered."

Vietnam.

"Out here anyone can speak out against the war and it makes no difference. But if I get a professorship in the States, I won't just be working; I'll be able to directly influence U.S. academics."

My mother thought it was bullshit, another of her husband's idealist fantasies; she'd learned to live with them, but they still drove her up the wall. Nonetheless, she gave in. Within months, we had packed a few belongings, sold everything else, and boarded a plane to Boston.

What happened next is irrelevant: high school, college, boyfriends with acne, ten million comics read beneath the covers, psychopathic snipers, political correctness, thermoses filled with gin, overweight couples holding hands, distant wars, unreliable condoms, ecstasy, the Cure, discovery of a voracious sexual appetite that would lead to good times and more foul-ups, an arrest or two, Dostoyevsky and Bukowski. My life moved beyond the mundane when I finally found a way to link my true interests with an academic and professional pretext that justified them. After years of denial, I accepted that my true passion was comic books: reading them, drawing them, writing them, and—why not?—researching them. I realized they could be seen as a means of pop expression, as the sketchy realizations—with their low cost and unique accessibility—of people's aspirations, ideals, and fears.

I spent my childhood obsessed with the comics that I was forbidden to read. Any book with more than five pictures was suspect, from the lowbrow Adventures of Kaliman and Mickey Mouse to Tintin, Superman, Astérix, and Corto Maltese. It made no difference; anything with thought bubbles was instantly condemned, even thrown out the window.

"It's entertainment for imbeciles and illiterates," my father said.

This forbidden aspect was part of their allure.

I concentrated on studying and writing my thesis. While comics were often used for the most base and mercenary ends—as propaganda tools, vehicles for consumer and religious training, mechanisms for controlling the masses, and systems of sentimental education—I postulated that they could also be used to break the information monopoly of mass-media consortiums, the ideological oppression of the state, and the mental laziness of those incapable of opening a book. It's not that I thought humanity would free itself from its chains by reading the funny pages; but I fervently believed that they had something valid to say, even if it was in the most basic sense. The first time I read something about Marx, Freud, or Ho Chi Minh, it was in a comic by the Mexican cartoonist Rius. He may not have spurred me on to communism, but his work opened my mind to a different avenue of learning.

Okay, I'll admit my theory was nothing out of this world. Similar stuff had been said by dozens of others. Many simply wanted to justify their juvenile passions. I wanted to take it further. So I started digging through art history, and without having to look too hard, I rediscovered the Mexican muralists: Diego Rivera, Siqueiros, and Orozco, and the artist José Guadalupe Posada. Adding a dash of the ancient pre-Columbian pictographic tradition, I had a set of visual criteria that offered an interesting portrait of Mexican culture. Armed with these concepts, I returned to Mexico and contacted several groups that made underground comics and zines. I spent months researching and documenting their work. By the time I had enough for a decent thesis, I was already collaborating on a strip for the magazine *Gallito Cómics*. I had also moved in with Alberto Mejía, an artist who dreamed of becoming a famous painter but drew comics and political cartoons for a newspaper for a living. Alberto and I didn't last much longer than the time it took us to illustrate a few pages. That's when I met Joaquin.

I didn't go to Mexico looking for romance, but I didn't foresee meeting Joaquin. The day I met him began so strangely.

I woke that morning with an odd vision. A series of letters arranged in a very specific way filled my mind. I wrote them down on a sheet of paper:

E

N

I

T N U J A A

B

N

I stared at them. They had no meaning that I could determine. No relation to anything I could think of. Yet they seemed important. Very important. I tried to work on one of my comics, but the letters obsessed me. Every few minutes my eyes would return to the pad. It was as if these letters, in this pattern, possessed an almost religious significance. An undeniable, transcendent power. It was unlike anything I'd ever experienced before.

The letters appeared to be completely random. They didn't form words; they didn't even suggest sounds. They were just letters. And the pattern didn't seem to have any obvious significance. But I knew it meant something.

I felt this was the most important thing I'd ever seen in my life. I would kill for these letters. I would build temples to these letters. If these letters could talk, I would do anything they said.

It was bizarre. I had never been excitable or fanatical. My love of comics was deep and powerful. But it didn't even touch this. This was huge.

I took a shower hoping the feeling would wash away. But as the water pounded against my skin all I could think about were those letters. They had a hold on me. I wanted to jump out of the shower, run back to my desk, grab that pad, and cradle it in my arms like a baby. But I fought the urge, turned up the hot water; maybe I could steam these crazy urges from my soul.

Slowly, as the vapor filled my nostrils, the urge dissipated. By the afternoon I returned to work on my comic, and by evening, guests started arriving for a party Alberto had arranged. The letters were all but forgotten.

chapter 19

FINDING ALONDRA

Finding Alondra completely changed my life. I met her at a party thrown by some acquaintances who created underground comics. I was sleep-deprived and unenthusiastic at the thought of going out. Every time I went to one of these things, I'd ask myself the same question: Why bother? Usually I returned home bearing the same answer: Next time, don't bother. Friends I hadn't seen in months would greet me from the bottom of bottles and roach ends of joints. I'd see desirable women on the arms of total jerks, stave off hunger by eating potato chips and drinking liquor so noxious I could feel my liver corroding before it even reached my stomach.

On this particular occasion, I found a chair in a corner of the kitchen, next to an artist who wrote and drew a comic about a zombie superhero. I pretended to be interested.

"Zombo is like a classic superhero, with foibles, anxieties, and problems. You know the whole Stan Lee thing," he told me.

"What are his superpowers?" I asked.

"Well, he's immortal because he's already dead. He lives in a grave and only comes out at night. He defends democracy and he protects his girl."

"Why would a zombie care about democracy?"

"Because he's a modern vigilante."

"Oh, of course," I said, suppressing a laugh.

A woman dressed head to toe in black, with full lips painted the same color, approached.

"So what's Zombo up to these days?" she asked with a smile. She had a subtle accent I couldn't place.

"Defending the world from injustice."

"And protecting democracy from its enemies?" she added, giving me what seemed like a conspiratorial look.

"Have you met Joaquin? He's a disc jockey."

"A disc jockey?" she asked, considering me coolly.

I let the question go unanswered. I didn't want to talk about my job.

"I knew a disc jockey once. Killed himself by jumping in front of a train," Alondra said.

I didn't know what to make of this comment. Hostility? Ridicule? I wasn't sure.

Unable to think of a rejoinder, I asked her name.

"Alondra," she said. It sounded like a challenge.

"Are you also an expert on zombies?" I asked, hoping to sound witty.

"I'm an expert on a lot of things. But zombies aren't a favorite."

Zombo's creator grasped Alondra's sarcasm and his face fell. I seized the moment.

"Frankly, my main problem with Zombo is that he has a really stupid name," I ventured.

He stared at me in confusion; he was obviously trying to hold in the anger that would make him look like what he was: a ridiculous, easily offended cartoonist. He decided to laugh instead.

"It's meant to be stupid," he said limply.

"His name's the least of his worries. Believe me. I've read most of his adventures," Alondra said, moving closer to me.

"Well, it's a work in progress."

"Progressively decomposing. But for a zombie, that might be a good thing."

Crestfallen, the artist got up and limped away.

I already liked everything about Alondra: her face, the black dress she wore trimmed with antique lace, her hair, her hands; the accent that seemed ripped from the soundtrack of an old Superman cartoon.

"So, what do you do?" I asked.

"Guess," she said, a hint of playfulness dancing in her eyes.

"Well, you dress like you're in a Goth band, which means you're not."

"Good."

"Too sarcastic for an actress."

"Much too sarcastic."

"Too independent to have come here on someone's arm."

"Yes, my arms are free."

"And since this is a party for underground-comics people, you must be one of them."

"Nice deduction, Sherlock."

I gave her a courtly bow.

"The guest list kind of tipped my hand."

I nodded.

"What might you have guessed without that?"

"Serial killer?" I blurted out.

She laughed and some of her armor slipped away.

The conversation shifted, becoming easier, looser.

We talked about comic books and hip-hop, politics and food, Web sites and the crime rate in Mexico City. She told me a little about the trajectory that had carried her to the Federal District.

"You hungry?" she wanted to know.

"Hardly at all now. I ruined my appetite with a rancid bag of something I found lying around here," I answered.

"Let's go eat something more substantial."

Without another word, she headed for the apartment door. I followed. Just as we were crossing the threshold, Alberto came up to us.

"Where you going?" he asked Alondra.

"I'm having dinner with my friend Joaquin here."

I'd known Alberto for some time. In fact, I'd invited him onto my program, back when it followed the conventional cultural broadcasting model. He was upset, but keeping his cool. Barely.

At the time, Alondra's bluntness, while refreshing, seemed a little cruel to me. I couldn't help identifying with poor Alberto. I'd been "that guy" more than once. Hell, we all have.

"You want me to come along?" he asked feebly.

"You should stay with your guests," Alondra said, but in a tone that made it sound more like "fuck off."

"When will you be back?"

"Not sure. I'll have to come back eventually, my stuff is here. Don't wait up."

I said good-bye, but Alberto didn't answer. We left silently, not speaking until we climbed into my car.

"What was that? It seemed like you were a little mean."

"I behaved impeccably," Alondra responded. "Where are we going?"

I took her to Charco de las Ranas for tacos. It wasn't easy for us to pick up the conversation again, which was mostly my fault; I kept expecting an explanation.

For a while I feigned interest, but I couldn't focus on what Alondra was telling me about popular myths and traditions in Papua, and eventually I interrupted:

"It seemed like something serious happened with Alberto back there. Do you have any idea what it might have been? He acted jealous."

"Yeah, I suppose so."

"Does he have any reason to be?"

"People have reasons for a lot of stupid shit," she answered.

"I guess it might be because you've been with him and his group for a while. He must feel a certain attachment or affection for you. Maybe he was disappointed that you left in the middle of his party," I said, choosing my words carefully so they wouldn't sound like an accusation.

"Maybe."

"But you don't think so."

She shook her head.

"What do you think it is?"

"I fucked him a few times," she said, biting into her beefsteak taco.

I nearly choked on my glass of horchata.

"Pardon?"

"I thought you knew. But don't worry, it's meaningless."

"Where I come from, doing something like that to another man can end up costing you your life," I said, although inwardly I doubted that this would be the case with Alberto and me.

"Don't be dramatic. That's the way it goes. I'm crashing at his place. I got bored. It happens."

"But still . . ."

"I'm not cheating on anyone, Joaquin. Eat your tacos."

I didn't have an answer for this woman, who seemed more attractive, fascinating, and dangerous with each passing moment.

At this point, Alondra changed the subject. Clearly she wasn't interested in talking about Alberto anymore. And, I have to admit, I was grateful. We finished eating, and on the way to the car, she asked me where I wanted to go. I suggested a bar, and she agreed, so I decided to take her to a hole in the wall over on Medellín Avenue: a ruined garage where musicians, artists, gang members, politicians, and other bums came to drink and dance until dawn. The noise was overwhelming but the ambience was worth it; Alondra seemed to enjoy herself.

It was hot in the club, so I took off the jacket I'd been wearing all night. Alondra noticed my forearm. I have an odd tattoo that often raises an eyebrow or two, but nothing prepared me for Alondra's reaction.

She grabbed my arm and pulled me into a corner of the club where the lighting was better. She studied the tattoo; a look of concern, even fear, marked her face.

"You don't like it?" I asked feebly.

"What does it mean?" she said, her eyes wide and her lips trembling.

"Would you believe me if I told you I don't know?"

"How can that be?"

"I used to raise quite a bit of hell. After one of those hell-raising nights, I woke up with this on my arm."

Alondra looked deep in my eyes. And after what seemed like an eternity, she said:

"Do you believe in premonitions?"

"I don't know, maybe."

"Well, I didn't. But I do now," she said, and kissed me on the cheek.

All this because of my crazy tattoo? I looked down at it, wondering what it could possible mean to this girl. It meant nothing to me, just an odd collections of letters:

E

N

I

T N U J A A

B

N

Around four in the morning, we left. I didn't have to say a word. We climbed into the car and drove toward the National University campus sculpture garden, where we waited for the sunrise, telling each other our dreams and nightmares.

At eight in the morning, I took her back, having done nothing more than talk to her. Well, I did get that one kiss on the cheek. I doubt Alberto slept that night.

In the following days, I saw Alondra several more times. We visited all the little-known spots in the city that interested her: temples and ruins, old cantinas and dilapidated stores.

We spent our second afternoon together in my bed, and after that, we found several cheap hotels and motels in different parts of the city. We could have gone to my apartment, but the hotels fit well on the list of urban attractions Alondra wanted to explore.

Every day, I tried to convince her to come live with me, to leave Alberto's house once and for all. It wasn't long before it felt like Alberto and I had traded places. Now that she was with me, I was the one suffering anguish and nightmares about the two of them together. Alondra was still sleeping under his roof, and although I believed there was nothing between them, there was always a nagging uncertainty. Alondra told me living with him was convenient because they were collaborating on a comic book, but eventually she finally had enough of Alberto's tearful pleading.

One morning, after we returned from a trip, she showed up at my apartment with her two suitcases. We took a quick shower together. I couldn't believe my luck, but a voice inside my head kept saying, "Be careful." Alondra didn't make any promises, but she delivered no warnings either. Our relationship was nonjudgmental, but also noncommittal. I told myself I was content, but really I wanted more. My night shift was wonderfully convenient for both of us, and she continued to be active in the underground-comic scene, where she created, edited, and published various books.

I'd told Alondra about my job in general terms, about my program and the unexpected turn it had taken. I explained how my vocation as a professional broadcaster was thanks, in large part, to my nighttime callers, who contributed the material we discussed every evening. By then, I trusted Alondra enough to start telling her how, sometimes, the stories I heard on the show resonated strangely with my personal life. How, in a way, I didn't believe it was sheer coincidence the program had taken this course.

I know that in the beginning Alondra thought I had a screw loose, or, more likely, was inventing macabre stories in hopes of appealing to that little necrophile all Goth women carry within them. However, her aesthetic tastes didn't translate into an interest in ghost stories or supernatural phenomena. As for myself, convincing anyone of the importance or veracity of the stories I heard each day was not a priority. In the beginning, it didn't seem relevant to me whether what callers said was true or not; finding rational explanations or dissecting their errors of perception and judgment was beside the point. The interesting thing was unraveling the worries, fears, and ambitions these tales embodied. Sometimes, the stories were of a purely social or economic nature; others were flagrantly oedipal. Of course, I had learned to weed out the pranksters, and each night, there were a few disturbed individuals who injected their own insanity into the show. Something that could be both entertaining and exasperating.

The real problems I ran up against, though, were my own; I had trouble identifying them largely because I didn't understand them well enough to articulate what they were. It may sound pretentious but I've always been courted by death.

chapter 20

TATTOOED

One might think the coincidence of the tattoo would have scared me. I've never been a fan of fate. And this felt like fate. No, it was more like: Destiny. But for some reason I wasn't afraid.

Joaquin seemed intelligent, laid back, and unconventional, a combination I've always found attractive. And there was the destiny angle, which made him seem dangerous. No woman, whatever crap they tell you, can resist that. But despite all of this, I wasn't anticipating a long relationship. I planned to continue traveling across Mexico and I wanted to do it alone. I had no intention of bringing anyone with me, and I wasn't going to modify my itinerary. I certainly didn't want commitment, or anything else to distract me from my goals. So, when I told him I was going to Oaxaca to see Monte Albán, Mitla, and Zaachila, to interview artist Francisco Toledo and maybe work in his studio, I was caustic, almost abusive. Joaquin seemed to get it at first. But his silence didn't last long. Even now I'm not sure how he did it, but he convinced me that we could travel together without getting in each other's way, with the understanding that I could split from him at any time without explanation or drama. Ultimately, our journey extended far beyond Oaxaca. We continued traveling cross-country and went to Chiapas, across the border into Guatemala and Belize, and back to Mexico through Quintana Roo. After a few days in Mérida we went into Campeche and finally Veracruz.

Joaquin was taking time off from his radio show, which had just won some prize and was, unexpectedly, developing a following, both on the Web and the conventional airwaves. I made no secret of the fact that the premise seemed absurdly old-fashioned to me. Was there still an audience out there interested in listening to ghost stories? Especially in an era so predisposed toward the visual, the spectacle, special effects, it seemed bizarre that anyone would have the patience and—I don't know—the naïveté to respond to them.

Of course, who was I to talk? Comics were also hopelessly retrograde. But comics possessed a charm, while radio just seemed tawdry. Or so I thought.

I was wrong, both about Joaquin and about his program. I enjoyed his company during the trip; I fulfilled all my research goals while discovering many aspects of Mexico I'd never known. Meanwhile, I found myself becoming fond of even Joaquin's weirdest habits.

The odd way he coughed when nervous. The adamant way he argued when drunk. I even succumbed to the gooey-eyed way he looked at me. I missed him when he wasn't around. Yup, I was in love. Wholly and completely. Though I hated myself a little for it.

When we got back, I didn't pause for even a moment to consider whether it was time to move in or not. I leaped in headfirst. Going back to his apartment to stay seemed like the most natural thing in the world.

During the trip we talked a lot about the show. He told me how it had evolved and transformed.

"But why would people listen to ghost stories over and over again?" I asked him.

"You have great eyes," he replied.

"Frankly, I don't get it. They're all the same."

"Like a tiger's."

"You'd think they'd get bored."

"Shining in the jungle."

"I'm trying to talk about your show."

"My subject is more interesting," he said, raising his eyebrows flirtatiously.

An hour later, our clothes strewn across the floor, I got him to talk about the show.

"Our interests are similar. What you're looking for in comic books isn't so different from what I'm trying to do with radio. They're both examples of low tech that's seductive. And speaking of seduction, I think —"

"C'mon, I really want to hear your take."

"Okay, okay, I think of what I'm doing as a sort of confessional, or, if you prefer a less religious metaphor, a psychoanalyst's couch. People call in to talk about their fears and phobias, things they've imagined or that have really happened to them, things they wish had happened. If the story's good, we all enjoy it. If not, at least the caller is getting it off his chest. And our listeners are looking for that element of surprise—the power of spontaneity, the unexpected, the limitless possibilities offered by other people's secrets."

"I don't want to disappoint you, but that sounds like the same logic that Dr. Phil uses to justify his brainless talk show. Is that what you're after?" Part of me was just trying to provoke him, but I was also authentically curious.

"Oh, you want to argue. I say we settle it with a wrestling match."

"Joaquin."

"Best two out of three falls wins."

"Answer my question."

"Of course the loser wins too," he said, his eyes doing that gooey thing.

"How about some verbal wrestling?"

"Mine sounds better."

I got up off the floor, and slipped back into my clothes.

"Now she's getting dressed."

"Might be talked out of them."

Joaquin smiled.

"Okay, I'll answer your question," he said, then laughing: "What was it again?"

Some days and orgasms later, I finally got an answer.

"Generally, I'm just letting people talk; it's great if it helps people resolve their issues. But I think I'm a lot like the audience, I like to listen to them."

"But you told me that sometimes the callers make a sport of tearing everything apart—mistrusting, mocking, even outright insulting those who share their deepest intimacies and fears. How do you expect to resolve a conflict in the midst of so much animosity?"

"I don't, that's up to the callers themselves. Most of the listeners know what they're getting into. I can't do anything other than ask for a certain level of respect and do my best to filter the nastier calls. In the end, if confrontations arise, that's part of the package. I doubt anyone is so naive that they would tell their story on air and not expect some criticism."

I questioned Joaquin aggressively for several days, between bouts of equally aggressive sex. I wasn't trying to convince him that the show was immoral, exploitive, or inconsequential, nor did I really question his convictions. Curiosity drove me, and he disarmed me through simple logic and an implacable sincerity. And that damn gooey-eyed look. He had it all clear in his head and his own brushes with death had bolstered his determination. Even if he was often skeptical about the stories he heard, he obviously felt a kind of respect for those who called in.

"Whether *I* believe them or not is what matters," he'd always say.

In our talks, Joaquin never missed a chance to point out the parallels between his work and the underground comics that obsessed me. Both forms of media were opening up new channels of expression, and each spoke its own language, an argot that was at once popular, spontaneous, vibrant, and raw. Each was an irreverent take on an old genre, each could be provocative, and both used shock as a means of communication.

Little by little, almost without realizing it, I settled in Mexico permanently. I'd traveled a lot, but this was the first time I'd chosen a home of my own volition, not because it was imposed on me or for practical reasons. After a few interviews I was hired by the political-science department of a private university. It wasn't a spectacular position and it didn't pay much, but I didn't care. I still worked with several comic-book artists, including Alberto. Because he had been my lover, he thought he deserved certain privileges, which annoyed me and drove Joaquin crazy.

I hate jealousy. Never understood it. But Joaquin even made that charming. His eyes found a new shade of gooey.

Love and her odd magic.

Yes, we were in love. But how do you talk about it? All those terrible clichés.

There's something indecent about talking or writing about love. It cheapens the feeling. And it's an emotion that none of us understand, even when we think we do.

If, in a moment of intimacy, someone asks if I love him, I find myself overwhelmed; I feel as embarrassed as I would publicly debating my innermost feelings in an auditorium full of strangers.

But I promised myself I'd try. Here. In this composition book. But I still can't. So I'll return to facts.

But, wait; I think there may be one word that describes my feelings for Joaquin:

Tattooed.

I'd been drawn in by a tattoo, then tattooed by love.

Okay, that's enough; if I write any more about it, this will take a hard turn toward cliché land. Back to the facts, I'm always better with facts.

Our daily life was unorthodox. Joaquin would return from the radio program at dawn. He almost always woke me up, and we would be together. Together in every sense of the word. And after an hour or more of that we'd have breakfast and sleep until noon. Then I'd head for the university, and when I got back, we'd be together until he went to the radio station around 10 P.M. Then I'd work on my projects, see my friends, and do the other things my life demanded.

We were perfectly synchronized, but one day Joaquin proposed that we make a change: He wanted me to start working with him on the show. I thought it was a rotten idea. We had something good. Why spoil it?

"I need you here," he told me. "You could make a huge contribution to the show. It's got nothing to do with spending time together. Your knowledge and skepticism, your perspective and humor—they would really enrich the program. Right now incredible things are happening; there's more and more interest, more sponsors, more money."

"Let's not ruin what we have."

I was sure he'd never convince me, and I pumped up the volume of "Deadship, Darkship," by Sorry About Dresden.

> *My eyes are threatening to open wide tonight (for the first time).*
> *I try to cover them up with a pillow's side.*
> *Twilight, made up and hated*
> *So bright like, shards of blood and rust and light.*

We went back and forth, back and forth. The more he asked, the more I fought it. And one night he became adamant, and I became cruel.

"You're just jealous of me having any life that excludes you."

And with that, I stormed out of the apartment.

But it was all an act. Earlier that day I had decided to say yes. I just wanted to make him suffer a little bit.

At first I thought *Ghost Radio* would be an interesting experience, a diversion from my work on comic books. I didn't realize then what had happened to Joaquin, what was still happening to him. To me, the program was just a job. It wasn't long before I discovered that, for him, it was more. Much more.

chapter 21

CALL 2305, FRIDAY, 1:35 A.M.
THE SOLDIER

The woman's voice was delicate and soft. But I liked it. I didn't want to ask her to speak up. So I had Watt boost the gain, hoping the lacelike tone of her vowels would be preserved.

My Ramón didn't want to go to Iraq. He said so all the time: those people haven't done anything to me, or my family, or anyone I know; I don't want to kill them.

Well, they sent him anyway, and he couldn't do anything about it.

On the night of April 17, I woke up screaming. My husband was asleep and he just mumbled:

"It's all right, go back to sleep."

But I was too upset. I walked into Ramón's room and he was standing there, as if he was waiting for something.

"Son, what are you doing here?" I asked him. I imagined the worst.

"I just came by to say hi, because I missed you a lot, Ma."

His voice was calm. I could sense that he didn't want to scare me.

"Don't give me that. Tell me the truth. Why are you here?"

"Oh, Ma. Aren't you glad to see me?"

"Don't play games with me," I told him. "You've brought me bad news. People don't just appear out of nowhere."

"If you keep it up, I'm leaving, Ma."

"Don't leave, just tell me the truth."

"No, Ma. You're way too suspicious, I better go back."

Then I heard a really loud noise coming from the kitchen. I turned to see what it was, and when I turned back, my son wasn't there anymore. He'd gone away. I threw myself on his bed and cried for the rest of the night. The next morning, my husband asked what was wrong with me. He could see that I'd stayed in Ramón's room all night, and my eyes were swollen from crying so much. I started to tell him what I'd seen, but I hadn't said more than ten words when they knocked on the door. They were two military officers dressed up real formal-like, looking serious.

chapter 22

HABIT AND CHANGE

"The whole Goth scene bores me to tears," I told him.

I didn't feel like saying any more. My black lipstick added the appropriate irony.

Creating the look had been a real triumph. But that was years ago. I maintained it more out of habit than anything else. It had become my uniform.

Sometimes I think I'll wear my black clothes, combat boots, and corsets right into old age. Sometimes I think I'll chuck it tomorrow.

The boredom I referred to stemmed from the fact that to many these aren't just clothes. They are an ideology, an attitude, urban paganism, second-rate Satan worship, and all that crap.

This discussion began one afternoon when Joaquin stopped what he was doing, looked at me, moonstruck, and tried to rationalize why he liked my style so much.

He told me the significance he drew from each article of clothing, its Victorian heritage and its sadomasochistic connotations. He expounded on the contrast between the soft, feminine lace and the hard, military accessories; the sensual warmth and the cold, mortuary appearance; the pleated, Catholic-schoolgirl miniskirts and the inverted crucifixes. His eye for detail impressed me. I was interested in the social history of the Darksider wardrobe too, but I'd heard it all a hundred, no, a thousand times before. So, I stopped him.

"You like it because it makes me look hot."

I felt a little guilty about it, but I had to set certain boundaries and I decided to start then and there.

Our relationship was about to spread beyond intimacy and private space, making us into media celebrities, and I needed to establish strict rules about the way we portrayed ourselves through our microphones. Joaquin didn't have a problem with that; he'd developed an alter ego who was sometimes maniacal but sometimes restrained, who could listen patiently, and didn't treat every public appearance as an opportunity to show off. But I was more interested in ensuring we wouldn't turn the program into a farce, a grotesque vaudeville show starring us as one of those monstrous couples who put themselves on display. I couldn't shake the image of Jim and Tammy Bakker. But when I mentioned this to Joaquin, he just laughed and said:

"I think secretly you want to be Tammy Faye."

I know I was exaggerating; maybe I was even being a little hysterical. But anyone who values their independence feels threatened when they embark on someone else's project.

It's a basic survival instinct.

I agreed to be on *Ghost Radio* because I thought it would give me material to work with once I got back to the university. Plus, it might be fun. But if my guard went down, I was lost.

As a matter of fact, it was fun. For me, sessions on the air were like living *Star Trek* episodes. We listened to stories in isolation from the world; we commented on them, we argued to the point of shouting. Most of the stories were really about loneliness, primal fear, maternal abandonment, Electra complexes, sexual frustration, spiritual suffering. You didn't have to be a genius to figure out that these were the things our callers were really afraid of. It didn't matter whether we imagined them as transparent specters, *chupacabras*, mummies, tentacled monsters, or any other malformed creature; in essence, all these beings were reflections of everyday fears and traumas. Discovering this, which was obvious to so many, was a revelation.

Joaquin understood where I was coming from. But didn't always agree.

"Sometimes a ghost is just a ghost," he'd say.

Perhaps he needed that attitude to make the show work. You can't be psychoanalyzing all your callers, and still create entertaining radio. And Joaquin created entertaining radio.

I loved watching the different emotions he went through, from enthusiastic, to arrogant, to bemused, to excited. Occasionally, he went into a trancelike state. Those episodes made me nervous.

At first, I was convinced it was theatrics, that he was putting on an act to impress me. But I soon realized that it wasn't that at all, he was truly entering an altered state—and when he did so, he was oblivious to the world around him.

I eventually got used to his sporadic trips into the world of unexplained phenomena. He was able to wade through the mist covering the borderland between the normal and the paranormal. Although it scared me a little, part of me admired it. But I had concluded it was just one of those things better left alone. I chose to ignore it, but that wasn't always possible.

In time, *Ghost Radio* became my home, a space where I felt comfortable, where I could express myself without fear. Our little program was a tunnel, a highway of voices: Sometimes I was behind the wheel, sometimes simply a passenger. I'd earned my slot on the program. I got along well with the staff, and participated in the decision-making process. That was already several times better than the relationship I had with my fellow professors at the university, with whom anything more personal than an exchange of "good afternoons" was unthinkable.

As always in my life, I assumed from the beginning that this was just a passing phase, that at some rapidly approaching moment everything would change. I couldn't imagine any other outcome, even though, unlike practically every earlier stage of my life, I was really satisfied. I didn't feel like going through another change, lugging my suitcases somewhere else, saying good-bye to people, and filling garbage bags with the things I couldn't take with me.

One afternoon, I was having a coffee at Joaquin's apartment, which was now my apartment too, and thinking about this, when I looked out the window and saw a couple fighting in the park. He was trying to hug her, but she pushed him, gently at first, and then with more force. He gestured emphatically, trying to make her stay. She didn't seem convinced, and walked off, but he ran after her and stopped her. Once again, he waved his hands around, speaking in a voice that, although I couldn't hear through the closed window, was obviously growing louder and louder. I could almost hear him through the closed window. I didn't want to eavesdrop, though; I didn't want to know what he was saying to keep her from leaving him. He didn't seem to care that passersby were watching. Shame and discretion had vanished; there was only his desperate attempt to conquer this woman. She dug in harder, looking at the ground, not like someone who's embarrassed, but sternly, refusing all contact. She raised her hands to keep him from even touching her. Finally, she turned and walked away. He watched her, his shoulders drooping.

Their separation affected me in a way I had difficulty understanding. I couldn't stop thinking about them, about his enormous sadness and her detachment. I walked through the apartment, appreciating it more than ever, its wide windows that let the sunlight in, its wooden floors, its kitchen and cozy bedroom. It was going to be hard work leaving this place; it was going to be even more difficult to peel myself away from Joaquin. When he returned the next morning, the first thing he said to me was:

"How'd you like a change of scenery?"

It seems he had a chance to test *Ghost Radio* in the United States, possibly leading to a syndication deal.

The notion of going back to the United States didn't seem very attractive at that point, but it wasn't something I completely ruled out either. I figured I'd have to return eventually, but going back now felt like cutting off something vital, sacrificing important experiences, abandoning ideas and projects. Above all, leaving Mexico made me think of my mother, who'd followed my father to America and was never happy there. Was this history repeating itself? Fate, genetics, emotional programming?

"You're going to have to go alone. I'm staying," I told him. I didn't get emotional.

I didn't know if I was right. I had to take this position. But I also had to hear his arguments.

We spent weeks debating the advantages and disadvantages of moving. It was a major opportunity for Joaquin and it made me feel guilty to think of him sacrificing something so big. He was in the same situation. He didn't want to leave me, but he didn't want to pressure me to go. It seemed that no matter what, we both came out losers. Joaquin spoke of the violence, the kidnapping, the misery, and the pollution in Mexico.

"And you really want to live in a country at war where you're an ethnic minority? You want your program to target the marginalized and dispossessed?" I asked him.

"Don't go all intellectual on me."

"I'm stating facts."

"But avoiding the real one."

I stared at him, trying to diminish the anger in my eyes.

"What are you afraid of, Alondra?"

I was about to challenge him. But I knew he was right. I was afraid. But why? And of what?

I shook my head slowly, and looked at the floor.

Nothing was resolved. The discussions continued. Joaquin became more convincing and I faltered. I conceded certain points, but held fast on others. He hadn't won yet. But a tiny voice inside me told me he would . . . eventually.

Adding to the mosaic of issues that came with a return to the United States, Joaquin was counting on me to form part of the *Ghost Radio* team. I didn't find out until later, but the corporation buying the program did not want the format changed, and my presence was fundamental because I was American; I was the link between both cultures. Joaquin didn't dare tell me that they were pretty much buying *me*. He was afraid, and rightly so, that this would be too much pressure. At any rate, he said:

"They want the entire team. They want to reproduce the program's formula exactly."

"Well, I guess you and Watt will have to find someone else."

I asked Joaquin not to talk about it for a few days. I wasn't interested in hearing any more about moves, changes, or cultural transplantation. I needed to weigh the pros and cons myself. I needed time to think.

chapter 23

THE CONTRACT

I sold my soul to the devil.

That old cliché never felt more apt. I won't go into detail. When you're talking about business, the minutiae of contracts, unions, safety, and benefits bore me to tears. After all, it all boils down to one question: How much?

I know it might sound mercenary, even flat-out selfish, but what can I say? For the first time in my life, someone had managed to stir my ambition. It began, like so many other things, with an e-mail. The message was signed by a guy named Dan Foster and sent from an address at InterMedia Enterprises. I answered courteously, as I always do. Dan kept sending me messages for a few weeks, like he was just another fan commenting on the program and giving his opinion on my hosting. Then one day he traveled to Mexico to see me, and tossed out his proposal. He didn't waste time.

He offered me a nationally syndicated program, a fabulous salary, an apartment, and a car. But Dan Foster, who it turned out was president and CEO of the media conglomerate, presented all this as if it were a mission, an unprecedented adventure in social upheaval.

"We're going to break barriers in every sense of the term—not only because they'll be able to listen to you across the United States of America on the radio and around the whole world on the Internet, but because on top of crossing over into the afterlife, you're also going to be crossing linguistic and cultural barriers that no one's ever been able to penetrate. Can you imagine what this will mean to the Hispanic community?"

I could imagine and nodded my head, but it all seemed abstract to me.

Besides, I wasn't interested in being a pioneer in my field. My life wasn't what you would call chaotic, but I considered it well stocked. The way Foster was talking, this program was going to turn me into the general of a Hispanic broadcast revolution. I told him this.

"You're going to pave the way for your countrymen."

"To be honest, I didn't get into radio to change the world."

"You're gonna be a hero."

I won't deny having ridiculous delusions, but becoming a hero wasn't one of them, and certainly not from a broadcasting booth.

"Dan, it's a little program about ghosts and horror stories; we're not writing declarations of independence here."

"I know, but believe me, it'll be revolutionary anyways."

It didn't make sense to argue; to him, a Mexican hosting a successful radio program was groundbreaking. To me, it didn't seem any more relevant than the fact that there were Mexican actors and directors like Salma Hayek, Guillermo del Toro, and Alejandro González Iñárritu in Hollywood. Apparently, to him, this was not only more important but more subversive.

Next, we talked about money.

I didn't go into radio for the money. What I earned allowed me to live well, but the InterMedia offer was very impressive. We're talking serious cash.

He did say I'd have to go through a "test period," but suggested with their promotional backing I'd pass through that with flying colors. I wasn't so sure.

I originally developed an interest in radio after I accepted that I'd finally reached the inevitable age where I was too old for rock and roll, and too young to die. I played with lots of bands and recorded hundreds of tracks after the dissolution of Deathmuertoz, but I was never satisfied with the results. I had never been able to recapture the kind of sound I'd had with Gabriel. None of what I'd done afterward seemed like it was up to the standards of our music.

And Gabriel wasn't there.

Without him, making music felt like work.

For me, radio was a space for reflection. On the air, I submerged myself in music and literature. I listened along with my audience; I read to myself and to them, I discussed all kinds of ideas with total strangers. It was the perfect medium: intense, warm, interactive, and highly volatile. From my very first session in the broadcast studio, I felt like I was in a time capsule, a sensory-deprivation chamber. It was a protective bubble where nothing and no one could touch me. The semidarkness, the illuminated panel, and the on-air light combined to create a cozy, womblike environment, a sort of cosmic solitude. I had the sensation of floating in space, completely isolated from the real world. My only human contact was with the disembodied voices of callers. Everything seemed dusted with an ethereal—yes, I'll say it—ghostly quality. I could touch and hear the whole world, while no one could be sure of my existence; I was just one more voice in the teeming concert of hertzian waves. It was a land of the blind, where we were guided by sounds and voices, and space took the shape our words gave it. We transformed it with every description, comment, insult, or digression. It was almost like death, floating aimlessly at night, listening to spectral voices that in turn spoke about specters, indifferent to their own condition.

One day, I read a fragment from Edgar Allan Poe on the air: "The Telltale Heart." My audience responded well. The calls poured in. Some, who already knew the story, praised me for "elevating the abysmal level of discourse on that pigsty you call a program."

Others, younger or more ignorant, wanted to know more about Poe. Did he teach at a local university or sign autographs at shopping malls? The surprising thing was that a few, inspired by my reading, started calling in with anecdotes, stories that seemed to them mysterious or inexplicable.

"Hello, my name's Manuel. I work as a security guard at a building downtown that's under construction. I couldn't resist the temptation to call, because I really liked what you read. I already wrote down the author; I'm going to buy the book. But what I really wanted to tell you is something that happened to me.

I'm forty-two years old, and about twenty years ago I worked in construction, you know, as a builder. Anyways, one night I was working overtime with my uncle at a site. I had to push wheelbarrows full of mixed cement up to the third floor on top of some wooden planks. One night my uncle, who got me the job, showed me a bottle of tequila. "How 'bout it, nephew, want some? It'll warm you up!" I said no, it was a bad idea. I could get into trouble or even fall. He said: "Don't worry, just take it easy. We aren't getting drunk, we're getting warm."

Back then I drank. Not anymore.

The last time I had one was about five years ago and I don't intend to fall off the wagon. But back then I thought my uncle might be right. Besides, he was almost as important as the foreman, so I figured nothing would happen. I took a drink and started up with a load. When I got back down, I walked past my uncle again. He told me to take another shot, and I did. By the fifth round, I was real tipsy, singing and talking shit. And then I fell. I fell into the wheelbarrow, rolled a few yards, and then dropped about six feet. I was covered in liquid concrete. Everything hurt; I thought I'd never be able to move again. Then I heard my uncle's booming laugh. His guffaws echoed on the naked walls of the construction site. He finally stopped laughing and came down to see if I was still alive. He wiped the cement off of me and helped me up.

"What a fuckin' idiot you turned out to be, nephew," he said over and over again.

I'd had enough and I was really hurting, so I told him a few times to knock it off, but he'd have none of it. He thought it was the funniest thing in the world, me falling like that. He kept making fun of me as we climbed out, but then he slipped, hit his head, and landed in the same place where I'd fallen. I limped down there to take a look. He wasn't moving. His eyes were open but it looked like he wasn't breathing.

"How 'bout that, motherfucker, who's got the last laugh now!" I shouted at the old bastard.

I was so angry I threw the wheelbarrow down after him. But it wasn't long before I sobered up and realized that this was serious business and I could end up in jail. I brought more cement and poured it over my uncle. By the second full wheelbarrow, though, he started moving. Terrified, I ran for another full wheelbarrow and threw it on him. Then I carefully smoothed it over. By the next morning, the cement was dry and the floor looked pretty good, maybe a little higher than it was supposed to be. Luckily, it was hardly noticeable. When the architect arrived that day he asked me why we'd poured that floor already. I got nervous. I said my uncle had told me that it had to be done so they could put in the stairway. He looked at me curiously, and asked how my uncle was doing.

"I don't know, last night he went home by himself," I answered.

"When you see him, tell him to please come and see me."

"What, the floor isn't good enough?" I asked him.

"It's fine, but I need him to hurry up with the stairs."

No one ever saw my uncle again. Some thought he'd run off with a woman. His wife couldn't understand it, because he'd never been a Don Juan and he always checked in. After some months, she accepted that he'd either gone up north or been killed during a mugging.

I continued working at the site. One night, I woke up tasting blood and tequila. I washed out my mouth several times, but it wouldn't go away; on the contrary, every time I passed the place where my uncle was buried, the taste grew stronger. Sometimes, I thought it was going to choke me; sometimes it even made me throw up. I went to see several doctors, even a healer. No one found anything. I chewed mints all day long. I ate raw onions and garlic, but the tang of blood covered everything. I became

*desperate; I had all my teeth extracted, thinking that would cure
me. Nothing. It pursued me long after we finished that building.
The people living there now would never imagine that they walk
over my uncle every time they climb the stairs. Yesterday, in fact,
I almost went over there to yell to the whole world that my dead
uncle is buried in the cement down below. My nerve failed me.
But when I heard that story just now, I knew it was a sign. Finally, I must confess.*

"Well, thanks for sharing your story on the air, although I don't really know how to handle a case like this. Are you going to turn yourself
in to the police?"

"No. Why should I?"

"You murdered your uncle."

"I didn't murder anybody. He fell by accident."

"Well, you covered him with cement."

"He wasn't dead at the time."

"I know, but the cement killed him. How do I know you're not pulling my leg?"

"That's your problem," said the man. I imagined the taste of tequila
and blood in his mouth as he hung up.

This definitely wasn't the kind of response I'd expected from the public when I decided to read Poe on the air. I never thought it would turn
my audience into "radio witnesses" to a crime.

"But while we're researching that, keep those calls coming," I said.

The calls didn't stop. At first, we only got a few each night, but it
quickly became a deluge. Thousands of people wanted to talk about their
experiences or put in their two cents about the stories of other callers.
Soon I couldn't keep up with all the calls pouring in. This piqued the interest of the radio station; first, they assigned me a permanent sound engineer (up to that point, I'd worked with whoever was on the clock), and
then they started adding assistants to take calls and attend to the growing
needs of the program. Most remarkable of all, I gained the respect of my

colleagues and bosses. My placid oasis of calm, the pitch-black ocean of tranquillity where I had floated aimlessly, became a frenetic anthill of activity. There were still dead hours, and slow days, but *Ghost Radio*, as we started calling the program, consistently registered the best ratings in both its genre and its time slot. Calls flooded in from across the nation and other parts of the world; Latinos residing in the United States bombarded me night after night with their stories, but soon they were also calling in from as far away as Australia and Namibia. My bosses were happy, and so was I. I wouldn't have changed a thing, but change came anyway . . . with a vengeance.

chapter 24

A PECULIAR EXCHANGE

The new show with InterMedia was certainly different from those early days. The office was nicer, the coffee was better, and the paychecks substantially larger. But one thing was the same: the callers. They were the same mix of bizarre, sincere, and ridiculous.

Joaquin liked this mixture. His fears about being in America slowly disappeared. But they would return one night when a peculiar caller lit up line two.

"We're here with a caller who won't give his name," said Joaquin, pushing the button for line two. "Go ahead, anonymous friend, you're on the air."

The silence seemed endless.

Usually in situations like this, Joaquin would jump in, yelling: "Caller, are you there?" If the caller didn't respond instantly, he'd be cut off. This time, though, Joaquin sat quietly. He didn't rush the caller and didn't check to see if the line was still active.

"Dead air!" hissed Watt.

Joaquin didn't respond. Alondra opened her mouth to say something. Joaquin signaled her to wait.

Silence.

The seconds passed.

Tick . . . tick . . . tick . . .

A raspy voice resonated through the speakers.

"Joaquin. I'm glad we can speak to each other again."

"Speak again?"

"We're old friends."

"I usually recognize my friends."

"I saw death."

"Tell us what happened."

"Just what I told you. I saw death. Nothing happened to me; I wasn't pulled from death's grip; I didn't lose my will to live. I simply saw death's face, its poisonous snout squealing a few inches from my own."

"Like *Alien 3*?"

"No, nothing like that."

"The first *Alien* film?" Joaquin said, suppressing a laugh.

"You've seen him too, Joaquin. He remembers you."

Joaquin was intrigued.

"And how do you explain this apparition?" asked Alondra.

"Let's just say at this point I wouldn't consider it to be a solitary apparition, but rather a recurring event."

"So you see death often?" asked Joaquin.

"Often."

Joaquin felt a chill run down his spine. This call was making him very uncomfortable. It wasn't the usual. It demanded attention. He looked at Watt, who had stopped eating and was motionless, staring at the monitor. Like a cat thinking it's heard a mouse.

"I am something special. Unlike anyone you've ever talked to before. I am *Ghost Radio*'s beginning and end, its alpha and omega. I am a transformed and transfigured being, waiting for you in the night."

Joaquin's arms felt numb. He wanted to stretch or maybe stand up, but he could barely move. Out of the corner of his eye, he noticed a change in the shadow that the table cast on the wall. It looked different, as if it were illuminated by another source of light. For a moment it seemed to transform into . . . a tombstone. He blinked, and it was the table again. But now he was aware of the shadows playing tricks with his peripheral vision. Before his eyes, matter transformed into shadow and shadow into matter.

Meanwhile, the anonymous caller continued.

"It's a privilege to be in this position: between life and death . . . heaven and hell."

"Purgatory," said Alondra.

"No, sweetheart, that's a bedtime story for religious freaks. From where I am, I can make phone calls, watch TV, eat junk food."

"Some would say that's the best of both worlds," remarked Alondra.

"And the worst, of course," added the voice.

Joaquin saw a cadaverous face: flesh hanging from bone, muscles exposed. He winced.

"Try to imagine an animal is eating you alive, chewing on your head. You're conscious. You feel its fangs dig into your scalp, feel strips of flesh pulled from your skull. For the past ten years, I've lived with that sensation."

Joaquin was startled. His palms were sweaty. He glanced around, half expecting to find somebody watching him.

"Now, are you interested in listening to me, Joaquin?" asked the caller.

"Completely," he answered. "But I think you're lying."

"Just think what it would feel like to burn in an ocean of fire forever, to be cooked alive for eternity, suffering every instant as if it were the first moment you felt the flames touch your skin, without the slightest possibility of growing accustomed to the pain."

Before the voice had finished speaking, Joaquin saw the shadows in the studio become a window looking out on an infernal landscape, one worthy of a famous illustration by Gustav Doré for the *Divine Comedy* that had given him childhood nightmares. He couldn't understand what was happening. Blinking nervously, he looked around trying to gauge whether he was the only one tormented by these images. A sense of anguish overwhelmed him—he had never seen or felt anything like this. It was true that after his parents' deaths, extremely vivid nightmares had caused him years of sleepless nights. But he had overcome these long ago. One day he decided that he wouldn't be afraid again, that he wouldn't allow it, that instead he would respond coldly to everything. The worst thing that could happen to him already had, and so he unshouldered his emotional burden.

At that moment, however, flanked by his girlfriend, Alondra, and his friend Watt, the old fear returned.

"Did you hear my question?" Joaquin asked, trying to regain his composure.

"What do you think I'm lying about?"

"I don't think you can watch TV, I don't think you can eat junk food, I think you're lucky to even make this call."

The caller was silent. But this time Watt didn't warn Joaquin about dead air. Finally, the caller spoke.

"What do you think of this fairy tale? Once upon a time, there was a young man, barely past childhood, who lived in a perfect world of privilege, a world where his sexual awakening was experienced with the most beautiful girls, where he only needed to wish for something and it would come true, and where everything indicated that his talent and intellect would take him to the top of whatever mountain he chose to climb. Then his universe fell apart; he was left abandoned and alone in a world of shadows and danger, at the mercy of criminals and depraved minds. The young man, no longer a child, was transformed into a swan, saving him from that bleak world."

"A swan, huh? Like in Andersen's story 'The Wild Swans.'" Joaquin recollected it vaguely.

"Exactly."

"Why don't you just cut off this asshole," whispered Alondra in his ear. She was covering the microphone, but it was obvious she would have preferred to scream it out on the air.

Joaquin shook his head.

"For our listeners who don't know it, this is yet another children's tale, so of course it's macabre, sadistic, and sordid. As it should be.

"In this one, the king's eleven impeccable and well-behaved sons were the victims of their evil stepmother's jealousy. She forced the king to expel them from the palace. It was through some strange magic that they were transformed into swans," explained Joaquin.

"That's right, the swan is a symbol of the ethereal state of salvation. What appears to be a horrible punishment is, in fact, redemption.

"At night, the swans once again took on human form. In the end, their only sister made the sacrifice of sewing linen nightshirts for them, woven from nettles taken from a cemetery. When the swans were draped with these nightshirts, the spell was broken and her brothers were set free. I don't care what it is; I find this story sinister, a sad tale of injustice with an absurd moral."

Watt and Alondra were making frantic signals, drawing their index fingers across their necks as if slashing their throats. Alondra slipped him a piece of paper:

"You have to cut him off. Now!"

Joaquin again gestured for them to leave him alone.

"Well, my friend Joaquin, since you're having some sort of rebellion among your staff, I'm going to let you go for now. But before I leave, let me just say this: Joaquin, we'll talk soon. Best wishes."

And then everything fell silent.

Once again, they had dead air.

Joaquin shivered just as he had that night, months earlier, when he received the same message flashed in Morse code by a helicopter. But strangely, he also tripped back to another night. A night of destiny.

chapter 25

A NIGHT AT THE STATION

A massive electrical storm was brewing. The sky turned from gray to mustard yellow, and the smell of ozone filled the air.

Joaquin knew the plan was hasty and premature. But he couldn't turn back. Gabriel wouldn't let him. He didn't even want to, because he'd never seen Gabriel so excited about one of their projects. *Deathmuertoz Live from Radio Mexico* was the makeshift title they'd given the concert, performance, and media intervention. They'd crossed the border like illegal aliens in reverse, from the United States into Mexico, the notion being that the trip itself was part of the show—everything had to be a transgression. They carried a few instruments, and bags filled with the paraphernalia they planned to use during their jam session.

On the Mexican side, three fans awaited them: Colett, Feliciano, and Martin, who had faithfully followed their music over the past year. They originally proposed the concert and offered to help with logistics. Gabriel took Polaroids along way: new pages for his visual diary. Each flash reminded Joaquin of the night before: a raid on a convenience store, sliding packs of Polaroid film into his oversize coat, Gabriel played lookout.

The border crossing was no big deal, other than the intermittent rain. According to the plan, they rendezvoused with Colett, Feliciano, and Martin at a gas station along the highway. The rain had stopped. But the blacktop was slick, and water collected in the potholes.

Martin sat in the driver's seat of an old Volkswagen van. Feliciano paced in front. And Colett leaned seductively on the hood; her dyed black hair still damp from the recent rain. They greeted Joaquin and Gabriel warmly. But Joaquin sensed a reticence in Colett. Behind her smiling eyes lurked a wariness that he found alluring.

A few months ago, Colett and her friends helped set up an illegal feed of an Armenian punk concert broadcast from a jail in Ankara. Martin worked at the university-owned radio station, but its employees had gone on strike two years before, and the conflict was still unresolved. Gabriel and Joaquin had given him the impression that they knew how to operate the station's equipment. In reality, they didn't have a clue.

Martin told them what to expect once they got in.

"The station's operational, but it's been abandoned for some time," he said, showing them a diagram that explained how to broadcast a signal. He gave them some more drawings of electric circuits, pointing out that all of it ought to be ready to go. "You shouldn't have any trouble getting the ball rolling."

He'd originally said he would come along, but there had been a change of plans. It would be better, he said now, if he kept an eye on the guards at the gate and picked the others up when they were done.

Feliciano expressed concern. They hadn't had enough time to prepare. It was going to be risky and complicated to air the concert that night.

"It'd really suck if we didn't do this because we're afraid."

"We've been working the grapevine for two weeks, letting everyone know the jam session's tonight. So it's gonna be tonight," said Gabriel, who was taking Polaroids of everyone. "And besides, nothing seems more perfect than playing on a night like this."

Joaquin didn't say much. He couldn't keep his eyes off Colett. He lost himself in her dark, bitter eyes and juicy lips. She spoke with a strange accent. There was something familiar about her that he couldn't quite place. Although she smiled provocatively at him from time to time, on the whole she seemed somewhat detached.

They decided to go for tacos and wrap up any unfinished business. Over dinner, Gabriel explained that taking over the station would be a great leap forward in their career. They'd burn CDs of the concert and package them with a booklet of all his Polaroids.

"We want stations taken over everywhere: a full-scale rebellion, giving radio back to the people. Away from the corporate suits and their bean-counting Top 40 shit."

Joaquin agreed with the concept, but he was surprised to hear Gabriel trying to talk like a militant. It sounded artificial. He realized that much of it was aimed at Colett. This was flirting, Gabriel style.

After finishing their tacos, Feliciano, Martin, and Colett went over their part of the plan: Feliciano would drive them to the station, where they'd scale the outer fence. Martin would take care of security, and Colett, who knew the station well, would accompany them inside and act as their engineer.

"You know how to use a soundboard and all that?" Joaquin asked her.

"Yeah, I worked at a station in Boston for a summer. I learned a few things," she said as she brushed her hair from her face with the back of her hand.

Joaquin vowed not to leave Mexico until he got to know her more intimately.

"That'll do. It's gonna be perfect," Gabriel said, taking another photo of her.

Yup, Gabriel liked her too. He was certain. If Joaquin wanted to nip in ahead of him, he'd have to act fast.

Near the end of their meal, a drunk approached them, selling flowers.

"For the little lady," he said with a drunken grin.

Gabriel took one, tossing him a dollar; his eyes never left Colett.

"In Aztec society, flowers were an offering reserved for goddesses," Gabriel said, handing her the flower.

Joaquin rolled his eyes.

Colett wasn't impressed. She questioned the accuracy of Gabriel's statement.

"Aztecs offered flowers to their goddesses? I don't think so."

An argument ensued. Gabriel was a good debater, but Colett parried every thrust. She knew her stuff, and Gabriel's bluffs withered.

During this exchange, Joaquin sketched a rose on a napkin. He paid careful attention to the stem; halfway down, it morphed into electric cable, ending in a two-pronged plug.

He offered the finished drawing to Colett.

"In modern society, drawings of flowers are given by broke guys trying to impress superhot girls," Joaquin said, mocking Gabriel's tone.

"That's a fact I can't dispute," Colett said, taking the drawing.

She studied it, furrowing her brow. Joaquin thought it made her even cuter.

"Very cool. Would make a nice tat," she said, offering the highest of Goth compliments.

She folded the napkin and slid it into the back pocket of her alluringly tight jeans. They left the restaurant. Gabriel's rose lay forgotten on the table. Round one to Joaquin.

They split up as planned. There was so much electricity loose in the desert that Joaquin's hair stuck to the van's interior. They got out of the VW. There wasn't anyone guarding the station. Joaquin jumped the fence first. Colett followed, leaping like a dancer: a dancer in combat boots. Gabriel went over last. They heard barking.

"Martin said there weren't any dogs," Joaquin said.

"That's because there aren't any," replied Colett.

"Something's coming this way, and it's barking," Gabriel said.

"Okay, maybe there *are* dogs," Colett said.

As she spoke, two enormous mastiffs leaped out from around a corner, barking and drooling. The group took off running. Joaquin felt an odd sense of joy in this moment. Gabriel sprinting ahead of him, the sound of combat boots on gravel behind him. And the growl of dogs farther back.

This felt like life. Real, immediate, powerful.

Gabriel reached a ladder set in the wall; he grabbed the bottom rung and scampered up. Joaquin let Colett go next, then sped off in the other direction pursued by the dogs.

He ran toward a brick wall at the back of the building, calculating on the fly that he could probably reach the top. When he jumped, though, his backpack shifted, he lost his balance, slipped, and hit his head against the wall. One of dogs pounced on him, biting his head, near the ear, then released him and backed away. Joaquin raised his head, disoriented, in pain and terrified; the mastiff's jaws hovered inches from his nose. A low growl emerged from deep in the beast's throat. Joaquin froze. He tried to think of a way out, but any movement would only provoke the dog further; this time, he was sure his face would be the target. He was completely vulnerable, his life hanging on the instincts and the caprices of an animal.

It's great to be alive, he thought strangely.

Then, looking at the dog, at his slavering jaws and into his cold eyes, he had an idea. It was so absurd it just might work.

"Home," he said in a commanding tone.

The dog cocked its head as if it were listening. Its growls changed frequency.

"Home," he repeated sternly.

It slowly retreated, closed its jaws, and trotted off. Joaquin smiled and stood, the adrenaline mitigating the pain of his wounds. He returned to the ladder, where Colett and Gabriel still clung.

"What happened?"

"The dogs are gone," he said.

Colett jumped down, and gave a start when she saw Joaquin's wounds. She gently caressed his face.

"The dog?"

"He tried to kiss me, and missed."

Colett chuckled, and then shifted gears.

"I don't think we have any choice but to stop now. Just look at the poor guy," she said to Gabriel.

"It's just a scratch; Joaquin's very resilient. One little bite isn't going to hold you back—right?"

"I'm okay. Let's go inside."

"How'd you get rid of those dogs?"

"I have a way with animals," Joaquin said convincingly.

Though, before tonight, he hadn't been aware of it.

"There never used to be any dogs here," Colett said again.

"Maybe the strikers brought them to watch for people breaking in. Like us."

Gabriel opened the door with ease. Picking locks was one of his many talents. All three entered the building. It was a mess: Windows were cracked and broken; puddles of water were everywhere; and documents, books, and folders littered the floor. This place had been abandoned for some time.

"Well, if those were watchdogs, they're a fucking failure," Joaquin said.

"*We* realized how incompetent they were when they let you go with that little scratch on the head," Gabriel remarked.

Colett guided them through the darkness, following Martin's instructions, until they reached the transformer. Gabriel gave the electric cables the once-over to make sure they corresponded to his diagram. Once he'd finished, he snapped a few Polaroids and they headed for the broadcasting booth.

"Martin said we shouldn't turn on any lights on the ground floor."

When they reached the booth, they were greeted by the stench of humidity and rot. The toilets had been torn out, but no one had bothered to shut off the water. The carpet was wet and the walls were covered with mold. Colett nervously flicked on the light switch and the whole room lit up. Gabriel and Joaquin got their instruments out of their backpacks. Everything was wet, but seemed in good working order. They hastily set up a crude altar, composed of a range of bizarre objects.

Joaquin hadn't understood when Gabriel expressed the need for an altar. But now, as it took shape, it seemed essential. As if the whole exercise would be pointless without it.

Joaquin helped Gabriel carefully position the articles they'd brought with them: the flashlights, the old Kwik Kleen bottles filled with suspect liquid, the toy soldiers, old coins, a dollhouse, a strange headdress, a knife, carved wooden symbols, drawings, and other items.

"What are you doing?" Colett asked.

"Can't you tell? We're asking the gods to watch over us."

"Shit, you and your crap ideas about the Aztecs. Fucking thing looks like an Aztec altar, designed by a retard, or a senile old lady."

"Awesome! Exactly what we were going for," Gabriel responded with a laugh.

When Gabriel connected his guitar, he got a shock; a bolt of electricity arced from the instrument to his hand.

"Sonofabitch!" he yelled.

"Tonight, the guitar will become an instrument of torture," Joaquin said.

"We'll feel a little of the dead warriors' pain in our fingers."

"I can assure you it won't just be in our fingers."

"Those warriors would have preferred a few electric shocks to the obsidian knives they used to cut out their hearts," Colett said through the control booth speakers.

"Better to have your heart ripped out than to smell the sewage water flooding this goddamn studio," Joaquin said.

"Actually, the Aztec sewage system—"

"Okay, girl, lose the Aztec history lesson and show us some of your broadcast expertise," Gabriel said, cutting her off.

Colett moved over to the console, powered up, and played with the sliders—mixing the signals from the guitars, tapes, synthesizer, and drum machine.

Watching her, Joaquin was turned on. The way her hands danced across the controls. How she cocked her head when something didn't sound quite right. And the sly grin that snaked across her face when it did.

Everything was ready at around one thirty in the morning. Gabriel took over the mike. On his first word, the amplifiers popped and the lights went out. It didn't take them long to find which fuse they'd blown, but they couldn't find a replacement. Joaquin sat down in the dark, defeated. His head was still bleeding. The dog bite throbbed, and they didn't have anything to clean or cover it. But Gabriel wouldn't give up. He found a thick cable and used it to bypass the fuse. The lights came back on. By 1:49 A.M., they were on the air.

A red light went on in the studio.

"As promised, we are Deathmuertoz, and we're liberating the airwaves of Mexico," Gabriel intoned.

They started playing. They opened with "Voices Gone Unheard," a classic punk challenge filled with rage, mounted on an intense percussion track composed entirely of insect sounds. It was the perfect opener, and it invariably left their audience turned on and hungry for more. Joaquin wasn't satisfied; he thought they sounded flat, and he signaled for Colett to adjust the bass, lower the monitors, and up the reverb. She did so, brushing the hair from her face with the back of the hand.

They continued with "Death Concealed Among the Civilians," a fusion of Afro-Caribbean elements with scratchy, aggressive vocals that gradually formed a counterpoint to synthesized string attacks inspired by Mahler. By then, both Joaquin and Gabriel had entered a trancelike state, playing as if possessed by the spirits of fallen warriors.

chapter 26

EUPHORIA

A group of around a hundred, maybe a hundred and fifty youths had gathered in a small plaza. They had an old Mazda car radio connected to an amplifier. Some had been there since midnight. The locals couldn't figure out what they were waiting for. There were about ten cops anxious to intervene, but with orders not to. It was clear that those attending this mysterious, improvised meeting were consuming alcoholic beverages and a wide variety of drugs. The cops could have started arresting people whenever they wanted.

Suddenly someone jumped up on the roof of the Mazda and yelled:

"They're on, motherfuckers!"

As soon as the first chords were heard, all hell broke loose. An enraged, delirious mosh pit started vibrating to the music exploding from the speakers. It was so powerful that the cops were frozen with dread. They could only stand aside, contemplating the crowd as if they were watching a UFO landing. The mob was like a rhythmic, hungry beast threatening to attack the handful of pedestrians looking on from the streets nearby. Someone threw a bottle. It was followed by several more, then a rock went through a shop window. That was when the cops took action.

The same scene played out in other cities. Some said ten. Others, over a hundred. It would be difficult to know for sure. What's certain is that the energy unleashed in those few minutes of the Deathmuertoz concert via Radio Mexico left an indelible mark. Politicians, activists, parents, and commentators all condemned the delirious outbreaks of violence. But no one who was there that night could deny that they'd remember those minutes of complete euphoria, mayhem, and release for the rest of their lives.

chapter 27

MISCALCULATION

Colett was livid.

"The cops are outside. We've gotta leg it. Now!"

"Sister, this jam is too hot. I ain't going anywhere."

"I'm staying too," Joaquin said. "But you should go. Shove a couple of those cabinets against the door. Then climb out the bathroom window."

Joaquin watched Colett, her eyes wide with fear and confusion.

"Go," he said calmly, as he pounded out another power chord.

Colett moved to the double doors, pushing a couple of cabinets in front of them.

"Enough?" she asked.

Joaquin gestured to a large wooden shelf unit. Colett nodded and pushed it toward the doors. It squeaked and barked on its journey. Joaquin liked the sound. He hoped the mikes were catching it.

Colett tipped the unit over; it smashed against the doors loudly. The mikes certainly picked that up.

Colett shot Joaquin another questioning look. He nodded and watched her run toward the bathroom, its tiny window, and freedom.

Now alone, Joaquin and Gabriel played "Chismes y Deadly Legends," using a collection of noises that sounded like a funeral procession to add texture to the already vertigo-inducing 180-beat-per-minute composition. Their music had never sounded so vital and powerful.

At 2:00 A.M., a surge in the electric system blew out their equipment. Joaquin had already felt several minor shocks that night, but this time his arms, then his back and neck, tensed up till all his muscles were hard as a rock. He saw smoke rise from his flesh, and a burst of flame emerge from his mouth, and then a blow to the abdomen and he was airborne. A moment of floating silence, then . . . WHAM . . . down onto the wet floor, the wind knocked out of him. Slowly, his vision blurred. The world faded, until he was left in darkness.

He heard the mastiffs enter the studio and sniff at him. Then he heard something else . . . distant . . . indistinct. Voices? Music? As he struggled to make it out, he felt his body rising toward the ceiling. He looked down, and saw Gabriel, supine on the floor. The dogs bit at his chest, tore at his face and crotch.

He also saw his own body lying on the floor . . . immobile.

The police burst into the studio. When they saw Joaquin and Gabriel on the ground, they called for paramedics.

Joaquin was strangely calm as he watched the scene below. Suddenly everything around him shifted. The damp station evaporated, replaced by a vast arctic landscape. Joaquin felt the snow crunch under his feet. In the distance, jagged glaciers stretched skyward.

Without knowing why, he began to climb the nearest snowdrift.

He shivered as he trudged forward, each step harder than the last. He'd barely made it twenty yards before he found himself sinking into the snow. First to his ankles, then to his knees, then it almost reached his waist. He pushed on, unsure where he was going, or why he found it imperative to continue. The snow was up to his chest now, and movement had become virtually impossible. He was using all his might to inch his way forward.

A loud crack filled the air, and snow tumbled down on top of him. He felt like hundreds of icy blankets were being hurled on top of him. A suffocating fear gripped him as he struggled to break out.

Suddenly he was free.

The snow beneath him gave way and he felt himself falling. He fell and he fell. And while he fell, he heard Gabriel's voice:

"Why do you always fuck everything up, Joaquin? This isn't your place. You're not meant to be here. You're not meant to see this."

He continued falling, and music replaced Gabriel's voice; a strange booming music that reminded him of pistons and steam engines. It clanked and hissed and pounded and screeched.

Then he hit the ground, hard.

He looked up and saw a paramedic crouched over him, defibrillator paddles in each hand. The paramedic said some calming words that he couldn't make out, and then he lost consciousness.

During the following week, a rumor circulated among their fans: Los Deathmuertoz would never play again.

chapter 28

CALL 3307, TUESDAY, 4:02 A.M.
THE GHOST BRIDE

"My name is Yang, but call me Joe."

"Hi, Yang-Joe. What do you have for *Ghost Radio* today?"

"Well, I know some people."

"And which people would those be?"

"Not, you know, good people. They're people who trade with the dead."

"What do you mean, trade with the dead?"

"I mean that they, um, provide some special needs for some dead people."

"Yang, or Joe, you lost me there. What needs? What are you talking about?"

"See, in western China, in the Shaanxi province, there's a very old custom that says when a young man dies unmarried, he should be buried with a bride, a dead bride. You've heard of it?"

"Now we have," said Joaquin.

"So these people, they provide women . . . um . . . female corpses for ghost weddings."

"Uh-huh."

"When an unmarried woman dies at the same time as an unmarried man, they speak to her family, offer them a small sum, and they bury the bodies together after a ceremony."

"And if there isn't some conveniently dead woman?"

"Then there are other options: They go to villages and buy young women or girls, claiming that they are preparing an arranged marriage."

"And?"

"They kill them."

"That might be a scary story, but it sounds like more of a matter for Human Rights Watch than *Ghost Radio,*" said Alondra.

"Well, here's the thing. A man that I know was in this business. He was doing nicely, providing brides all over the yellow-earth highlands and keeping the tradition alive by any and all means. He would buy a young woman for ten to twelve thousand yuan, that is, around thirteen hundred to two thousand dollars, and sell her dead body for double. Or even better, he and his associates would kidnap prostitutes and girls from other provinces and kill them. When the demand for corpses was low, they would take care of a few young bachelors, and later provide the ghost brides for the poor fellows.

"So, this man called me at home in San Francisco. I needed money, and he offered me lots of it. I accepted, so he flew me to China, my ancestors' homeland, to help him."

"How do you know this guy?"

He's my uncle. Anyways, last summer was busy for us. I mostly took care of the business side; he and his associates would deal with the brides. On one occasion, though, my uncle asked me to go to a remote farm in Inner Mongolia to buy a girl named Li. He explained what I should do, and soon I found myself in a hut making a deal with the girl's father. I told him I would marry his daughter; finally, we reached an agreement. I paid eleven thousand yuan and took her with me. From our first meeting, I'd been noticing a disgusting smell of yak's milk.

As soon as we started the long trip back, she said, "I know what you're going to do with me." I tried to be like my uncle and ignore her, but I felt uncomfortable. When we got home I tied Li up and called my uncle to come take care of her, but he told me he was too busy and ordered me to do it myself. I felt queasy, but I gathered my courage and strangled her. They preferred that method of killing because it didn't damage the body. I put her in a big icebox, and the next day she was buried with her ghost groom. Usually that was the end of the story. That night, though, I heard strange noises coming from the icebox. I grabbed a stick and walked over to it, thinking that a rat or something might have crawled inside. But as soon as I opened it, Li popped up like a jack-in-the-box. I fell back, terrified. Her ghost stood before me and spoke: "I reject my groom; I have already chosen a different one." She approached me. "I choose you." The smell of fermented yak's milk coming from her mouth was unbearable. I stood up and ran from the house screaming, but the aroma stuck to me. It followed me on the buses and trains I took to get to Beijing, and on the plane back to San Francisco. The passenger sitting in the seat next to me asked the stewardess to move him because of the stench. By then, I didn't care what people said, because my body was slowly rotting, my flesh was decomposing, my organs turning to mush. I am only thirty-two, but by the time I arrived in the United States, I looked sixty. I could hardly see and my hands were trembling uncontrollably. Every time I turned my head, I saw Li out of the corner of my eye. I went home, but I was too scared to be alone. I don't know why, but with my remaining money I took a room in a hotel. I turned on all the lights, the TV, and a radio that I bought at a drugstore. I sat on a chair with my back against the wall hoping against hope I would be safe from Li.

But it didn't work. I realized Li was in the bed, lying there stiffly. I was terrified, but I didn't move. All she said was "I will be waiting here for you." I was so exhausted and miserable and hopeless that I just sat there, looking at her, knowing that eventually I would have to join her in a deathly embrace.

"And how did you get away, Joe?"

"I didn't. I'm still in the chair looking at Li. I just wanted to tell someone."

The line went dead.

<< < < *chapter 29* > > >

THE POLICE OPERATION

One night, during an electrical storm out in the deserts of northern Mexico, Joaquin died and came back.

It sounded like something out of a B movie or maybe even a horror bestseller. But the Mexican feds weren't impressed by these apparent wonders. Even though Joaquin was carried out of the radio station unconscious and seriously injured, reeking of burned leather, they still handcuffed his right wrist to the stretcher. Just in case.

Despite the sporadic protests of a doctor or two, they kept him handcuffed either to the bed or the plumbing for most of the time between his arrival in intensive care and his assignment to a private room.

The weekend before, Irineo Pantoja had attended the funerals of two of his officers. He knew he was fighting a losing battle. He had neither the resources nor the guts to go up against the drug cartels that were using his city as a hub to channel their merchandise to U.S. cities. Pantoja had risen to the rank of police chief only through a lack of other candidates. One by one, all the bravest, most competent policemen, the ones least likely to take bribes, had been murdered. Pantoja narrowly escaped several attempts himself. He'd gotten used to saying good-bye to his face in the mirror every morning because he knew he might never see it again.

When, at 1:40 A.M., they informed him that someone had taken over the university radio station, he jumped out of bed. It's a sign, he thought. A patrol car picked him up a few minutes later, and he rushed off to spearhead the operation. The report he was handed said that the people responsible for seizing the station were rock musicians, "probably gringos," who were "just screwing around." That information didn't register. Pantoja had a totally different interpretation: this was a bluff orchestrated by his enemies in order to humiliate him. It wasn't just about breaking and entering. It wasn't a teenage prank. It was evil forces taking over the city.

The police chief saw this as an opportunity, maybe his last, to show the drug lords that they couldn't use the city as their playground. He decided not to wait, not to negotiate. His subordinates were surprised, but no one objected when the order came:

"Shoot to kill; these are extremely dangerous criminals. Have the paramedics ready and waiting,"

No one believed him, but most of the agents went in ready for a fight anyway. Paradoxically, instead of bullets they were met by an explosion, caused by the same short circuit that had electrocuted Gabriel and Joaquin.

Hours later, Pantoja made a statement to the press. He claimed that the survivor, whose name and identity were unknown, was an international hit man; he confirmed that this man had been hired by the Pacific cartel, and that invading the station was part of a conspiracy to take control of the broadcast media. No further explanation was ever provided.

The press didn't question his absurd logic. It was a good story, so they ran with it.

chapter 30

THE RESCUE

When Joaquin opened his eyes in the hospital, he expected Gabriel to appear at any moment, burned, in bad shape, but alive. He imagined Gabriel smiling and tossing off some jokes about "escaping another one." Gabriel was dead, of course. Joaquin knew this. But he couldn't shake the feeling of an impending reunion.

He'd known it from the moment the surge blew him off the ground in the radio station. However, they hadn't *officially* informed him. And he clung to this, hoping against hope that someone would come in to announce that Gabriel wasn't dead after all. He knew it was a pointless fantasy, but it was the only thing that kept him going.

When he'd first come to, he'd discovered he was mute. With his hands bandaged, he couldn't write either. This set off an attack of hysteria, and several orderlies had to hold him down and administer a strong sedative. This confirmed the generalized fear around the hospital that he was a violent killer.

Joaquin didn't know what condition his hands were in, or whether he'd even be able to use them again. He knew it was possible to lose extremities from an electric shock; he'd once heard of someone losing an arm; he imagined the worst. Often, the doctors spoke freely around him, as if he couldn't understand them. One said there was "no doubt his fucking vocal cords are scarred."

Joaquin desperately tried to shout, to scream, but it only irritated his throat, sending him into violent coughing fits while the indifferent doctors horsed around and made obscene jokes, and the two attending nurses howled with laughter. In his confusion, Joaquin found himself joining in their amusement. If he ever got out of there, he thought, Scarred Vocal Cords would be a good name for a band.

One day, Pantoja paid Joaquin a visit. He had spent most of the morning straining against his handcuffs, reopening the abrasions on his wrist in the process. Two officers accompanied Pantoja. They wanted to know what Joaquin's name was, where he lived, and where his accomplices were hiding out. They demanded that he confess.

"Better do it now. The longer you wait, the more it's gonna hurt," one of the cops said with a smile.

Pantoja kept silent, staring at Joaquin. Joaquin wondered what he might be thinking. He couldn't tell. Pantoja's eyes were too blank and cold. They stared past him . . . through him. And he stood stock-still, waiting, as his subordinate continued questioning. Then, finally . . .

"Give me a minute alone with the suspect," Pantoja calmly told the two officers.

After they left, Joaquin noticed a hint of animation entering Pantoja's eyes.

"Who *are* you?" he asked.

Joaquin tried to return the icy stare.

"I asked you a question," Pantoja told him.

Joaquin didn't blink. Two could play this game, he told himself as he tried to inject some hostility into his expression. He knew his eyes didn't match Pantoja's steely weapons, but hoped he could make up for that with a mute passivity.

Pantoja held his gaze for several seconds, then turned and left the room.

Joaquin sighed, reveling in this small victory. But then the crushing strangeness of his situation pressed in on him. Here he was, injured, in pain, and accused of being part of a drug cartel. All he wanted to do was grieve for Gabriel, but circumstances wouldn't let him. He had a new battle to fight. But maybe Gabriel would like it that way. He'd never been one for maudlin displays. This situation would be a new entry in his Polaroid diary. *Joaquin the master criminal*. For a moment this thought made him feel alive again. Gabriel's joking, irreverent soul felt very near.

Joaquin sighed again. This time not with relief or satisfaction, but at the enormity of his emotions.

He wished he had someone to talk to.

But, unlike his last hospital stay, this time Joaquin found no friendliness or complicity among the hospital staff. Most of them avoided him. The nurses who brought him his food didn't say a single word. They left the tray and scurried out as if they feared he hosted some horrible contagion. At times, feigning sleep, he heard them whispering that the cops had said that he was a notorious, sadistic drug trafficker, the kind who cut off people's heads and murdered whole families with hammers and hacksaws. One nurse even worried aloud about a squad of hit men armed with AK-47s storming the hospital, guns blazing, kicking down doors, tossing grenades, and killing doctors in order to free their boss. He even heard rumors that hospital officials had requested security backup from the city, the state, and federal government.

Joaquin wasn't sure what was going to happen, but he knew that the most important thing was to protect his identity. For the time being, they referred to Gabriel as "The Rat," a known local thug, and gloated over his death; they hadn't picked a name for Joaquin yet. However, it was clear they were using him as a scapegoat, and he was in no condition to defend himself. All he could look forward to was a long stay in a high-security prison, unless things changed drastically and the authorities recognized they'd made a mistake.

After two weeks in the hospital, Joaquin was able to walk and talk again. However, he was very careful not to show any sign of his progress. He thought it gave him a small advantage. Of course he was still gravely injured, weak, and fragile, but he was already planning his escape. He'd considered several options; all were equally dangerous, unrealistic, and, lamentably, more inspired by Houdini than by reality. He thought maybe he could disguise himself as a doctor and walk right out the main door, or even rappel out the window using a rope made of knotted sheets.

He tried to keep track of those moments when he wasn't under the intense gaze of the guards, as well as when he wasn't handcuffed or tied down. The time he spent in the bathroom seemed like the best option. Every chance he got, he tested how much they'd let him get away with while he was alone. Unfortunately, it wasn't much. On the contrary, every day there were more and more guards, and lately, elite cops complete with bulletproof vests, helmets, machine guns, their faces hidden by ski masks.

One morning, while eating breakfast, he heard an explosion in the hallway. At first, he thought it must be demolition or remodeling. Then another, louder explosion, sounded closer to his room. Shouts and gunfire followed. And then more explosions.

Through the door, Joaquin heard howls, orders, and cries for help, some of it filtered through the beep and crackle of walkie-talkies. Instinctively, he launched himself from the bed, but the handcuffs stopped him, leaving him dangling off the edge . . . the cuffs cutting into his wrists. As he struggled to pull himself back onto the bed, the sounds of battle moved closer.

They were horrific noises. Primordial animal sounds. Not clean or easy like an action movie, but jumbled and desperate and ugly. They told him two things. One: Outside his room, people were fighting for their lives. And two: They were headed his way.

As he dragged himself back onto the bed, he tried to assess the situation. Who were these people? Why were they fighting? But his mind wouldn't work. The sounds in the hallway pushed away rational thought, replaced it with the desire for survival. He screamed and pulled at his restraints. But it was hopeless. He wasn't Houdini. There was no way out. Finally, he just lay back on the pillow and closed his eyes, resigned to his fate.

For some moments he stayed like that, letting his mind drift away. Then he heard the door smashing open. He turned and lifted his lids slightly, and saw a man with a machine gun head his way.

Joaquin squeezed his eyes shut. He heard the sound of boots moving across the floor toward him, and then a voice saying:

"We've come for you."

He thought he recognized the voice, but he couldn't be sure about anything. He was so terrified that he didn't dare look the stranger in the face. He kept his eyes firmly shut. He heard the jangle of keys in the man's hand, and seconds later was released from his handcuffs.

"Open your eyes, you moron, and get up," the visitor demanded.

Joaquin complied, but wouldn't look directly at his rescuer. A backpack landed at his feet.

"Get dressed."

Confused, and so dizzy that he could barely stand, Joaquin pulled some pants and a shirt from the bag. He immediately recognized them. They were Gabriel's. As he was putting on the shirt, carefully because of the bandages, the door flew open again. Three police officers burst in, pointing their weapons in all directions. Joaquin threw himself on the ground, covering his face with both hands. The cops shouted out confused orders.

"Freeze!"

"Hands in the air!"

"Down on the floor! Now!"

Through his fingers, Joaquin saw each officer cover one flank as they moved step-by-step into the room, fingers on triggers. Then the guns turned on Joaquin.

"Where's the guy who released you?"

Joaquin had no idea where his mysterious rescuer had gone, but he was certain that he couldn't have gone far. Just then, Pantoja came in, accompanied by another agent.

The officers moved aside to let him through. All he said was "Where is he?"

Joaquin raised his head a little, trying to get a look at the chief of police as he drew closer. He felt a kick in the ribs.

"Don't move, asshole!" one of the cops hissed.

That's when Joaquin heard the first shot. Then the officer who'd kicked him collapsed, a jet of blood spurting from his neck. The other cops ran for cover, some of them firing randomly; one accidentally shoved Pantoja in his desperate attempt to find a hiding place. The chief of police fell on his back and, as he tried to get to his feet, took a bullet in the shoulder. The cacophony of bullets and screams was deafening. One officer was shot in the face, another in the leg. Joaquin dragged himself under the bed. From this vantage point, he saw another officer slammed against the wall by a bullet. With a grimace of pain and despair, he slid slowly to the ground, leaving a smear of blood. He twitched a few times and stopped moving. With no one left standing, the shooter reappeared.

"You better get out from under there, or the mice are gonna get you," he said.

But Joaquin was paralyzed. From under the bed, he couldn't see anything but the shooter's legs, heading for Pantoja. The chief of police was gasping for air, pressing down on his wound with one hand, trying to stop the bleeding. Joaquin could clearly see his face; the expression in his eyes changed quickly, from pain, to rage, to terror.

"Yes, Irineo. It won't hurt for very much longer. You knew—you knew from the start how this day would end. This morning, in front of the mirror, you were finally right. Isn't that a bitch, knowing when it's all gonna end?"

Joaquin thought he recognized Gabriel's voice, but he was too scared to trust his senses.

The shooter aimed at Pantoja's forehead and fired one, two, three times. Joaquin couldn't watch. He closed his eyes and waited. Just then a hand grabbed his shoulder.

"We've got to go now," the killer said.

Joaquin's eyes were still squeezed shut. When he opened them, he deliberately looked the other way. This was partly to show his unexpected rescuer that he hadn't seen his face, and therefore couldn't finger him if they caught him again, but it was also because he was frightened to look in the eyes of the man who could inflict so much violence, who sounded like Gabriel. He could never have imagined that this fear, which seemed so irrational at the time, would eventually become such a familiar feeling.

As he walked beside the gunman, Joaquin repeated words to himself like a mantra—"Gabriel didn't kill people, Gabriel wasn't part of a cartel, Gabriel is dead"—as if this way, he could ground his thoughts. The idea of escaping from a hospital with the help of a killer was already shocking enough without adding a heap of metaphysical concerns.

The shooter pulled Joaquin through the hallways. Chaos enveloped them; through the smoke and shouting, sirens could be heard. Joaquin wasn't in any condition to go anywhere, and he felt vertigo, pain, and nausea with each step. His vision tunneled. He was blacking out. He couldn't understand why no one was trying to stop them. Moments later, he felt sunlight.

They were outside, walking on the pavement. His rescuer shoved him into a Chevy Suburban, waiting on the curb with the motor running. He said something to the driver, closed the door, and the vehicle took off. In the rearview mirror, Joaquin watched the shooter's back as he walked tranquilly away. No one followed him.

Exhausted, all he could say was:

"Wake me up when we get there."

He didn't have the slightest idea where they were going.

chapter 31

RETURN TO THE CITY OF PALACES

Joaquin slept for hours. When he awoke, the first thing he saw out the window of the SUV was a sign reading: WELCOME TO MEXICO CITY.

But Mexico City was different than he remembered it. The capital had turned into a gigantic, indescribable monster, an amorphous mass of gray and ocher. The city of Joaquin's childhood had disappeared, buried under a mountain of toxic sludge. He barely believed what he saw. It was like the landscape in a fever dream.

He'd longed to return to the capital after his parents died; he'd dreamed of home, school, the Zocalo, the Zona Rosa district. He had imagined the feelings that would course through his body: feelings of nostalgia or dread or desire. But now, entering the streets of his city, he was just tired and hungry.

The driver handed him a bottle of water. After taking a few gulps, Joaquin considered the driver. He had a clipped moustache, cinnamon-colored skin, and blue eyes; he chain-smoked as he drove.

His cell phone rang several times, and each time he glanced down at it but didn't answer.

Joaquin refused to speak to him. He didn't know what the relationship was between this man and the killer who'd liberated him from the clutches of the police, but he guessed the driver must be a subordinate. Another killer, no doubt, who, for the time being had been relegated to the lesser station of chauffeur.

Joaquin had grown accustomed to silence during his hospital stay. Silence was good, he told himself. Silence was comforting. Silence was his new religion.

Of course, this didn't stop his mind from racing. He couldn't stop the questions: Why had he been rescued? Who were these people? Where was he being taken? There was no point in interrogating the driver; he felt his only advantage lay in the fact that his identity remained a secret. If the drug lords thought he was someone else, he'd be in serious danger when they found out they had the wrong man. He didn't think these particular businessmen would take it lightly if they found out they'd made a mistake. Moreover, a lot of cops, and who knows how many others, had been killed during the rescue, and Joaquin was tortured by the thought that it was all his fault.

Then again, there could be no doubt that whoever had done this possessed a grim determination. After the events in the hospital, he knew that this was no game, knew they must think he was valuable in some way. His only consolation was the fact that he hadn't hurt anyone, and that in a way he was just another victim of these monstrous crimes.

Joaquin looked out the window of the SUV at this city of scars, of sad expressionless buildings. Where was the famed City of Palaces, the flower-filled capital of gardens and majestic structures? Maybe the Mexico City of his memories had never really existed: a childhood fantasy that had accreted over the years, finally achieving mythic proportions. This disappointed him, devastated him even. But given his current condition, there were more important things to worry about.

Just as he'd spent every moment in the hospital trying to devise a way to escape, now he considered the question of how he could jump out of the moving vehicle—or should he wait until they reached a street with heavy traffic, get out at a light, and lose himself in the throng? He wondered if the driver would fire into a crowd. Then he remembered the hospital, and his doubts evaporated. These people were capable of anything.

They drove past avenues that looked familiar. Gradually, in spite of the traffic, the atrocious pollution, the kids who cleaned off windshields at the street corners, he began to feel like he was back in his city. As they approached the downtown area, the Alameda, the Palace of Fine Arts, the Mining Palace, and all the other postcard attractions, the wounded megalopolis recovered its mystique and charm. Joaquin felt a wave of optimism. Nothing bad could happen to him there; not even a cartel of drug lords and murderers could harm him in these streets. This was his city. Here he could be a king. These thoughts encouraged him and helped him keep his cool even as the SUV started winding through the narrow streets near Garibaldi Plaza.

Suddenly the driver stopped the car. He turned off the motor and lit another cigarette.

"We're here."

Joaquin looked at him, trying not to give himself away. He nodded his head as if he knew what the man was talking about.

"You're going to go to that hotel over there. Lie low for a few days, maybe weeks. Don't call any attention to yourself. It's most likely that in a little while, they'll stop looking for you. After all, you're lucky: they don't know anything about you."

"That's it?" Joaquin finally asked, unable to restrain himself from speaking any longer.

"Don't worry," the driver said through a cloud of cigarette smoke. "Someone's watching your back."

Joaquin wanted to ask what he meant, but he had already started up the SUV's motor. His stare made Joaquin understand that he didn't have any more time for him.

"They're expecting you at the hotel."

Joaquin got out, knowing that he could go wherever he wanted now. He weighed his options. As he moved away from the vehicle, he thought about looking up the house of some friend or relative, but no one came to mind, so he walked toward the hotel. The driver yelled a few parting words:

"He'll be in touch when the time is right."

He closed the windows and took off.

Joaquin went in and found the front desk of the hotel. An old man gave him a key.

"Room 303. They told me you needed some rest."

"Yes, I've got to lie down. But first I'd like some food," he said. Then he remembered he had no money.

As if he could read minds, the man handed him a fat envelope. "They left this for you," he said.

Joaquin opened it discreetly and saw a bundle of crisp pesos secured with a fat rubber band. There was also a note. It read:

Take it. You'll pay me back later.

No signature. But he couldn't shake the nagging, inexplicable feeling that Gabriel somehow had something to do with all this. Now, though, he was tired and hungry. Without wasting another thought on it, he put the money in his pocket, took the key, and headed for the restaurant.

chapter 32

QUANTUM FLUX

"Reality isn't my friend."

"What a great way to begin a call," said Joaquin, chuckling.

"Perhaps . . . but it's not a great way to live a life," the caller said, a note of controlled desperation in his voice.

Joaquin recognized the tone.

"That was a laugh of commiseration. Reality isn't my friend either," he said, hoping to relax the caller.

"I can't seem to get a handle on it. Most of the time I just accept that I'm crazy, dreaming of the day the insanity takes over, obliterating everything."

"What exactly is happening?"

"It began with my furniture. Each day I'd wake up to find it had changed. One day I have a leather sofa. The next day it's some ratty cloth job from the Goodwill. The tables, chairs, pictures on the walls, everything would change. One day I had no furniture at all: just a mattress on the floor of my bedroom and a few old lamps in some of the other rooms. And no matter what furniture I found in the morning, it always looked familiar. I could remember its history. A friend helping me pick it out. Or lugging it up the stairs. Or whatever."

Joaquin liked the caller's voice: a cool baritone. Perfect for radio. He wished more callers had good radio voices.

"But I also remember the old furniture. Even right now I have more than six hundred distinct memories of decorating this apartment, all memories from the same week: the week I moved in."

"And then what happened?"

"It began spreading to other areas of my life. First with friends, I'd wake and have a completely different circle of friends. And sometimes friends that were dead one day would be alive the next. Some days I was married, some single. Some days I was even gay. And all of these facts were tied to distinct memories . . . to lives I'd clearly lived . . . but hadn't. Then it was everything: jobs, family, even the city I called home. Everything changed. Everything. Every day I woke to an entirely different life, and went to sleep knowing I'd find a new one in the morning. One day last week I was on Death Row."

A man who lived in a state of pure quantum flux. Joaquin had never encountered a person like this. He'd never had a call like this. It always made him happy when he found a treat for his listeners. Even if this guy was lying, it was still a great story. It was also great radio.

"In the last few days, it has gotten worse. It used to be that one reality would maintain itself through an entire day. That was a small comfort. But a few days ago, that changed. Now the shifts occur suddenly. I barely know from minute to minute who I am, where I am. And yet part of me knows it all."

Joaquin sighed. This was getting tedious.

"Jack, we like your story. But you can't keep calling and telling it. You've already called three times this month with the same story."

"I know. I'm sorry. But when I began this call, I'd never called before; I'd never even listened to *Ghost Radio* before tonight."

"That's a nice spin. But it's not going to fly. Call back when something new happens, Jack."

"I didn't even give my name."

The line went dead.

Joaquin took a pull off his coffee and smiled. He liked Sam's calls and his weekly reports about his shifting reality. Joaquin hoped he would call again. *Ghost Radio* needed more callers like Bert. He hoped the next time Tim called he'd put his wife, Phyllis, on the line. Sarah made for good radio too. He hoped she'd never call again.

chapter 33

MISS WIKIPEDIA AND
THE URBAN LEGENDS

There were nights when, no matter how insistent the calls, how heated the debates, and how tearful the confessions, I had a tough time maintaining my focus on my callers' voices. I drifted, losing my concentration. My mind wandered, filling with thoughts unrelated to the show: thoughts of women I'd slept with, great meals I'd eaten, and cool summer evenings on the beaches of Chiapas. What kind of life was it, to grow old in some decrepit broadcasting booth? To become a radio institution, or, more likely, one more disgusting old goat who stays on the air until he's dead? When this happened, I drank dozens of cups of coffee, splashed water on my face; all the tricks one uses to stay alert. But nothing worked.

Well, that's not true. One thing always worked: a great call. A call that electrified the entire studio. That night I felt a bit dizzy; I thought maybe I was coming down with a cold.

A call came in. Not great. Not electrifying.

He told a story about a "friend of a friend" who'd met a gorgeous blonde, taken her to a club, and after a few hours of passion toasted her with champagne in which she'd dissolved some kind of narcotic. The next morning—

"He woke up in pain with a strange scar on his side. Right?" I said, cutting him off.

"No way. Yeah."

"Because they'd removed one of his kidneys to sell on the black market," I continued impatiently.

"Yeah."

"That's what we call an 'urban legend,' a story passed down orally through the naive complicity of people who believe the phrase 'it happened to the friend of a friend of mine,'" I said, emphasizing the last few words.

"No, it's true. It really happened to my friend's friend."

"Anything can happen to that mysterious friend of a friend, because it always happens far away from us and there's never any way of proving it. It's the folklore of our era, the constant reappropriation of grotesque anecdotes."

"No, I'm telling you, it really happened. You don't believe me?"

"What I can't believe is that there's still someone out there who believes this crap. I've heard this one before, with a couple of variations. In one, the gorgeous woman writes a message to the friend of a friend on the hotel mirror that reads 'Welcome to the world of AIDS' or something along those lines. In others, like the one about your friend's friend, it's all about organ trafficking. If one percent of these stories were true, this blonde of yours would not only be an active threat but an authentic serial offender. So, I guess I have no choice but to warn our listeners to never, *never* trust a gorgeous blonde who is ready to hop in the sack with you. Fortunately, in the real world, at least the one I live in, the danger of that happening is extremely low."

"You're making fun of me."

"Yes," I said.

"Jeez."

"I'd make fun of anyone who believes this crap. Because if you buy those stories, I can't imagine the other kinds of bullshit your friend and your friend's friend are gonna make you swallow. And people like me might suffer the blowback. People who aren't total morons."

"To some extent, these stories have a lot in common with jokes," Alondra interjected, trying to lighten the mood. "They're passed around and we can repeat what we've heard without necessarily having to cite our sources. The objective is to trigger a reaction. In both cases, there's often a moral, a twist; in jokes, obviously, it's comical, and in urban legends, horrific."

But Alondra's interruption did not change my mood. I entered what she called the "Annoying Spiral": an intensifying state of fury, in which the whole planet conspires against Joaquin to drive him up the wall. Or so I think.

"Bullshit, bullshit. It's for real, it really happened. And Miss Wikipedia can just keep out of this," the caller said.

"Miss Wikipedia?" Alondra repeated in a low voice, her finger on the "cough button."

"I'm sorry to inform you that you've been conned. In fact, now that you mention it, it might not be a bad idea for you to consult Wikipedia before calling. And by the way, my colleague Alondra has a Ph.D. in urban folklore."

Alondra grimaced. She didn't like to be defended when she could do it herself, nor did she like her credentials to be flaunted as if they were medals.

"Goddamn stupid broad!" the caller exclaimed.

"In other words, in addition to suffering from a pitiful, childlike gullibility, you also hate women. Tell us how it all began," I said. "Your mommy didn't nurse you?"

"You're a major asshole. Go and get yourself—" *Bleep.* Watt cut off the caller's last words.

I engaged in conversations like this every night, sometimes several times a night. Usually I'd just let it go, but other times I'd take it personally, as if the caller had picked a fight directly with me and not with my disembodied voice. I wanted to hit, to punch, to kick. I wanted to take something beautiful and make it ugly.

This was how I felt when a call came through on line two.

"Joaquin, I want to tell you about something that happened to me.

My wife and I had our first child, Edward, a year ago. When he was eleven months old, we decided to have him sleep alone in his own bedroom. It's a transition that's difficult for all parents; it took us several tries until we were able to stand hearing him cry without rushing in right away to pick him up. At night we'd turn on the baby monitor and we'd listen to him babble, call out to us, and, eventually, fall asleep. One night, I woke up to what sounded like an adult voice on the monitor. I thought my wife had gone in to check on the baby, but there she was, sleeping beside me, and the voice I'd heard didn't sound like hers. I thought I might have dreamed it, but I went into my son's room anyway. Edward wasn't asleep. He was awake, on his knees, grabbing on to one side of his crib. I was a little scared when I saw him wide-awake and motionless like that. Usually when he opened his eyes it wouldn't be three seconds before he'd start crying or calling out to us. This time was very different. He seemed calm, like he hardly even realized I was there. The episode surprised me, but so many other things surprised and worried me every day: whether he ate or not; whether he walked or crawled; whether he repeated words or played with his toys in a safe way. I brushed the strange voice aside as a single memory among countless others. Until I heard it again.

I was awake this time and heard it very clearly: like a strange gibberish, forming unrecognizable words. I don't know what language it was, but I can't forget the rasping, inhuman quality it had. I was immobilized for a few seconds, unable to stand up or even speak. I ran to my son's room. Before I'd even looked at the crib, I knew something terrible had happened. Then I saw a sort of shadow thing scurrying into the corner. And Edward wasn't there. I starting screaming, calling for help, completely out of my mind. My wife ran in, and without even knowing what was going on, she started screaming too. We haven't stopped looking, we haven't given up. But I know that what I heard was the voice of whoever or whatever took Edward away.

None of us spoke for several seconds. Several long seconds. Any of us could have said this was another urban legend, one more tall tale passed on along "biological vectors" by people who circulated it, enriched it, added credibility by including emotions and an element of spontaneity. But no one said so, because we knew this wasn't the case.

I offered clumsy words of compassion for the caller's loss. The caller had already hung up.

The tone of the show changed at that moment. It became darker, more serious, and remained that way for the rest of the night. It felt like a funeral parlor rather than a radio station. The link between the inhuman voice and the child's disappearance was tenuous, unbelievable, and barely justifiable, and yet, it seemed unquestionable.

It felt true.

chapter 34

CALL 2412, FRIDAY, 2:15 A.M.
ICY CLIFF

"I want to tell you about something that happened to me last year. It's not a ghost story, strictly speaking. Then again, maybe it is."

"Sounds like fun. Lay it on us," said Joaquin.

A long sigh came over the speakers, then the caller spoke:

I've sailed the seas my whole life. I learned the trade when I was a boy, from my father, as he'd learned from his father. We lived in the icy waters of the North Pole, and from the time I turned sixteen it was my responsibility to steer shipments between enormous icebergs and floes. Nothing thrilled me more; I came to know the most treacherous routes of the Arctic by heart. I was one of the few sailors who'd venture out in small boats, without the considerable advantages provided by satellites and GPS navigation. After the Soviet Union disintegrated in 1990, new markets opened up and a lot of unprecedented trade opportunities emerged for those of us who knew these waters. I stopped working for other people, and I was able to buy one vessel, then another. I couldn't believe my good fortune. Although it wasn't just luck, it was due to my fearlessness toward the ice and the fact that I'd take routes few others dared to attempt. Everyone in the business considered me an expert in navigating the narrow labyrinth of channels that forms between the arctic floes. But even though I impressed colleagues and clients alike with my dexterity and skill, I could never convince my wife that I knew what I was doing. She tried everything in her power to get me to follow the example of my competitors. She didn't seem to realize that by doing so, I'd lose my clients and the privileges we enjoyed. She also didn't understand that, more than any economic incentives, what really motivated me was the excitement of competing against the ice, creating new passages where no one else dared to go, feeling the ship escape the frozen jaws of the icebergs time and time again. Determined to convince her that there was no real danger and also partly, I admit, because I wanted to impress her, I took her along on a voyage. She'd never sailed those waters or set foot in an arctic seaport, and was terrified; I had to resort to every sort of pressure, deception, and blackmail you could imagine to get her on board. Before long, I was showing her how I could knock a day off the trip by traversing a passage between the floes so narrow it looked like a piece of string. The sound of ice rubbing against the ship's hull always gave me pleasure, but naturally, it filled her with fear. My crew knew me and trusted me, even though they all understood the constant danger of becoming trapped in the ice.

Joaquin sank down into his chair and covered his face with his hands, listening to the call with his eyes closed. Suddenly he felt a deep shiver rock his body. He realized instantly what was happening; it wasn't the first time he'd found himself in this situation. He slowly, apprehensively, opened his eyes to find himself on the deck of a ship. The broadcasting studio, Alondra, Watt, the radio station, the building, the city had all disappeared. Next to him, the captain looked around, visibly concerned. It was cold. Joaquin couldn't move, couldn't control his body in any way. He breathed deeply, trying to remain calm. The narrator stood only a few steps away. But he looked right through Joaquin. I'm a ghost in this world, Joaquin thought, finding an eerie pleasure in the notion.

Our second night out of port, we found a sinuous corridor that seemed safe to me. I estimated it would remain navigable for at least a couple more hours, more than enough time to run the gaunt-

let and save myself the trouble of a long detour. When we advanced into the passage, though, the ice started shifting much more quickly than I'd expected. I evaluated our options and decided our best shot would be to press on, full steam ahead. My wife was asleep. The ship struggled for a while, and then suddenly halted. Everyone ran around on deck. I knew all too well what would happen next, but I couldn't bring myself to accept it. I pushed the engine hard. It rumbled and screamed. We didn't budge. But the ice did, pushing in on us from all sides.

Joaquin watched the narrator come up on deck, seeing and hearing the ice that surrounded them on all sides. The narrow corridor of water had disappeared. The ice pressed up against the sides of the ship, which groaned under the strain.

I ran down to find my wife. I longed to believe that the ice would stop moving, would open up again, but I knew it wasn't going to. People were shouting everywhere. When I reached the cabin, she was sitting on the bed frozen with panic. I wanted to calm her down, to reassure her, but I could only gaze at her helplessly. Things were happening much faster than I could have imagined. The ship started to cave. I tried to run to my wife, to grab on to her, but I wasn't able to. The cabin had suddenly split in two; the geometry of the space changed in an instant. It turned from a rough cube to a parallelogram broken down the middle. The bed rapidly sank into the crack, disappearing under the water. The staircase on which I stood pushed upward, until my legs lodged between the timbers. I heard the hull crumpling around me. The sound was like a scream and gave the impression that a gigantic sea monster was slowly devouring us all. The beast screamed again, the timbers shifted and broke, pushing me upward. Then I felt something . . . something like giant fingers wrapping around my body.

Floorboards exploded around Joaquin, showering him with tiny splinters. He heard the rumble of other explosions belowdeck, it vibrated under his feet. Some crew members leaped over the railings, jumping out onto the ice. They knew the danger. They would not last more than a minute if they fell into the icy sea.

Another explosion rocked the ship. It knocked Joaquin off his feet. Jumping up, he rushed to the railing. The captain lay on the ice, his feet splayed out awkwardly beneath him. And moving away from the captain was the shadow of something . . . something like arms. The ship pitched, sending Joaquin over the railing. He tumbled through the air, and landed on the ice next to the captain. Joaquin rolled on the frozen surface and remained motionless, looking up at the starry sky.

> *I saw these long skinny arms coming out from the water, I know it sounds ridiculous, but they grabbed me and threw me to the ice. This thing saved me, although I didn't want to be saved. The fact I didn't go down with my ship that night, that I spent two days unconscious on an iceberg, seems to me like a kind of cruel punishment. A Norwegian icebreaker rescued me; they never found my wife. My crewmen all lost their lives, even those who survived the shipwreck and were scattered on the ice. They say I'll walk again someday. I hope I can, so I'll be able to walk all the way back to the Arctic. But even if I can't, I'll drag myself into the sea first chance I get, to pay off my debt from that night.*

At the sound of the caller's closing words, Joaquin's out-of-body experience came to an end. In the blink of an eye, the arctic night gave way to the soft lights of the broadcasting studio. After announcing his plan to take his own life, the narrator fell silent. Watt and Alondra looked at Joaquin expectantly. But Joaquin couldn't speak, could barely move his hands; he would have had trouble shooing away a fly.

Finally, he spoke.

"What a devastating story. But the fact that you survived is a privilege, an opportunity to start over again, not a punishment. Even when all is lost, you can never give up."

He didn't believe a single word he was saying. In fact, he thought the caller was right, but he knew he couldn't say something like that on the air. Anyways, the caller probably knew he was lying; the whole world probably knew.

He felt numb, as if he really had been exposed to the subzero temperatures of the North Pole, and he was shivering—discreetly, but uncontrollably. The caller said he didn't want to die without telling his story first. He said the only thing that mattered was that someone else hear it, so his story wouldn't disappear along with his wife and his ship. The caller hung up. Watt went to a commercial.

Still Joaquin couldn't stop shivering.

"What's wrong with you?" Alondra asked.

"I was out there, on the ice. It's happening again."

"You've got to see a doctor."

chapter 35

GHOST RADIO GENESIS

It's late and I don't know what I'm doing. These waking dreams are beginning to unhinge me. But tonight, rather than dwelling on my confused emotional state, I find myself thinking back to the events that led to the creation of *Ghost Radio*.

It began during a strange period in my life. Although years had passed since Gabriel's death, the pall of that event still hung over me, lending a darkness to even the brightest days.

I was living in the Mixcoac neighborhood of Mexico City and working a variety of radio jobs, ranging from gigs as fill-in producer or guest announcer to grabbing the occasional disc-jockey or talk-show slot. I felt directionless. I wandered through the murky bars of Mexico City, daring the world to attack me. I inhaled the darkness and all that came with it.

I drank every night, trying to erase my memories of Gabriel, our musical ambitions, and the events that brought me here. Numb and alone, my days blurred together. But my warrior instinct pushed me onward. It pushed me toward my destiny.

I had just left an after-hours club, and was stumbling down the street in search of another, when a limousine pulled up beside me. A man leaned out the window and called to me in a vaguely familiar voice. I couldn't make out the face. The man urged me to get into the limousine. I mumbled something about wanting more alcohol and lurched off down the street. The limo's doors opened behind me, and before I knew it, strong arms grabbed me in a viselike grip and dragged me toward the vehicle.

I found myself in the back of the limousine. The man introduced himself as "The Rat," but something about him reminded me of Gabriel.

I cannot remember what happened during the rest of the night. I have murky recollections of bars and women and pain. I remember singing and playing an instrument. I remember the Rat's voice, talking, encouraging me.

"Your life is about to become real. The past is a prologue. Prepare for the future, my friend."

It seemed as though he repeated this over and over again. But maybe he only said it once. I can't be sure.

I awoke the next morning, at home in my own bed with a dull pain in my arm. I looked down and saw a bandage. I ripped it away and was shocked to find a strange tattoo. A collection of letters arranged in an odd pattern:

<pre>
            E
            N
            I
      T N U J A A
            B
            N
</pre>

Shortly after that night I was offered a regular gig as a DJ on a local radio station. On my first night, I received a telegram that read:

JOAQUIN,
    CONGRATULATIONS ON THE NEW JOB. THE PAST IS A
PROLOGUE.

                                          —THE RAT

Several months later, I took my first call about a ghost.

chapter 36

WHY WATT?

Before he met Alondra, Joaquin had dated Elena, a beautiful, aspiring TV personality and former tennis pro. They met at the radio station, during a promotional tour. The moment Joaquin saw her, he knew he had to meet her. The pair didn't have much in common, but whenever they were together they enjoyed themselves a lot—especially indoors.

Elena was athletic and extraordinarily sensual, but she possessed a superficial streak a mile wide. Sustaining a conversation with her was a drain on Joaquin's patience, and he always found himself suppressing exasperation. In short, things worked out marvelously for both of them as long as the relationship stayed between the sheets.

One night, she called him, terrified. She said a strange man had been harassing her, was pointing a rifle or some other kind of long-barreled weapon at her. It was Sunday, which meant Joaquin didn't have to go to work. Sunday night was one of the few times during the week he could get a good night's sleep and was, therefore, a time he relished. He didn't feel much like running off to rescue Elena, or anyone else, unless it was an authentic emergency. In this case, he had a hunch it was a false alarm, a panic attack brought on by Elena's vanity.

Despite the fact that she appeared only occasionally, stammering through the weather reports on an afternoon news program, and doing comedic banter on a morning show, she imagined she had an army of fans who devoted their days and nights to stalking her. She thought that whenever she showed up at a busy restaurant and removed the enormous sunglasses she wore in public, it was enough to make the maître d' scurry off to prepare a special table for her. In reality, more often than not, he gave her the once-over and put her name at the end of the waiting list.

This wasn't the first time Elena had called Joaquin for something like this; in fact, it was the fifth. She'd even done it a few times when he was on the air. Although the police had also responded to her calls on several occasions, they had never found the alleged stalker.

He wanted to tell her to go to hell, then roll over and fall back asleep. Each time he calmed her down and got her off the phone, she'd call right back. After the fourth call, he had no choice but to go to her. He dragged himself out of bed, climbed into his car, and drove to her house. After spending several hours searching the neighborhood, in vain, for a threatening stranger carrying a weapon with a telescopic sight, he had nothing to show for it but a bad mood and a stiff neck. He was tired and ready to tell Elena he was sick of dealing with her neuroses. But the moment he entered her apartment, she jumped up and wrapped herself around him. Her body was warm, as if she were running a fever. Joaquin wanted to push her away, but before he could, he felt her pelvis rubbing against him. He tried to tear himself away, but he couldn't. Her sensuality overwhelmed him. He spent the rest of the night with her. It was fair compensation; he'd gotten out of bed for much less. But even though the sex was great, Joaquin told himself that he wasn't falling for the imaginary stalker story again.

Around four in the morning, he woke up thirsty. As he was going for a glass of water, he heard a strange noise. When he looked out the window, he saw a man clinging to one of the trees outside, barely concealed behind the sparse foliage, and holding some sort of recording device.

"Son of a bitch! What the fuck are you doing there?" Joaquin yelled.

The guy in the tree was apparently half asleep. When he heard Joaquin he lost his balance, slipped, and was left dangling about three yards from the ground, his recorder hanging from one shoulder.

"I'm gonna kill you, motherfucker!" Joaquin howled, running to look for his pants so he could give chase.

When he came out of the house, the guy was still hanging there.

Joaquin jumped up and grabbed his legs; the stranger fell on top of him. As Joaquin lay there, barefoot and dazed, the man started to run off, but Joaquin tackled him. Once he was down, he didn't put up a fight.

"Don't hurt me, I only recorded the audio," he said.

"You've got to be kidding. I'm gonna have you arrested, you perverted bastard! You should be grateful I didn't plug you while you were in the tree, and that I'm not whupping your ass right now."

Out of breath, Joaquin sat down beside the man, whose recorder still hung from his shoulder. Joaquin guessed from his behavior that he wasn't the violent type.

"I know this looks bad, but really it's not. I'm just collecting sounds."

"Collecting sounds?" Joaquin was truly surprised.

"I record people's sounds, their movements and activities."

"Secretly?"

"It's gotta be in secret. I want the true sounds."

Of course, this immediately struck a chord with Joaquin. A great deal of what he and Gabriel had done was just that: collecting "found" noises, often in a clandestine way. While they'd dedicated most of their research to nature, insects, birds, and animals, they recorded people, machines, and street sounds as well. They had also gotten into trouble for it.

They would compile and classify their finds, then polish, edit, and rework the best clips in order to sample them. Over the years they accumulated quite an impressive collection. This sound library was a source of pride and gave a unique quality to the music they played.

Joaquin couldn't maintain his fury; he was much more interested in the stalker's project than in putting him behind bars. This was too much of a coincidence; it verged on conspiracy or witchcraft. How was it possible that in Mexico City, with a population of over twenty million, and thousands of criminals of all shapes and sizes, he ended up dealing with an audio fiend just like he and Gabriel had been? What were the odds of something like that—one in ten thousand? One in a hundred thousand? It was *beyond* improbable. He thought of all the other coincidences in his life. Sometimes he almost believed that there was a kind of "unseen hand" behind it all, his fate manipulated by someone or something with an unknown purpose. Joaquin wasn't religious. But he couldn't deny that often his life seemed ruled by strange laws. Order in the chaos. Sense in the senselessness. Destiny.

Without asking permission, Joaquin grabbed his captive's backpack and started going through its contents.

"Be my guest, make yourself right at home," the stalker told him.

"I want to see what you've got—what your tools of the trade are."

He had several recorders and microphones, one of them with the formidable telescoping boom that Elena had seen, as well as high-quality earphones and a notebook.

"May I?" Joaquin asked, brandishing the notebook with a grimace.

"Go right ahead."

Joaquin leafed through pages of notes and comments. It was a field notebook with details of the recordings: descriptions of every situation, individual, and time of day. The notes were accompanied by diagrams of locations and various technical annotations. His handwriting was uniform, with firm, decisive strokes. Somehow, this inspired trust in Joaquin, who couldn't imagine that someone who wrote so stolidly would do him any harm.

"Are you aware of how risky this is?" he asked.

"It's worth it."

"How do you choose your subjects? How do you decide who to record?"

"I observe people until I see something that resonates. It might be how they walk, eat, talk, laugh, anything. I can't explain it. I have very flexible criteria."

"But you're harassing my girl, and that's gotta stop."

"I didn't want to bother anyone—I'm just taking her sounds. She doesn't need them, and it won't bother her if I keep them."

Joaquin wanted to explain that he understood, that what he really felt like doing was asking to hear his collection. However, he remained firm.

"If I hand you over to the cops, you'll probably spend the night in jail.

They'll confiscate your sounds and your equipment. They might even prohibit you from going anywhere near a recorder for the rest of your life."

"I'll stay away from your girlfriend. I'm not interested in her, I swear."

"If she finds out about this, it'll be even worse for you. Up till now, she's been convinced that you're an out-of-control fan, one of her countless admirers who lose sleep over the idea of catching a glimpse of her in a camisole. And, believe me, you're better off if she thinks that, because if you add a sprinkle of disappointment to this mess, she won't rest until you're punished."

"I'm real sorry," the guy said.

"Sorry isn't good enough. What do you use these recordings for?"

"To create soundscapes."

"Music?"

"I wouldn't call it that. I'm interested in building landscapes using different layers of audio. I try to create minimalist, abstract textures where the protagonists weave narratives with their movements, voices, and noises."

"I'm not sure I get it."

"It's really basic. Think of them as movies that you can't see."

"Have you done many of them?"

"No, just a few. It takes months of hard work, assembling sounds, finding narratives, setting up counterpoint. . . . Anyways, it takes a long time. But I do have a couple of things ready to go."

"Ready to go where?"

"Anywhere someone besides me can hear them."

"Let me guess: You don't have many friends, do you?"

"I got some."

"Sure you do," Joaquin responded with open sarcasm. "Would you be willing to show me your work?"

"Of course I would. Now?"

"No, not right now. Crafting soundscapes . . . can you make a living with it?"

"Of course not. I've got a day job as a customer-service executive with an international marketing corporation."

"And what do you do there?"

"Basically, I talk to potential clients on the telephone twelve hours a day, from a room that holds another thirty-nine customer-service executives just like me. I call people at all hours, but the company asks us to try to do it at particularly inopportune moments. It makes it easier to sell them objects and services that they never thought they'd want or need."

"Telemarketing?"

"Precisely."

"Lady stalker, telephone predator. You wouldn't happen to be a serial killer or cannibal too, by any chance?"

"Well, I haven't killed anyone, and I can't say my hunger has ever reached those extremes."

"I think I see a pattern here. Your thing is to take stuff away from people who you can hear, but never really see."

"Yeah, I guess you're right. I never thought of it that way. But you gotta understand, my work in the marketing company isn't something I do for pleasure. It pays the bills."

"Sure it does—but even so, it's probably not worth it."

"You can get used to anything, even making an old lady with Parkinson's or Alzheimer's invest her life savings in shares of a pharmaceutical company the night before it tanks."

"You used to do that?"

"I didn't say that."

"So you didn't?"

"I never said that either."

"You're a professional crook."

"Everything I do is legal. Not especially ethical, or nice, but legal. That is to say, strictly speaking, I don't break the law; I just create the conditions necessary for my bosses to abuse the trust of naive and defenseless people."

"Disgusting. Forget all that and come work for me."

"How? You want me to steal for you?"

"I need a sound engineer for my program."

"Program?"

Joaquin told him about *Ghost Radio*. He listened with interest.

"I've never done radio."

"Even better. We can start from scratch."

"But what about jail and your girlfriend?"

"Never mind that. Quit working for those con men, come with me, and all is forgiven. Although I am going to have to think up a good excuse for Elena."

"Tell her I got away."

"Or that I killed you, cut you into little pieces, and threw you into the sewer." That would get me more hours of grateful sex.

"Whatever."

"Nope, I'm gonna have to tell her the truth. Which means I'll probably be left without a girlfriend. So I hope what I'm doing for you is worth it. Here." Joaquin gave him one of the business cards the station had had printed up for him. "Show up on Monday at eight P.M., we'll talk then."

"You know, if you want some memories of her, I have a bunch here."

"Don't test my tolerance."

"Thanks. So you're really offering me a job?"

"Yep. What's your name? Mine's Joaquin." He offered him his hand to seal the deal.

"People call me 'Watt.'"

chapter 37

CALL 1904, MONDAY, 4:01 A.M.

THE TRANSLATOR

"This story is about me," said the caller, "but even more it's about a man who was my friend for many years, Norbert Gutterman:

This happened a long time ago when I worked in downtown New York. This would be around ten years ago now, and at the time I was still trying to make it in middle management at Emigrant Savings Bank. We usually worked from eight to five, but I would stay longer on most days, trying to impress my bosses, you know. I rode a packed train at seven in the morning, and came home on a nearly empty one, at eight or nine in the evening.

I rarely had free time, and when I did I usually spent it at bars or at home watching soccer games on Telemundo. One Sunday morning, on a whim, I decided to head into Central Park, I'm not sure why. Fresh air, maybe. I was carrying the newspaper under my arm; I figured I might find a nice spot in the sun and read the financial section. As I made my way down one of the paths, I noticed a man sitting by himself at one of those outdoor chess tables, kind of isolated in a small plaza under a couple of oak trees. He was thin, older, wearing a brown suit that was threadbare but clean, and he held an old-fashioned briefcase on his lap. Even though he was outdoors, he conjured up images of thick leather-bound books and wood paneling. You might even say that with the crisp creases in his trousers and the defined shadows and lines in his face, he resembled a well-preserved antique book himself.

He looked up as I passed, and waved me over, which surprised me. I hadn't found people to be that friendly in the city, and except for the women professionals I occasionally dated, I tended to avoid contact outside of work. I wondered if maybe he was looking to hustle me. Something about him, his posture or his hair that curled a little at the neck or his shoes, reminded me of premature unemployment, living alone, and for a reason I can't explain, of pickles and onions floating in a jar.

I needn't have worried. He looked down at the chessboard in front of him, the pieces all laid out and ready, and asked, "Care for a game?"

I almost shook my head and walked away, but something made me stay. Pity or curiosity maybe.

So we played chess. He tested my game, let me joust a couple of moves, and then beat me with a simple queen pin. He told me his name was Norbert. He was a Polish immigrant, a translator by trade, specializing in Eastern European poetry and history; I asked him if he'd done anything I might have read.

"From the look of you, I doubt it," he said.

It was embarrassing, but true. I hadn't read a good book since college, and as for poetry, well, I didn't think nursery rhymes counted.

It was actually fun, but at last I excused myself. One of those chance encounters, I figured, a story that would be remembered for a few weeks or months and then forgotten. As I walked away, Norbert called after me: "Next week, then?" I laughed and waved patronizingly.

The following weekend, I was busy, on a conference call most of the day. Afterward, I was exhausted, drank a six-pack watching football, and went to bed. But I couldn't stop thinking about that chess game, half in, half out of the shade, my opponent considering his moves carefully, the way I imagined he picked words out of the back of his mind before he laid them down on the page. The next week, I went back. Norbert was there, reading; he didn't mention our missed appointment, and after that, I went to the park every Sunday. Sometimes I would even beg out of weekend meetings or put off projects until Monday. That weekly game was like a tropical island in a sea of work. It was my one genuine human contact, a time when I could sit in the quiet of the park, reveling in the shouts of children, the sprinkle of fountains in the distance, and just live and breathe and think. It was a friendship with no strings attached.

It seemed like Norbert didn't do much work anymore, but every week, he'd be sitting there, with a book in a different language, or maybe a sandwich, always on rye bread with raw onions. We'd talk about poetry and history; he'd tell me stories of his childhood in Poland. And we'd admire the women that jogged or walked past us. Norbert, you see, was a great lover of women. He had so many different anecdotes that I often accused him of fabrication; inside, though, I didn't doubt him.

After we got to know each other better, I occasionally invited him to join me outside of the park, for dinner, for coffee, for a local poetry reading or play. He always said he was busy; although it was obvious he was being evasive, I figured that maybe there was a part of his life that he wanted to keep private, whether it was a dingy apartment, a wife—maybe he lived in a rest home. Or maybe, he didn't even have a home. I didn't have his phone number, or address. We only met in the park at that table. Now and then we took a turn around the pond to watch the fish rise to catch flies as dusk moved in.

Eventually, I quit my job. I think my meetings with Norbert had a lot to do with it; I started to dread going to the office; I lived for those days in the park. I'd applied to graduate school, and a place in Baltimore accepted me into a writing program. The weekend before I was to move, I sat down at the chess table and told Norbert that this would be the last time I'd see him. He took the news quietly. We played chess in silence and sat for some *time, until I had to go. I looked back at him as I walked away; he was sitting with his hands in his lap, looking after me, wistful, as firmly planted as the oak that hung over him like an awning.*

It was in my second year of school that I found myself searching the aisles of a used bookstore; I needed an obscure text for an independent-study project, and I hadn't been able to find it in the school library. As I was browsing, I came across a small, yellowed book, the kind that they used to print in the seventies. The cover read, The Minsk Publishers in 1952, *in black on white. This volume didn't fit in with the cloth- and leather-bound hard covers next to it, and I flipped through the first few pages. The author was Ignacy Chodźko, an unfamiliar name, but underneath were words that caught my eye:* "translated from the Polish by Norbert Gutterman." *I was thrilled. It felt like I had been looking through a keyhole for years and the door had suddenly been thrown wide in front of me.*

I leafed through the book that night. It was on odd history of Poland, but I could hear Norbert's voice in its words, the careful pacing that imbued everything he did. It felt like a window into his mind, a validation that he had a rich, vibrant history of which I was only the latest chapter.

In the back, I noted with some excitement, was a page titled "About the Translator." A moment later, the book fell from my fingers and landed, pages spread, facedown on the floor. I picked it up again, my hand shaking a little, and reread the first few sentences:

Norbert Gutterman (1901–1984) was one of the most prominent translators of the twentieth century. Born in Poland, he lived in countries all around the world, making his home in New York for many years. He moved to Cuernavaca, Mexico, in the 1980s, where, in June 1984, he passed away of natural causes.

That was ten years ago. Since then, my experiences with Norbert are never far from my mind. At worst, I thought I'd gone crazy. In my better times, I think fondly about the man I'd met and wonder who he really was.

Well, I moved back to New York two years ago. What can I say? I just couldn't stay away. My first weekend back in town, I hurried out to the park. I had to know whether my Sundays in the city had been a dream.

I return to our table often and just read books and wait. I have started many games waiting for him. Sometimes I catch the faint odor of pickles and onions and think he has come to play chess.

chapter 38

THE CALL

At eight in the morning (which, by Joaquin's schedule, was midnight), the telephone rang.

"Yes?" Joaquin roared, with what little energy he could muster.

"Hi, I want to share a story with you," the voice said, imitating the style of *Ghost Radio*.

"What?"

"A story. I've got a story for you."

"Wrong number," he said. He moved to hang up, but his arm stopped when he realized he recognized the voice.

"No, Joaquin. I've got the right number. I want to talk to you and I prefer to do it in the intimacy of your home, but we can continue to follow the program's format. Would that make it be more comfortable for you?"

"Who is this?"

"Someone who wants to share a story with you."

"Look, I don't know how you got this number, but this isn't the right time or the right person. Have a nice day!" Joaquin slammed down the telephone. He felt sure that hanging up that way would solve things.

He couldn't get back to sleep. Alondra raised her head.

"Don't tell me that's what I think it was. Someone found our number and wants to give us a little home delivery?"

"It looks that way. Let's hope he doesn't keep calling back."

"Let's hope," she said, her head dropping back down onto the pillow.

The room was almost pitch black thanks to the heavy curtains they had installed so they could sleep late. Joaquin stumbled away from the bed, smacking his knee on the way. His hands felt puffy; his face like a giant scab ready to fall off, and an acrid, acid taste filled his mouth.

He entered the bathroom, flipped on the light, and looked at his face in the mirror. It didn't look like a giant scab; but two-day beard, baggy eyes, death-white lips, and tightened skin made him look about fifteen years older. Not much of an improvement.

"At least fifteen—maybe more," he said out loud.

Quietly, he left the bathroom and stumbled into the kitchen. He fired up his latest toy, the Saeco Primea Touch Plus, a gift from the station. While the espresso dripped into the cup, the telephone rang again.

This time, Joaquin checked the caller ID: *J. Cortez*, followed by a number that meant nothing to him.

He quietly thanked technology for making it possible to catch red-handed all the imbeciles who harassed people from behind the anonymity of their receivers. Imbeciles too stupid to know that any phone could block caller ID.

"I believe in the microchip," he said to himself as he picked up the receiver, "and you are now officially *fucked*. Yes?"

"Joaquin, it seems we were cut off."

"Yes, we were. Because I hung up the telephone. Look, Mister"—he glanced at the display again—"J. Cortez, I don't know you, I don't feel like talking to you, especially at this time of day."

"I just want to tell you a story."

"Can't you understand that this is neither the time nor place? Be so kind as to never call here again."

"A friend of mine had a terrible accident when he was a teenager. His life was left in tatters. It seemed like the end, like they'd seal him up in a wooden casket and bury him next to the rest of the victims. Instead, he recovered and life went on. Years later, he had another close call and was left pulverized, burned to ashes. But just when everyone again thought they'd be sweeping him into a little box and putting him away with all the other relics, he got back on his feet and kept going. They thought this guy was either very lucky, or had a guardian angel, but actually he had a secret. He was a vampire who sapped the life energy from others, a parasite who could survive anything by stealing the inner flame of those around him."

Joaquin listened, disconcerted, furious, and afraid, all at the same time. Was this nonsense? A biting accusation? Or the truth about his life?

"All right, you've told your story. Now what do you want?"

"Not my story. Yours."

"I don't like people invading my privacy."

Thousands of his listeners knew that Joaquin had survived the automobile accident in which his parents had died, and those who dug a bit could easily find out about the events surrounding Gabriel's death.

"What do you want?" Joaquin asked again.

Then he heard a click as the caller hung up.

Joaquin tossed the cordless handset onto the counter.

"Fuck you very much," he said under his breath.

The perfect espresso he had prepared for himself was cold. He hated cold coffee. He watched its thick layer of *crema*—not too light, not too dark—dissolve. The coffee was dying.

He took a sip of it anyway, as he analyzed what had just occurred. But his thoughts were muddled, too many strange things had been happening to him. None made sense.

He'd never received a call like this one, and no matter how enraging it was, all he felt was a big hole in his chest.

Alondra came out of the bedroom. She held on to the doorframe as if the building were shaking.

"Was that the same idiot?" she said, shading her eyes, which carried traces of mascara.

Joaquin nodded.

She walked into the kitchen, pulling down her T-shirt until it covered her belly button.

"Your coffee."

"What?" Joaquin shook his head.

"Your coffee, it's cold."

"Yep."

He raised the cup and drank it in one swallow.

The whole time they'd lived together, Alondra had never seen Joaquin drink a cold espresso. This time, he didn't even blink.

Then he took a pen and wrote down the number next to *J. Cortez* on the caller ID.

"What are you going to do?"

"Look for the guy."

Alondra shook her head.

"Alondra, I have to do this."

Alondra said nothing. She sat down beside him and waited. He stared at the piece of paper as if it were a code he could crack, or one of those "Where's Waldo?" pages.

"Are you going to make me a coffee, or will I be forced to go to Starbucks?" she said.

Joaquin leaped to his feet and prepared her an espresso with impeccable *crema*, worthy of a commercial with a living room bathed in morning light. His mind was elsewhere, not distracted or absentminded from drowsiness. Truly elsewhere.

Alondra's warm and sensual body and the intimacy of their home looked unreal to Joaquin, as unreal as the set for that imaginary coffee commercial. He felt cut off from this modest paradise, expelled by J. Cortez. Somehow that man's words had penetrated his hard shell. The shell that protected him during his communion with the dead. The call crushed all this with a single devastating blow.

When she'd finished her coffee, Alondra stood up.

"I'm going to take a shower. Want to join me? It'd do you good; it might even wash away those bags under your eyes."

Joaquin hesitated, but he really couldn't waste any more time. He needed to go.

"No, you go ahead. I've got something to do."

He dialed the number. Let the hunt begin.

The telephone rang around nine times before a harsh voice with a strong Spanish accent answered.

"Hullo."

"Who's speaking?"

"Pastor Cuahtémoc Illuicamina, at your service."

"Pastor whatsit, what did you say your name was?"

The voice on the telephone patiently repeated itself.

"I believe you called me a moment ago," Joaquin said, although he knew it wasn't the same voice.

"And you are . . . ?"

"Answer me this: Didn't you just call me to tell me a story?"

"I haven't a clue what you're talking about."

"I've got your number on my caller ID. 'J. Cortez'; that's you, right?"

"I already told you, I'm Pastor Cuahtémoc Illuicamina, of the Temple of Christian and Toltec Redemption."

"Of what redemption?"

The pastor repeated himself again.

"Well, you won't find redemption by making crank calls."

"I didn't call you. I don't even know who you are."

"Then someone used your phone to call me. Who was it?"

"No one's used this telephone."

Joaquin didn't want to argue. He had proof the call came from this number. He'd go there and show J. Cortez the proof. With a little luck, showing up in person would end the harassment. He'd confront the pastor and warn him not to mess with him anymore.

Armed with both the name and telephone number, he easily found the address for the Temple of Christian and Toltec Redemption with a couple of quick Google searches. It was just an apartment, located in one of the slums at the edge of town.

He dressed quickly, not waiting for Alondra to finish her shower, and in five minutes he was in his car, driving toward a rendezvous with Pastor Illuicamina.

The building was in an enormous block of housing projects. Joaquin went up to the seventh floor in an elevator covered with graffiti and looked down a dark hallway for number 713. The apartment's front door was ajar, and he heard voices coming from inside. As he approached, a small boy, maybe eight or nine, peeked out. Behind him, Joaquin saw two overweight women sitting at their kitchen table, listening to the radio. Joaquin smiled at the boy, but as he got closer, the boy slammed the door. It was strange; Joaquin felt sure he had heard Watt's voice in the apartment, although there was no *Ghost Radio* broadcast at that time of day. He shrugged; he had bigger concerns at the moment.

He knocked firmly on the door to the improvised temple. A short, portly man wrapped in an old bathrobe, who looked about fifty-five, opened the door.

"Can I help you?" he said with the tone of a decadent mariachi.

"I'm the guy who called a while ago."

"Uh-huh," the man said skeptically.

"I want to solve the mystery of the calls I received. I say mystery, because according to my caller ID, they came from your telephone, and since you say you didn't make them, I'm going to help you find out who did. It's for the good of both of us."

"But no one here is going around making obscene phone calls to people."

"Let's talk," Joaquin said, brusquely entering the temple-apartment without asking permission. Caught off guard, the man let him pass.

Inside was a small, one-room apartment. Dusty furniture sat in odd places, and covering all available surfaces was a a strange array of objects: porcelain figurines, Kwik Kleen bottles filled with suspect liquids, dollhouses, plastic soldiers, blank paper, unsharpened pencils, myriad flashlights, old religious magazines from past decades, a partially disassembled radio, fruit, crucifixes, dried tortillas. As Joaquin took in the chaos, he thought to himself: What a pathetic and embarrassing place. Who could live here?

However, he quickly realized that the paraphernalia and arrangement of the furniture followed a specific pattern. There was logic in the chaos. The bric-a-brac had been organized with maniacal, childlike precision, with the delirious fervor of one who supposes that objects have secret powers if you combine them correctly. And something else about it grabbed his attention. It reminded him of something. Something he could not name.

"My friend, you've arrived at a bad time. As you can see, I was about to have a bath and then give a service."

"This won't take much of your time. May I sit?"

The call had put Joaquin into an implacable mood; he had never behaved like this with a stranger, much less a man of the cloth—even if in this case that cloth was Toltec-Christian.

"I've no idea who might have called you," said the pastor.

"Try to think. If I can't figure this out, I'm going to have to go to the police," Joaquin replied, picking up a disgusting headdress covered with ketchup stains. Ketchup stains . . . or blood.

"Might have been the boy, but I don't think so. Doesn't do such things."

"Boy?"

"One of the members of my congregation. Sometimes lends a hand with administrative matters."

"There. We already have a clue. What's this boy's name, and where can I find him?"

"Barry. He'll be here soon."

"How soon? Maybe we should to go get him," Joaquin said, continuing to pick up and fidget with the items on the table, chairs, and floor.

Even as he kept touching them, he felt certain that he should leave them alone—not just because his hands were getting dirty, but because by intervening in the order-disorder that presided over them, Joaquin thought he might unleash something he couldn't fully comprehend: something evil. Why would he have such a thought? It seemed crazy.

Joaquin wasn't prone to credulousness or fear of charlatans, but as he spoke to this pastor, he got the distinct impression that very strange things could happen in this place.

"I have no idea where he might be."

"Well, we're going to have to find him."

At this point, the preacher's tone of voice changed. He took on a mournful expression and said:

"You've come to kill me. I've seen this in my visions."

Then his eyes rolled up in his head and he recited what sounded like a prayer.

"I didn't come here to kill anyone; I just want to be left alone."

The man raised his head and continued his strange prayer, incantation, or whatever it was.

"*Sholotl, xelatl, dominum budadl . . .*"

"Enough already. I haven't come here to hurt anyone."

The man ignored Joaquin, raising his voice and repeating a mantra of strange words that sounded vaguely familiar. Joaquin went over to him. When he was only a step away, the preacher sprang up onto his toes and punched him in the face.

Joaquin moved, but not quickly enough. The man's fist glanced off his cheekbone with enough force to knock him off balance. He fell back, slamming hard into a drawer filled with broken toys, and pain shot through his spine.

As he stood up, the preacher kicked him; first in the ribs, then in the gut. This guy's done this before, Joaquin thought as he curled away from another blow. Then age and weight caught up with the pastor. He stopped kicking, and took a short wheezing breath. This might be Joaquin's only chance.

He leaped to his feet and charged, throwing his right shoulder into the pastor's abdomen. The pastor hardly budged, raining a series of blows on Joaquin . . . mostly to the gut and kidneys. Joaquin reeled.

Where the fuck did this guy learn to fight? he thought. And why is he fighting with me?

These thoughts running through his mind, Joaquin dodged and blocked the blows—looking for a way in. A knee to the balls. A forearm to the throat. Something to stop the pastor in his tracks.

Finally, he found it. Ducking under a hail of fists, Joaquin grabbed the pastor around the waist, tightening his grip. Not what he hoped for. But it did the job.

The pastor wriggled and twisted, trying to break free. No luck. Joaquin held tight, increasing his viselike hold. The smell of the pastor's cheap soap and aftershave wafted into Joaquin's nose, and he wondered how he'd gotten himself into this situation: a mysterious phone call, and less than an hour later, he's wrestling with a reverend of Toltec Christianity.

Life takes some odd turns.

At that thought, the pastor broke free, pushing himself away from Joaquin, clasping his hands together, and bringing them down hard on the top of Joaquin's head.

Joaquin reeled, watching the floor wobble and turn to Jell-O. It looked so inviting: soft, gentle, and welcoming. He wanted to collapse into it.

The door swung open. Joaquin righted himself and glanced toward the door. His blurry vision could just make out a rough shape.

"Maestro, I couldn't find—"

The pastor turned toward the voice, and Joaquin sent a right cross speeding toward his jaw—hoping his hazy vision could be trusted. A sharp crack and a thud as the pastor's body hit the floor told him it could.

"What the fuck?" exclaimed the blur at the door.

Joaquin glanced toward the blur, shaking his head. The shape resolved itself into a blond boy holding packages. Just as the image became clear, the boy dropped the packages and ran off.

"Get back here!" yelled Joaquin.

Pulled by strings that seemed beyond his control, he went after the young man. He remembered what the pastor had called him.

"Barry, hold up. I just want to ask you something."

But the young man kept on running. He took the stairs, jumping down, sliding, and bouncing hard off the walls. Joaquin followed him at top speed, losing contact with the ground, stumbling and leaping as he went.

On the ground floor, he almost caught up with the young man in the foyer, but Barry made it into the street, expanding his lead. Joaquin wasn't thinking, he was only running, possessed by a force he'd never felt before. His feet seemed to float above the sidewalk; he dodged people as if they were moving in slow motion.

The fresh air and intensity of the pursuit cleared his head. It filled him with energy. It felt almost as if he were playing tag with Barry, whom he knew he'd reach any moment now. Meanwhile, Barry kept bumping into pedestrians, struggling to give Joaquin the slip, until finally on one corner he tripped, lost his balance, and fell to the ground. Joaquin came to a stop over him and stuck out his arm to help him up, but with enough force so he'd understand that there was no escape. Barry's knee was bleeding. When he saw Joaquin leaning over him, he covered his face.

"I just want to ask you a few questions," Joaquin said, out of breath from the chase.

chapter 39

DRAINS AND LADDERS

The speed wasn't working. The coffee wasn't working. I was a ghoul, plunged into the land of ghosts. Nothing felt real. Maybe it never had.

I did the only thing I could.

"Caller, you're on the air."

My voice sounded odd, echoing distantly in my headphones.

"They're in the pipes, you know."

"What?" I asked. The echoing intensified.

"Well, it's one of their hiding places. One of the places you can corner them."

"Caller, what exactly—"

"I think they're there all the time. But we don't see them. They're too quick for us. Too smart."

The walls of the studio began to shimmer and bend. It's happening again, I thought.

"You have to be quiet. Patient. I was special ops back in 'Nam. So I can be quiet. And patient. Very quiet. And very patient."

Silence and patience. I wished I had some of that. The studio walls shifted toward translucence. The only thing that connected me to reality was the sound of the caller's voice.

"Last night I sat on the top rung of a ladder in my kitchen. About six feet from the kitchen sink. But I was high enough that I could see down into it . . . into the drain. I sat there for hours. 'Becoming one with the night,' as the top kick in basic used to call it."

I saw the bottom rung of the ladder in front of me. Splatters of white paint dried to the tread.

"Your body disappears. The limbs, trunk, neck . . . everything . . . somewhere else. You're only eyes . . . looking . . . waiting."

I looked up. The caller perched at the top of the ladder. His body impossibly still. It barely seemed three-dimensional: a shadow in black military clothes. I put a foot on the first tread, and pulled myself onto the ladder.

"And there I rested. Still. Eyes on the sink . . . on the drain . . . waiting."

Reaching the top of the ladder, I looked over the caller's left shoulder and down at the drain: a black abyss in a sea of burnished aluminum.

"I was there for hours. But I don't mind it. It reminds me of happier times: steamy nights in the Mekong."

His breath shallowed beneath me. It was unlike any breathing I'd ever heard. An autonomic function camouflaged by years of practice. Had I not known it was breathing, I might have confused it with a summer breeze, or the flap of a dragonfly's wings.

"Sometime around three, I began to hear something: something struggling to move through the pipes."

I heard it too. It reminded me of one Gabriel's more bizarre recordings: the amplified sound of two slugs mating. A sound suggesting viscous undulations and the faltering demands of an alien sexuality.

"Then I saw it."

Something glinted in the drain, catching the pale moonlight that lapped into the kitchen from the window over my right shoulder. I couldn't believe what I was seeing. It was impossible.

"A single limpid eye stared back at me from the drain."

The eye darted back and forth, moving from the caller to me. Then it stopped, blinked, and started scanning again.

"There's an intelligence in the eye."

The caller may have seen intelligence. I didn't. It appeared vaguely human, but its gaze suggested experiences vast and nameless. No, not intelligence, something much more frightening: knowledge.

"And as quickly as it came, it was gone. I would think that it was a dream or a hallucination had I not seen it so often."

As the studio began reappearing around me, I heard Alondra's voice.

"Caller," she said, "you never told us what these things were. Do you know? Do you have any idea?"

"Some think they died out. Or left to return to some forgotten homeland in the stars. But I think it's them, they're in the pipes."

"Caller, who are they?" Alondra asked again insistently.

"The Toltecs."

chapter 40

WHERE'D EVERYBODY GO?

Barry was an optimist, or at least that's how he saw himself. He was a political science major deeply committed to Latin American causes. He was a tireless seeker of spiritual stimulation.

For a year he lived in a tiny, poverty-stricken community in the Guerrero Mountains. There he caught a brutal stomach infection that had nearly cost him his life; he worked in sugarcane fields in the Dominican Republic, where he experienced the near-slavery conditions of the plantation workers; in Peru, he joined an association of workers and university students in their struggle against a local Ayacucho despot.

However, Barry always tried to take time out from his social crusades to spend the summers at his family's home in the Hamptons. His parents set up a trust fund for him so that he'd have everything he needed during his college years; but now he believed that using any of this money was immoral, and he opted to support himself by other means. He took odd jobs doing construction work; as a salesclerk in a pet shop; as a waiter. His main source of income, though, was "cultural commerce." Almost every day he stole a dozen books: bestsellers, art books, high-priced first editions, illuminated manuscripts, and other gems that he later auctioned on eBay or sold on Amazon.com. Under his complex system of religious logic, this was an act of justice, reparations for centuries of oppression. Unsurprisingly, Barry led a fairly paranoid existence. He kept an eye out for the authorities, alert to anything suspicious, anything out to end the logic and order of his life.

That was why, when Barry saw Joaquin fighting with the preacher, he assumed that *he* was Joaquin's real target.

Once Joaquin assured him that he wasn't a police officer, bookstore security guard, or library agent, Barry stopped trembling and started to relax.

Looking down at Barry, still catching his breath, Joaquin explained that he'd received a bizarre and especially undesirable phone call from the pastor's telephone.

"Although, like I said, the voice on the telephone definitely wasn't his," Joaquin concluded.

"Of course it wasn't. The pastor has much more important, vital things to do than make crank calls. But if you know it wasn't him, then how come you two were slugging it out?"

"I don't know; I told him my problem and he said that I'd actually come there to kill him." Joaquin's voice was colored with sarcasm.

"And is that what you came to do?"

"Please. Do I look like a murderer? I was only trying to defend myself because he attacked me."

"I know Pastor J. Cortez very well, and he is not an aggressive man."

"Let's go back there and clear up this whole misunderstanding. Maybe there was an error in the caller ID."

Joaquin didn't really want to return; he didn't think it was possible to get anywhere with these two. However, he did want to apologize for having imposed so aggressively. Clearly he'd made a mistake. He thought about giving Alondra a quick ring to fill her in on where he was and what had happened, but when he checked his pocket, he realized his cell phone was gone. He'd probably lost it in the fight or during the chase. The cell phone was extremely valuable to him. It went beyond possession and loss. Beyond the fact that he depended on it. This small electronic device was a necessity for him. He really did believe in the microchip.

Suddenly he wasn't sure of his own telephone number, the number at the station, even Alondra's cell phone. He always used his stored numbers and now he felt cut off, handicapped, lost.

"I lost my phone," he said

"Not surprised, you probably dropped it while you were in 'hot pursuit.'"

"Keep your eyes peeled. Maybe we'll find it."

They reached the building. Joaquin went up the stairs, slowly, carefully—looking at each step, hoping he'd find the phone there. No luck. He realized that in the last few minutes his priorities had changed; he wasn't as worried anymore about the call that had so deeply disturbed him earlier. Now his cell phone was the pressing concern. Its absence hurt . . . physically. He reached the seventh floor and went down the hallway, followed by Barry. Joaquin kept his eye on the ground, still hoping his precious phone would appear.

The door of apartment 713 was open, which seemed to worry Barry since he hesitated and gave Joaquin a look. Then his face twisted into a strange grimace and he gestured for Joaquin to enter first, as if he were afraid to walk in on another intruder. Joaquin entered slowly. His eyes scanned the floor nervously. He really wanted to find his cell. Amid the mess he saw red stains and puddles of red liquid. He remembered the ketchup he saw in the headdress, but this was something different. Then he heard Barry scream out.

"No! Murderer!"

Joaquin's eyes leaped to the center of the room, where he saw the pastor's body lying behind the table, bathed in blood. His dirty bathrobe lay open. Dozens—no, hundreds—of stab wounds decorated the torso, and his jaw hung limp, half torn from his face.

Barry picked up a blood-covered knife and brandished it at Joaquin.

"Stay away from me, you son of a bitch, you . . . murderer!"

"What are you talking about? You were with me when we left. And he was alive!"

"Don't come any closer, or you'll end up worse than him."

Joaquin's first instinct was to run. It wouldn't be easy to convince the cops that he'd only beaten the preacher up, especially when he'd had the knife, apparently the murder weapon, in his hands before the fight. Barry picked up the telephone and raised an index finger over the buttons, but his hands shook, he couldn't seem to find the right numbers.

"Use you brain, Barry. He was alive when we left. And we've been in sight of each other ever since."

"Shut up, you motherfucker, you murderer! You were beating the shit out of him when I got here. They're gonna lock you up and throw away the key," Barry said.

Running away was no solution. It wouldn't take long to catch him; any competent detective would follow the leads and find him. Joaquin's life hung by a narrow thread: a narrow thread with blond hair and a wild look in his eyes. What could he do? Either he waited for the cops to arrive, with everything that implied, or he ran away and hoped to prove his innocence later on. He had to decide fast.

As he glanced around desperately, he realized that the strange objects in the room had been rearranged. It's not that he recalled exactly where the small idols, papers, and pieces of fruit had been positioned. But the general impression those items exuded was different. Someone had moved them. It was like reading a paragraph after the word order had changed; it may convey the same idea, but the tone has shifted.

"Barry, listen to me. We were fighting and he was winning. Even when you distracted him, I could barely force him to the ground. I didn't do this. When you came in he was alive. Someone who got here after us did this. Maybe they took advantage of the open door."

Barry didn't respond. He continued dialing numbers on the telephone and hanging up, as if he were trying to crack a secret code.

How hard can it be to dial 911? Joaquin thought.

"It's not working! The telephone is busted and there are just voices and noises on the line," Barry said.

Abruptly, he dropped the phone and ran out of the apartment yelling:

"Help, the pastor's dead! The pastor's been killed!"

The thought of being lynched by a bloodthirsty crowd demanding justice should have frightened Joaquin, but he assumed a fatalistic attitude. He picked the phone up off the floor, cleaned off one of the chairs in the apartment, and sat down to wait. This all felt so abstract. A body splayed out on the floor. The strange objects littering the room. And this crazed, blond-haired boy screaming in the hallway.

"This is your life on *Ghost Radio*," Joaquin said to himself.

He looked down at the phone. Maybe he should call Alondra. But what would he say? The situation was confusing enough to him; to Alondra, it would sound like absolute madness. But still he thought he should call her, given the way he'd left the apartment. Who knew how long all of this would take?

He hit the talk button, but instead of a dial tone, he heard murmuring, a dry vibration that reminded him of distant voices merged into a single buzzing drone.

Barry ran back in, breathless and pale once again. He gave Joaquin a distressed look.

"There's no one here . . . no one."

"What do you mean, no one?"

"Either they're gone or someone took them away."

"What are you talking about?"

"Take a look. See for yourself."

Indeed, the building seemed abandoned. Minutes earlier, Joaquin had seen people in the hallways, heard children's voices, radios and TVs blaring, noticed the mingled smells of food and detergent. Now . . . nothing. Instead, there was a strange, surreal calm.

"Where'd everybody go?" he asked.

"I don't know. I've never seen anything like it."

"Is there an assembly, a residents' meeting? A parade that everyone went to?" Joaquin suggested, realizing how ridiculous it sounded.

The tableau suggested only one thing: a catastrophe. It was like the void great tragedies leave in their wake. The kind of mass exodus caused by earthquakes, wars, or full-scale alien invasions.

"The pastor is dead, and the whole building is empty."

Joaquin didn't have a reply. Barry had phrased his statement as if there were a connection between both events.

"I gotta call the cops," Barry said.

He left the apartment, looking around him perplexedly. He knocked on every door; he yelled; he called out to the neighbors. Joaquin followed him, silently. What more could he do?

When they reached the street, the scene was the same: total silence. Not a single person was in sight outside or in the stores. Not one car was in motion.

"The neutron bomb," Joaquin said, half alarmed, half fascinated by the prospect.

"Huh?" said Barry, looking more and more frightened. He turned in a panicked three-sixty, searching for signs of life behind the shop windows and inside parked cars.

"A bomb that destroys only living beings, while leaving nonorganic objects intact."

"What?"

"Nothing. Just thinking out loud."

After what seemed like a very long silence, Barry said, "'Neutron bomb to kill the poor,' like in the Dead Kennedys song."

"'It's nice and quick and clean and gets things done,'" Joaquin quoted.

They walked a few more blocks and Barry went into a cafeteria. Not a cat, a cockroach, or even a shadow. The tables were set. Some of the food on the plates still felt warm. There was no sign that people had fled, no traces of chaos or violence. It looked like they had simply vanished . . . evaporated. It reminded him of an episode of *The Twilight Zone*.

"It's like when the pastor died, the whole world died with him," Barry said.

"Barry, why do you keep connecting the pastor's death to all this," Joaquin said with a vague gesture toward his surroundings.

"It all was foretold in his visions: the deserted cities, the sandstorms, people lifting themselves up off the earth and embarking on a cosmic journey."

"The Christian rapture?"

"The pastor's visions," Barry said adamantly.

Joaquin hunted for words. None came.

"The dream disappears when the dreamer stops dreaming," Barry said distantly.

Joaquin decided he would go back home and leave Barry with his fantasies and his cadaver. This was all too weird—and he still didn't know who'd made the phone call. But right now that was the least of his worries. He started walking, quickly, back toward his car.

"Where are you going?" Barry shouted after him.

Joaquin just walked, not turning, not answering.

"Come back here! You can't leave me like this!"

Barry kept on shouting, but didn't try to stop him. It wasn't until he reached his car that Joaquin realized how much all of this had affected him. His hands trembled, and he broke out in a cold sweat. It took him more than a minute to insert the key in the ignition, and even longer to put it in gear. Then he drove away as fast as he could.

He cruised down silent streets, fearful and dazed. Instead of noon, it looked more like dawn. Joaquin desperately searched for signs of life. He felt the car sliding through the streets as if they were coated with ice. It floated, zigzagging, drifting aimlessly. He replayed the fight with the preacher in his head, he felt the blows again, but each time, the outcome differed. He imagined snatching the knife off the floor and plunging it into the pastor again and again. He watched a shadow slide into the apartment and throw itself on the pastor, jagged claws cutting him to pieces. He saw the pastor stab himself with tears rolling down his cheeks. He saw eyeballs considering him from every drain in the apartment. The death of J. Cortez had unleashed something expansive and uncontainable, something Joaquin barely understood.

"What happens to the characters in a dream after the dreamer wakes up?" he asked himself.

Ridiculous thoughts, right? But maybe they held some meaning. Maybe they were the clue. All of this was too much for him. A wave of anger ran through his body.

He honked the horn over and over again, pushing the gas pedal to the floor, slamming the dashboard with his fists, screaming as loud as he could. Several times, he reached into his pocket for his cell. He had a strange sensation that he carried a phantom cell phone; he imagined it was like the ache that amputees feel in their missing limbs.

He went the wrong way down one-way streets; he put the car in reverse; he drove on sidewalks; he jammed on the brakes over and over again. He let his disorientation take over, until he was completely lost. He couldn't remember how he had gotten here. None of the street signs looked familiar. Where was he? How would he get home? For all he knew, he might be in another city.

Desperate, he stopped the car in the middle of the street, beat his forehead on the steering wheel, and howled:

"What the fuck!"

Then a car behind Joaquin honked its horn. The spell was broken. The city had reawakened. Everything moved again. There were people walking here and there, entering shops, eating and talking.

The car radio came on with a strident burst of static, the noise beginning as a cacophony of voices until it resolved itself into a dialogue: two men arguing about the war.

"Where'd everybody go?" he said to himself. He slowly accelerated, overwhelmed by the uproar filling his ears.

He was relieved, but a nagging undercurrent of doubt lingered in his thoughts. What happened today? What *really* happened? Had he actually seen a dead body? Were the pastor and Barry real? The only thing he knew for sure was that his cell phone was still missing. He drove down streets and avenues that were familiar once again. Soon he was back in front of his apartment.

He glanced at his watch: 8:00 A.M. How was that possible? It was later than that when he'd gone out.

The moment took over. Joaquin sat in the car and wept.

chapter 41

RETURN TO THE PAST

Alondra awoke to the sound of someone trying to force the door open. She knew Joaquin hadn't come home that night, and she assumed it was just him, blind drunk. It wasn't a common occurrence, but it wasn't unheard of either. She stood up, barely able to keep her eyes open; covered only by a T-shirt a couple sizes too small and some underwear, she walked barefoot toward the door. Before she got there, it swung open and Joaquin stumbled in. He was sweaty and disheveled.

"Alondra, you've got to listen. I know what I'm going to say sounds crazy, but something completely incomprehensible just happened to me."

"I'd imagine it must have for you to show up at this hour. Go take a shower and get some sleep. We'll talk later."

Alondra wasn't fond of surprises, and she was even less fond of hysterics. Maybe it was her Irish blood—she tended to dismiss people who gesticulated wildly or raised their voices to say things that didn't seem particularly urgent. She had an especially strong aversion to excited men who acted like their enthusiasm and heightened emotions made what they said more important. She wanted to hear whatever Joaquin had to say, but he'd have to calm down in order for her to take him seriously.

"No, you don't get it. We've got to talk," he said.

"Now? Is it absolutely necessary?" she said, pushing her hair off her face with the back of her hand.

"I went over to the place where that call came from."

"What call?"

"You don't remember? The call that woke us up."

"What are you talking about? *You* just woke me up."

"I know it's eight o'clock. I'm not sure what's happening, but I got a weird phone call at eight, got the address from the caller ID by Googling. It was a priest or preacher or shaman or who knows what the hell he was; I got into a fistfight with him, and then Barry arrived and I had to chase him, and when we came back, he was dead."

"Who was dead?"

"The preacher. He'd been stabbed and Barry thought I did it."

"And who's Barry?"

"He's the preacher's assistant, disciple, friend, lover . . . how should I know?"

"Let's start over."

"Look, something really bizarre happened to me, and the strangest part of all is that now it seems like *nothing* happened."

"Come again?"

"You don't remember? Us having coffee earlier? You went to take a shower. And then I left."

"It was probably yesterday."

"No, it wasn't yesterday, it was today. If it never happened, then when did I leave?"

"You didn't come home after the show."

"So where did I go?"

"Joaquin, pull yourself together. I don't know where you went. I was hoping you'd tell me."

"I slept here, right next to you. The phone rang at eight in the morning and woke me up."

"I can say with absolute certainty that it didn't happen like that at all."

"This has got to have something to do with the waking nightmares I've been having. It's like my brain is being used by someone else; as if someone were hacking into my head. It's a downward spiral: the experiences are getting longer, more intense, more mesmerizing."

"Brain hacking?"

"That's what it feels like. I can't think of another metaphor that would explain it better. What's happening to me goes beyond simply hallucinating. It's like living in a parallel universe."

"What the hell are you talking about? Astral projection and out-of-body experiences?"

"I don't know what they are, but I can assure you they've been neither pleasant nor illuminating. I feel like I'm losing the ability to distinguish between what's real and what's not."

"They sound like bad trips—are they flashbacks from when you were doing 'shrooms or acid? Did you do something heavier?"

"No, I never did those drugs, and they can't be flashbacks, this is different. It's like they're coming from outside me, not inside."

"That's exactly what a flashback feels like."

"They aren't flashbacks."

"Then what's happening to you? Because I'm afraid that if these hallucinations aren't drug induced, the only other option is that you're suffering from acute psychosis." There was a certain condescension in her tone.

"I know there's no rational explanation for this, but I'm being sucked into the stories told by some of the callers. I mean, literally, all of a sudden their voices start dragging me in and my surroundings change. Just like that, I leave the radio station and become an unwilling participant in their terrifying episodes."

"You're taking your work at *Ghost Radio* too seriously. You're also taking your empathy with listeners to an extreme," she answered, still not really believing what Joaquin was saying.

"This goes beyond imagining what people tell us on the phone."

"Well, since you're not going to let me go back to sleep, let's have a cup of coffee."

"Another one?"

"No, the first one. Believe me, I know with complete certainty when I've had my first cup of coffee for the day."

They walked into the dining room. Alondra sat down, rubbing her eyes.

Joaquin made a beeline for the coffeemaker. It wasn't warm, and he prepared two espressos. They drank the coffee in silence. As he met Alondra's gaze, he felt a little ridiculous for having burst in the way he had. The preacher's body and the paralyzed city seemed remote, like something he'd seen in a movie. As soon as he sat down and relaxed, though, he felt the pain from his injuries. He ran into the bathroom to look at himself in the mirror. The blow to his face had left a mark, and he had several bruises on his ribs. He went back to Alondra, but didn't say anything. The apartment was more luminous than he had ever seen it. Everything glowed, like photos in *Architectural Digest*. The noise from the street grew louder, but he barely noticed.

"Your coffee," Alondra said.

"What about it?"

"It's getting cold, and you hate cold coffee. Or has that changed?"

"No. That already happened."

"Okay, we're going to continue this debate."

"No, forget it."

"Thanks."

"You remember I mentioned I'd been having a recurring dream about Toltecs?" Joaquin asked.

"Yes, and I also remember asking you how you could be so sure they were Toltecs, and not Olmecs or Nahuatls. Were there signs that said 'You are now in Toltec territory'?"

"No, of course not. But it was a dream. You just know things in dreams. I know they were Toltecs. And this preacher said he had a Christian-Toltec temple."

"You haven't been reading *The Complete Idiot's Guide to Toltec Wisdom*, have you?"

"What's that?"

"One of those self-help books whose system is inspired by Toltec philosophy. The author was some suburbanite woman named Rosenthal—no doubt from Long Island or Redondo Beach."

"And how do you know all this?"

"Don't ask. Just believe me, the Toltecs have been exploited by the shaman tourism industry, exoticist self-help gurus, and antiscientific anthropology for several decades now."

"Now I'm even more confused. Why don't you want to talk about it?"

"Let's just say it's stuff I knew about at some other time, in some other place, and I'm not the least bit interested in rehashing it." She sighed. "Besides, I try to steer my students away from it. If I didn't, we'd have more generations of little Carlito Castanedas running around the hills playing Nagual, and that, I can assure you, is something we don't need."

"You could at least give me a clue. What's this Toltec knowledge that even an idiot can master by reading some cheap paperback?"

"It's a series of techniques to following the 'Path of the Toltecs,'" she said, making a face. "Literally hundreds of books, CDs, and movies are available to indoctrinate anyone gullible enough in the secrets of alleged Toltec prophecies, gospels, and oracles."

"Barry mentioned prophetic visions."

"There are also guides to using Toltec wisdom for inner peace, personal transformation, knowledge, happiness, freedom, manipulation of body energy, and even for having the same glorious, magical sex the pre-Columbians had, which, as we all know, was truly spectacular," she said with a snort of laughter.

"Okay, this isn't helping."

"I don't know what you want me to say."

"Who were the real Toltecs?"

"Now that's the question, isn't it?"

"And the answer?"

"Complicated, complicated . . . complicated."

"Try me."

Alondra sighed deeply and ran a hand through her thick black hair.

"Where is this going to get us?" she asked.

"Humor me. I think it's important."

Alondra walked over to the refrigerator, pulled out a bottle of water, twisted off the cap, and took several long gulps. Taking a deep breath, she looked lovingly at Joaquin and told him the story of the Toltecs:

"The mistake most people make is to think the Toltecs were a people, a civilization, or a nation. For a long time those in Mesoamerican studies accepted this view, placing their civilization in Tula, Hildalgo. You can even find a book called *Art of the Toltecs*, which furthers this misconception."

"Okay, they're not a people. What are they?"

"They're really a mythology created by the Aztecs to lend quasi-religious weight to their quest to conquer the disparate peoples of Mesoamerica. It was one of the tools they used to build an empire."

"Wow! Really?"

Alondra nodded.

"Doesn't sound very 'New Age.'"

"Hardly."

"So how did it all work?"

"Well, the Aztecs claimed that there was an ancient civilization called the 'Toltecs.' And I could go into the myth of the Toltecs in detail. But what really matters is that they were an ancient civilization with vast cities and empires. So everything that suggested art, city development, or any centralized government was Toltec. Toltec equals ancient nobility. Hence, by supporting the drive for empire, you are noble."

"That's brilliant."

"The Aztecs were smart dudes."

"And it went beyond that, because the word *Toltec* meant 'artist' or 'artisan.' In common parlance, it could probably be stretched to mean 'bricklayer.' So the Aztecs used language to co-opt the very workers who were building the edifices of empire."

"Wait a second," Joaquin said. "We're all battling this today. We're becoming Toltecs even when we think we're fighting them."

"I'm not sure I follow."

"It's so clear. Don't you see it?"

"Not really."

"We think we're so smart and progressive. But when we idolize technology, even for good reasons, or for silly reasons, even for *Ghost Radio,* we're pushing forward the phalanxes of empire. We're becoming Toltec."

"I think you're right," Alondra said with a solemn nod.

"Wait, it goes beyond that."

Joaquin looked around the room. His eyes darted from floor to ceiling, they snapped into the corners, and traced the moldings.

"What's the matter?"

"They're here: sliding between day and night, light and shadow, dream and reality."

"The Toltecs? That makes sense," Alondra said. "The Toltecs supposedly believed that life is a dream."

Joaquin remembered Barry's words:

The dream disappears when the dreamer stops dreaming.

"They believed that our lives aren't real. We've been trained to believe in a reality that someone else has dreamed. That way, when we finally wake up, we can take control of the dream and be happy. I guess." She shrugged.

"That's what Barry said, that the dream disappears when the dreamer stops dreaming. What I hadn't mentioned yet is that after the pastor died, the world stood still."

"Okay, unless your pastor was Pope Benedict himself, I think we can assume that what happened was a dream of your own. Do you think everything really stood still?"

"After Barry said that, I left, and the streets were completely deserted—like an abandoned city. Tell me more about the Toltecs. Do you believe in that stuff?"

"I never believed in it, but someone else in my life did. Forget about it. You know how I hate talking about the past."

Joaquin leaned forward. "Right now I'm asking you to make an exception."

"I'm no expert on the Toltecs, but like I told you before, these cults exploit the concept of lucid dreams."

"Lucid dreams?"

"It's the notion that you can dream and be aware and in control at the same time, and thus experience your dreams as a sort of 'alternate reality' where you can do anything: you can fly; you can fulfill your most perverted, wild sexual fantasies without any danger."

"I feel like I've been living out the nightmares of other people, but not of my own free will."

"Joaquin, I think it's natural, up to a point, that when you listen to horror stories every day, your mind starts playing tricks on you."

"But where are my visions coming from?"

"No doubt the same place as the rest of our stimuli: the environment, TV, movies, video games. What do I know? Maybe *The Matrix*. Insisting on seeing that trilogy fifty times in a row couldn't have done your imagination any favors. You're turning into a Neo of the airwaves."

"This isn't funny."

She stopped smiling, but not very convincingly.

"Fine, fine, it's a matter of vital importance and not simply indigestion of the mind."

"They're not just images or visions or echoes of the media, Alondra. They're living experiences that drag me from place to place complete with smells, colors, filth, pain. Everything. Look at these."

Joaquin pointed at the mark on his face and lifted his shirt to show her the bruises the preacher's fists had left behind.

"What happened to you?"

"I fought with a fat man in a bathrobe on a today that never happened."

"Well, sometimes we psychosomaticize events. We can physically manifest things we've imagined. Or maybe you just hit yourself on something. It could be plenty of things."

Alondra carefully inspected the bruises on Joaquin's torso. They definitely looked like the marks of a beating and not the cutaneous symptoms of emotional disturbance.

"You didn't fall down some stairs?"

"At this point, I don't know what to believe."

chapter 42

INSIDE THE CANNIBAL HOSPITAL

The hospital had long, endless corridors. The facility had been army property, and during World War II, it had seen its share of action. Joaquin and Gabriel spent their first wheelchair ride without nurses slowly exploring the many wings on their floor. They read the commemorative plaque that hung in front of the administration offices and watched the nurses. Especially one who they both agreed had the most impressive breasts in the hospital. They did everything together as long as they could avoid talking about personal things.

After days of anxiety and loneliness, watching game shows, talk shows, and soap operas, Joaquin went looking for Gabriel again. He felt the need to be close to him, to get to know who he was, what he did, where he went to school, and what music he liked. What worried him the most, though, was the question he couldn't muster the courage to ask: What was going to happen to them after they left the hospital? At that time, he had no idea what arrangements were going to be made for him: How would his custody be resolved? Where would he live? It still felt as if his parents' death had never happened. He had to believe that Gabriel was going through a similar, excruciating process, coming to terms with a new reality.

As soon as he had permission to move about more freely, Joaquin searched for Gabriel in his wheelchair. One morning, he found him in one of the gardens reading a book. Joaquin stopped a few yards away.

"It's good to see you. I just finished this novel that I borrowed from the guy in the bed next to me," said Gabriel.

"What is it?"

"Stories by Stephen King. Do you like horror stories?"

"A lot. And I like Stephen King too."

"Do you want to read this one? Just give it back to me when you're done or my neighbor will hit me with his crutches. That was literally what he said."

"When you're in a wheelchair, that's a serious threat."

"Don't you have anything to read?"

"No. To be honest, I didn't plan on being here."

Gabriel chuckled.

"I didn't plan on this vacation either."

They talked a little about music, trends, the techniques used by certain guitar players, and the equipment used by keyboard musicians. They went on to discuss styles and reasons to make music at a time when the field was completely saturated. The conversation didn't end there; in fact, it became one of those critical elements in their relationship—a contentious point that was impossible to resolve but vital to the way they made music.

"I think that as long as you feel the need to express yourself with music, as long as you're having fun and like it . . ." said Gabriel, whose attitude was more relaxed.

"That's fine, but it's important to know that what you do is important, innovative. To say something that no one has ever heard before."

"Why would that be more important? First and foremost, you make music for yourself."

Joaquin was dismissive.

"That's bullshit. Everybody makes music for an audience. Maybe on a certain level it gives you satisfaction, stimulation, maybe you even need to do it, but I think that if you don't consider the listener, the whole thing is meaningless."

"No, that's secondary. First you have to enjoy it and feel the satisfaction that what you're doing is good. Then you can see if someone else likes it."

"Well, maybe that's fine if you play classical music where what matters the most is the technique. In that case you can view it like a sport that you try to perform with more and more grace, speed, and agility each time. Or I guess if you're a mariachi or studio musician, without any aspirations beyond playing a gig and collecting a paycheck."

"No, you're completely wrong. You have a very mercenary vision of music."

"And you're just talking nonsense. The only person who could fulfill your idea of 'playing music for yourself' is a retarded sixteen-year-old girl who's never had her period."

The argument was endless. It varied in intensity and typically lost coherence until suddenly one of them would lose patience, become irritable, and tell the other to fuck off. A minute or two later, they would be talking again as if nothing had happened.

Gabriel and Joaquin began conquering more territory within the hospital. They spent a lot of time together, and eventually arranged a transfer to a semiprivate room.

Most of the nurses were affectionate and gave them more attention and privileges than the other patients. They didn't force them to be on ridiculous diets, they let them use an old radio with a tape player, and one of the nurses even lent them a guitar as a friendly gesture. Of course she thought they would start singing popular songs for the rest of the patients. It was a bitter moment for her, hearing their first strange collaborations, in which they incorporated organic, metallic, guttural, even gastric noises. There was a lot of Zappa-like humor, but there was also a seed of what would become their future sound. Regardless of being the favorites, they soon lost their musical privileges; apparently it annoyed the patients, the medical staff, and the neighbors. Gabriel built a very simple synthesizer with electronic parts he'd liberated from a storage room full of old medical equipment. He used tape recorders to amplify the sounds made by his invention. Joaquin, for his part, constantly collected cans, bottles, pieces of metal and wood, and other objects he would use to improvise percussion instruments. Unfortunately, on several occasions he returned to the room to discover that his instrument had been tossed into the garbage. Gabriel had heard about the tape cut-up technique used by beatniks like William Burroughs; he explained to Joaquin the endless possibilities that existed if they incorporated rhythms, textures, and voices appropriated from the radio into their music.

"Sounds a little like what the Dadaists did," responded Joaquin enthusiastically.

"That's right. Something like that—like found art."

When your hours are long and idle, it's almost inevitable that you make your own entertainment, one way or another. A poor man with an advanced case of pancreatitis had a collection of cassettes; apparently his daughter preferred sending recorded messages to writing letters. Joaquin and Gabriel figured that given his condition, it was unlikely he would miss some of the tapes, so they "borrowed" a few. They recorded hospital noises, voices, radio interference, then used a sharp knife and cellophane tape to make some loops, and played them on the tape player.

One night, when they'd been up late talking, Joaquin was fiddling around with the radio. He turned the dial idly, searching for patterns that could be incorporated into a piece they had composed that day, when he came across *Ghost Radio*, a program in which the public would call in to retell all kinds of horror stories, unexplainable anecdotes, and macabre experiences. Some tales were fascinating, some unbelievable; some defied description. In general, the broadcast was enthralling and they were hooked from the first moment. After that, they listened to the show faithfully, every night. Change was important because it broke the stifling monotony of the hospital, but doing something regularly gave them a pleasant sensation of normalcy. Soon their horror session was the day's most exciting activity.

Of course, stories of horrible deaths, phantasms, and accidents seemed like the last kind of entertainment one would recommend for a couple of teenagers who had just tragically lost their parents. But in a certain way, the stories were like vaccinations that helped them share the pain. Most had a naive, camp element that neutralized the horror and transformed it into something acceptable, human—even ridiculous. Gabriel and Joaquin listened attentively to the callers and drank Cokes they'd smuggled into their room.

Every once in a while, a nurse would walk in and catch them. Most of the time the nurses just let the boys continue listening, although on occasion they objected and tried to impose their authority, turning off the treasured radio or even threatening to confiscate it. Fortunately, none of them ever followed through.

Sometimes, the boys even managed to get a hit of weed acquired from one of the janitors in exchange for the most diverse and unusual objects that they could get their hands on, from almost full boxes of chocolates to electric razors that they "found" while they were left unattended somewhere.

Gabriel often claimed that his school friends would visit him soon. He said that he would introduce Joaquin to the members of his band, but days went by and no one ever came. After some time, Joaquin realized that it was a delicate subject. He didn't know the details, but evidently Gabriel's friends didn't miss him that much. Gabriel made several calls to his friend Mike; each time, Mike promised that he would visit. Joaquin, on the other hand, had no expectations that any of his friends would come, but he waited anxiously for his grandmother to pick him up. The situation had been explained to her, and he had spoken with her on the phone, and it had been an extremely difficult conversation. Neither of them had cried. Both made a tremendous effort to be restrained, holding in their feelings, as if a single tear would unleash an uncontrollable avalanche of emotions.

One morning, Gabriel appeared.

"Come on, follow me. You're not going to believe it."

Joaquin followed him down the corridor and up a ramp; when they reached a doorway, Gabriel spoke.

"Here we are. What do you think?"

"What do I think about what?"

"The track, you idiot," he said, pointing to a path surrounding a part of the garden that was not well traveled.

Abruptly Gabriel lunged down the ramp, picking up speed and propelling himself with all the strength in his arms. Joaquin was startled; he had thought Gabriel was about to tell him something personal, and suddenly he was going full speed down an empty hospital corridor. His natural reaction was to race after him, trying to gain the fastest speed possible. He had no idea how strong the wheelchairs were, and the thought of what would happen if he ran over someone didn't even cross his mind.

The slope was quite steep, and soon Joaquin was speeding just a few yards from Gabriel. A nurse saw them and started to scream, "Stop! Stop!" Joaquin focused on reaching Gabriel. Suddenly a door opened, and Dr. Scott, a pediatrician, and one of the hospital administrators, Mr. Garcia, walked blithely out into the corridor. Gabriel swerved to the left, but Joaquin didn't have enough time. As the doctor saw the wheelchair speeding toward him, he covered his face and weakly cried: "Nooo!"

Fortunately, the wheelchair race didn't have any major consequences. The doctor just received a few scrapes and a bruised ego; Joaquin didn't run him over, even though he had to launch himself into a bush in order to avoid doing so. Mr. Garcia was not injured at all. The boys justified the incident by explaining that Gabriel had lost control of his wheelchair as he was going down the ramp; Joaquin, frantically following to try and stop him, had accidentally pushed him instead, causing the chair to accelerate. The offended doctor felt sure that it had not been an accident at all, that the boys had targeted him. He wanted to press charges against them for assault and property damage. The hospital's director, Dr. Friedman, pointed out to him that the assailants were simply two boys in wheelchairs who had recently lost their parents.

"Scott, I'm not sure that you'll be able to convince a judge that these young boys are guilty."

"But they assaulted me."

"Let's leave it at that. It was an accident, and they won't ever do it again. Right?"

Both boys nodded, holding back snickers.

Joaquin received a new wheelchair since his was completely wrecked. The pair started to get a reputation, which could have been a good thing since some of the nurses, especially the younger ones, were intrigued and interested in them. But at the same time other people were watching them more closely, so they had to be careful. Scott had decided that he was going to make them pay for what they had done; he followed them, spied on them, and did whatever he could to have them removed from the hospital. Friedman, who had defended them, was not particularly happy with the two bored and wild youths either, and would have preferred their transfer to another facility. Fortunately for the two boys, legally, there was nothing he could do. The bureaucracy was complicated and the process would take weeks or months.

At night, Joaquin and Gabriel continued their ritual of listening to *Ghost Radio*, and even though they had fewer opportunities to find the contraband that would enliven their evenings, they still enjoyed the program tremendously.

One night, they quietly left their room, gliding silently down the hallway. They knew that it would be difficult to reach the director's office without being seen, but Joaquin had succeeded once before. Stealth wasn't easy rolling down the hallways in the middle of the night in two wheelchairs that squeaked more loudly than the decrepit cots in a brothel.

They synchronized their movements to make as little noise as possible. The journey lasted almost an hour: an hour of barely suppressed giggles. At last they reached the door of the director's office. Joaquin tried the key he had gotten from an employee in exchange for a nearly full bottle of Aramis shaving lotion. It opened. They quickly went inside, closing the door behind them, and headed for the telephone. Gabriel got there first and dialed a number. It was busy. He tried again. Busy. And again, same thing. Disappointed, he dropped the receiver back onto its base. Joaquin placed his finger in front of his lips, motioning not to make any noise, and dialed the number himself. Busy. He tried again, and this time heard a young woman's voice.

"You're calling *Ghost Radio*. Do you have a story to tell?"

When he heard this, Joaquin quickly handed the telephone over to Gabriel.

"Yes," said Gabriel. "I want to tell a story."

"Sir, you're going to have to talk louder."

Joaquin started to laugh uncontrollably.

"About two years ago, I was admitted to St. Michael's Hospital in Houston. I needed an operation because I have a renal deficiency."

He suppressed another fit of giggles.

"My surgery was scheduled for the next day, but I couldn't sleep because of anxiety, so I took a ride around the hospital in my wheelchair. Then I heard a noise that caught my attention. I looked into an office with its lights on, and I saw some doctors and nurses devouring a bunch of raw, bloody entrails. The director of the institution himself, a Dr. Friedman, was at the head of the table. But it was Dr. Scott who was in charge of carving the human flesh and distributing it to the diners. The patient who had been operated on that day, my hospital roommate, who was there for a prostate operation, was lying motionless on the floor. The next day I told them that they couldn't operate on me because I felt dizzy and had been throwing up all night. Dr. Scott reluctantly postponed my surgery, and instead, they operated on a young woman with a huge tumor in her back. That night, I went out for a ride again. This time, I wanted to prove to myself that I had been hallucinating the night before. When I arrived at the office where I had seen the cannibals, I saw Scott and Friedman again, feasting on the young woman's still-pulsating organs. I've tried to escape but this hospital is like a fortress, so every day I have to make up new pretexts, hiding lab results, changing my bed, or blackmailing the staff so that they won't take me to the operating room."

Joaquin couldn't contain himself anymore. Finally, Gabriel hung up. They laughed until they fell off their wheelchairs. Then they borrowed some of the director's belongings and left with the same care as when they arrived. They were no longer two simple *Ghost Radio* listeners; they had become callers, and were very proud of themselves.

"If for some reason, I don't end up being a musician, I know what I want to be."

"A cannibal doctor?"

"A radio-show host."

They couldn't stop laughing.

Finally, the day came when Joaquin's grandmother was able to visit him. Joaquin was with Gabriel, reading in the garden, as the two did every afternoon. When he saw his grandmother, he tried to stand up. When he realized he couldn't, he wheeled toward her. Feeling awkward, Gabriel left. Joaquin and his grandmother talked endlessly, without any coherence and without saying anything specific.

Afterward, Joaquin returned to the room where Gabriel was waiting.

"I'm going to live with my grandmother when I get out of here. I'm not going back to Mexico."

chapter 43

THE NONEXISTENT SHOW

Joaquin went for a drive. He thought he might buy some CDs, maybe go to the supermarket and kill some time. His nerves were getting to him; he was starting to talk to himself. Then his cell phone rang, his new phone, which he still couldn't get used to. It was Prew, the *Newsweek* journalist; he sounded rushed and anxious.

"Sorry for bothering you, but I have a question. I was just talking with the fact-checker at the magazine; he's found a problem with the interview."

"What's wrong? I thought you canceled that article months ago when I refused to talk about Gabriel," asked Joaquin.

"Well, we did. But given your recent success, and some extra space in our next issue, we decided to run it. But, like I said, there's a problem."

"What is it?"

Joaquin was annoyed by the thought of this old interview being unearthed, and of a battalion of *Newsweek* employees methodically searching articles for errors, contradictions, or statements that could have legal consequences for the magazine.

"It's something minor, but he thinks you were confused when you said that you listened to a call-in program similar to yours when you were in the hospital with Gabriel."

"So what's the confusion?"

"Well, the program didn't exist."

His voice was worried.

"Of course it existed. Your fact-checkers are wrong."

"Joaquin, these are professionals. They've been working at the magazine for years and we've never had any problems with them. Could the accident have affected your memory?"

"No, I'm completely sure about what I said."

"That's impossible. There hasn't been a program like that in the Houston area for the last three decades—the records there were no shows about ghosts, ghouls, or monsters at all. I've reviewed the archives myself."

"Prew, there's been a mistake. It's not the first time that I've had to look for documents that have disappeared from libraries or archives. Give me a chance and I'll find it."

"Joaquin, you do not understand me. We really did search. We consulted many historic volumes and interviewed several experts. Nobody knew what I was talking about."

Joaquin stopped the car, feeling dizzy. He didn't need this kind of news right now; his grasp on reality was shaky enough.

"I know I might be confused about a lot of things from the past. But in this case, there's no doubt. That program saved my life; it inspired me to do what I do now."

"Could it be that you heard it in Mexico?"

"I'm sure I heard it at the hospital. There's no other possibility."

"Do you know of anybody else who might have heard the program at that time?"

Joaquin tried to remember, but he and Gabriel hadn't shared the experience with anybody else. Nobody was supposed to be awake at that time; it was against the rules to listen to the radio after nine o'clock at night; moreover, they didn't think that anybody else in the hospital would be interested in it.

"As far as I know, only Gabriel and I listened to it."

"Only you and your dead friend," said Prew, the disbelief in his voice palpable.

"I'm sure many people listened to it. It's just that I don't know who."

"Memories are just chemical reactions, simple electrical discharges. There's nothing more fragile."

"That could be, but this was a major part of my life at the time."

"Forget it. It's not a big deal; I'll just delete this part."

"No, don't, Prew. Give me some time . . ." said Joaquin, and hung up.

Joaquin accelerated and made an aggressive U-turn, oblivious to the traffic around him. Surrounded by honking horns and insults, he drove at full speed in the opposite direction. His first thought was that he should go home to rest; he still hadn't recovered from the pseudoshaman's death, which he wasn't even sure had really happened. On the one hand, he wanted to forget about it, to assume that it had only been a hallucination or a nightmare or a blackout. Yet he remembered, vividly, everything that had happened. And at that moment he had another, more pressing matter to sort out. He had to prove that that radio show really existed. If he couldn't, absolutely everything that he was certain of would collapse; that program was the cornerstone of his memories and recollections.

But where should he start looking? The solution was obvious. He must settle this now. He called Alondra. "I have to go to Houston, right now. I have to check on something or I'm going to go crazy."

Without giving her a chance to respond, he told her about the emergency. Alondra didn't understand at all.

"What difference does it make?"

"Right now it's the most important thing in the world."

"Calm down, Joaquin. Leave it to me. I'll check into it and in a couple of days at the most we'll know if it ever existed or if it's a figment of your imagination."

"I can't. I have to go now."

"You're being dramatic. Relax. Take a deep breath. Traveling right now isn't going to accomplish anything."

"Alondra, there's nothing you can say that will convince me not to go."

She sighed. "All right, but let me start checking into it and see who can help you. Are you coming back tomorrow?"

"Probably, unless I find something really important."

"Take care. Okay?"

Joaquin drove too fast. He felt a persistent heaviness in his chest, and a thick, abstract fog filled his mind. He arrived at the airport, bought a round-trip ticket, and walked toward his gate. His cell rang. The new one. The stranger in his pocket.

"I found out something for you. Max Stevens is the expert on radio broadcasting in Houston and all of Texas," said Alondra.

"Perfect. Give me his information."

"I spoke with him. Joaquin, you don't need to go there. He has a telephone. You can call him"

"Alondra, I have to."

"Do whatever you want. I'll text the number to you. Do you know how to use your new phone?"

"Yes, don't worry. Send it to me. I have to make an appointment."

"I did already. Stevens will see you today. I explained to him that it was an emergency. He was very accommodating."

As Joaquin boarded the plane, he realized that he hadn't been to Houston in a very long time. He didn't remember much about the city. This worried him. How could he forget a place where he had lived for so long? Then he remembered his return to Mexico City so many years ago. It had appeared unfamiliar as well. This calmed him. The memories returned then and they would today.

But this wasn't like that time in Mexico City. This was different. From the moment he arrived, he felt like he'd landed on an unknown planet. Initially, he thought that he'd be able to find his way with only a few directions; as soon as he started the rented 2007 Ford Taurus, though, he realized that he needed a map just to get downtown, which should have been relatively simple. He stared at the sunlight reflecting off the car's metallic green hood.

"My religion is the computer chip," he muttered to himself, reading the MapQuest directions to Stevens's place off the screen of his new phone.

The drive was uneventful. As he turned down Monroe headed for the freeway, he passed a café. At sidewalk tables sat a cluster of people huddled around a radio. Their eyes were vacant. They held cups inches from their lips, but didn't drink. He knew they couldn't possibly be listening to *Ghost Radio* at this time of day, but he couldn't shake the feeling that that was exactly what they were doing. He considered pulling over, rolling down his window, trying to listen, but he thought better of it and drove on.

The office was located in one of the luxury corporate skyscrapers downtown. Stevens had a secretary and a team of assistants who paced back and forth carrying files, boxes, and stacks of documents. In an anteroom there were posters advertising his books, photos of Stevens shaking hands with celebrities, and an oil painting of a sailboat on the ocean. Joaquin didn't have to wait long.

"Joaquin. It's a pleasure meeting you. As it happens, I'm very interested in you, because I'm including you in my next book. Your program has enjoyed a remarkable success."

Joaquin listened to a few more compliments, and tried to reciprocate by saying something positive about Stevens's books, which he had never read. Unsurprisingly, nothing came to mind. He said that it was a pleasure and an honor to meet him, and then added, "I flew here to see you, since no one knows this business better."

Stevens, a tall, thin man with sharp features and an impeccable appearance, looked pleased.

"I'll get straight to the crux of the matter. Sixteen years ago, I had a serious accident in this city. I was hospitalized for six weeks, and during that time I spent my nights listening to a radio program about ghosts and the supernatural, a program very similar to the one I host now. It was broadcast very late, maybe all night, and the public called in to tell horror and mystery stories, and talk about anything related to ghosts. Can you tell me anything about a show like that?"

"Nothing springs to mind," said Stevens.

"Are you sure?"

"Completely. Frankly, I think you may be in error. But I can double check. I have the most extensive and significant archive of radio broadcasting in the state, perhaps the country; allow me."

Stevens sat at his computer and keyed in something. Joaquin waited silently. As time passed, he sank deeper and deeper into his chair. He sensed that he wasn't going to get anything; it was as bad as a doctor breaking the news that he was suffering from an incurable disease.

Finally, Stevens spoke. "Joaquin, there must be a mistake. I have records here of overnight broadcasting, year by year, for the past three decades and I don't see any program like the one you describe, or even anything that deals with the subjects you mentioned."

"Mr. Stevens, I knew you were going to tell me that. That's why I came in person. I believe this show has been lost, so to speak."

"What do you mean by . . . lost?"

"For some reason, it hasn't been registered in the official archives."

"Why would that happen?"

"I don't know. But I can guarantee that it existed."

Stevens's eyes narrowed. Joaquin sensed this wasn't a man who liked being contradicted.

"Joaquin, I have a complete archive. It's impeccable. I won't tolerate any omission, and I don't understand what you mean by an unregistered program."

"I only want to know if it's possible."

"That's ridiculous. No. I have meticulous and exhaustive records"— Stevens emphasized the last words, verbalizing them slowly—"of *everything* that has been on the radio waves in the Houston area in the past thirty years."

"I have no doubt. But I'm completely sure that the program existed."

"Do you remember any other details about the program? The name of the host, the station, the days it aired?"

"No, I don't remember any of that. There were several people, both men and women, I think. It aired three or four nights a week, but I can't remember the station."

"Maybe the telephone number?"

"I don't have it, but I can probably get it," he said, remembering that when Gabriel and he had called, he'd written the number down in a notebook that might still be with the other mementos he had been dragging from place to place for decades. "Isn't it possible that there were underground broadcasts? Clandestine programs?"

"I suppose, that definitely wouldn't be included in my archive."

"Is there any way to research those types of programs?"

"I don't know."

"There has to be someone who's documented it."

Stevens was losing his patience.

"I'm sorry, but I can't help you," he said, standing up.

"I don't want to take more of your time, but this matter is tremendously important to me."

Stevens's irritation was obvious. He rotated his wrists mechanically, avoiding Joaquin's gaze. Joaquin wasn't willing to leave empty-handed. He needed something, anything.

"There's the Theo Winkler collection . . ." Stevens said reluctantly.

"Whose?"

"Winkler is a dilettante who over the years has compiled college, underground, and clandestine radio-broadcast materials. He's an ignoramus and a fraud, but he might have some idea of what you're looking for."

"I would be grateful if you would give me his information."

"My secretary will give it to you. Have a good afternoon, sir," Stevens said, directing Joaquin out of his office. It was obvious that he was offended by the fact that Joaquin had come to see him with an interest that wasn't related to him. Joaquin was most likely condemned to excision from his next book.

Joaquin thanked him and received a piece of paper from the secretary with a telephone number that he dialed as soon as he stepped outside.

Winkler answered. Apparently he didn't have a secretary. Joaquin explained where he'd gotten the number.

"Stevens? That supercilious despot told you to see me? Unbelievable, man."

Joaquin explained what he was looking for, and Winkler told him to drop by someday.

"It has to be today."

"It's late. I can't see you today."

"Please, Winkler, this is an emergency. I'm running out of time and I need to see you today. It won't take long."

Winkler accepted unenthusiastically; Joaquin downloaded a new set of MapQuest directions and started on his way. It turned out his destination was a dilapidated warehouse in a middle-class, residential neighborhood on the outskirts of the city.

"Thank you for seeing me," said Joaquin before Winkler could open his mouth.

Winkler's "archive" was a dining-room table surrounded by stacks of soundtracks, old tape recorders, and piles of ancient radio equipment. Inches of dust covered every surface; the whole place reeked of mold and marijuana. Winkler was a huge man dressed in overalls.

"Right. Since you called, I've been thinking about that program you mentioned. I think I know what you were talking about. I might have something, man."

He opened a file cabinet and searched through thousands of dusty papers. What seemed like an eternity passed. Joaquin felt the beginnings of desperation.

"Well, here it is," Winkler said suddenly, holding up a yellowed card with worn and soiled edges.

Joaquin couldn't believe it. It was too good to be true—his first positive news in a long time. Maybe he wasn't crazy, and he wasn't sinking into an absurd nightmare. Finally, with this record, his memories would be vindicated. He would call Prew and Stevens immediately just to show them that he wasn't lying or insane.

"Do you have any broadcasts in your archives?"

"Yes, I have something in the audio library. But you know, in order to support an effort like this one, I depend on donations."

"How much do you want, Winkler?"

"It's not that I'm charging you. My archive is available to everyone—but you can appreciate the expense that all this represents."

"I understand. Tell me, how much should I 'donate'?" Joaquin was ready to give whatever was necessary as long as he could listen to one of the tapes of that program.

"Two hundred fifty dollars," Winkler blurted out apparently at random.

Joaquin took out all the money he had in his wallet.

"I have one hundred fifty here and I can write out a check for another one hundred."

"Normally I don't accept checks," said Winkler, "but this time I'll make an exception."

Winkler searched through the moldy depths of what he called his "file" and some ten minutes later came back with an audiotape. He inserted it into an old Nagra tape recorder, fast-forwarding and rewinding until he finally managed to get a sound out of it. Not even three seconds had gone by when Joaquin recognized the voices.

"No, stop. You're mistaken, this isn't the program I'm looking for."

"This is *Ghost Radio*."

"Yes, I know. This is my program, that's my voice. That's me. What I'm looking for is a similar program, but one that was broadcast in the eighties."

"Look, man, this was taped more than twenty years ago. See?" Winkler said, pointing to the box the tape had come in. Written on it was "Ghost Radio, Sept. 13, 1983."

"That's impossible. It has to be a mistake. Maybe the box is mislabeled. This tape must have been made a few months ago."

Winkler looked at him blankly, as if he were speaking a strange language.

"It's been at least ten years since I stopped taping in this format."

"Then there has to be a mix-up. This is my program, *Ghost Radio*. Don't you hear my voice? And obviously I couldn't have done a program twenty years ago."

"I don't understand. You host a show called *Ghost Radio*, and this is a tape of that show with your voice, but it isn't the one you're looking for?"

"No, what I want is a similar program that was on the air twenty years ago. It was the one that inspired mine."

"Okay, whatever. This is the *Ghost Radio* that was transmitted in the eighties." He had a small box filled with tapes marked with the program's name and air dates.

Joaquin randomly grabbed another tape and replaced the first one; Winkler didn't interfere. He pressed the play button and, again, heard his own and Alondra's voices. In fact, he thought he recognized the broadcast.

"This is recent too."

Winkler looked at the box and checked the quality of the tape.

"Maybe, if you consider twenty years to be recent."

"Twenty years is nothing," said Joaquin, while he tried another tape.

The results were no different. He tried others; each one was the same.

"Okay, I think I've satisfied your curiosity," said Winkler finally.

"No! Now I'm more confused than ever! I need to figure out what's happening."

"Nothing's happening, man. You asked me for this show, here it is. There's no confusion."

"What's happening is that this place is a chaotic, confusing mess. Look around! It's impossible to imagine that you can keep any kind of order here. Stevens warned me about this."

"Stevens is an idiot; my archive is in perfect order. I don't give a shit if you don't believe me, but these recordings really are *Ghost Radio* from 1983."

Joaquin regretted blowing up. This was the worst possible time to lose his temper, but now he couldn't restrain himself.

"Well, as I see it, there are only two options. Either you don't know where your own asshole is, or you're trying to make me think that I'm crazy."

Suddenly Winkler pointed to the tape still playing.

"Listen to that," he said.

Joaquin listened. It was newsbreak. The anchor spoke of the publication of the *Hitler Diaries*. No mention of them being forgeries. And then an ad came on for *Return of the Jedi*'s "world premiere."

"Wait, wait," he said. "You put that stuff in there, didn't you? You're doing this to fuck with me, right? Who put you up to this? What is this about?"

"All right, I've had enough, man," said Winkler. "Get out of here or I'm gonna have to take you out one piece at a time. I thought I'd seen my share of paranoid conspiracy theorists, but I've never seen anybody like you." By now he was shouting. "Get out!" He turned to grab a bat that was leaning against the wall.

As Winkler turned, Joaquin slipped one of the tapes into his pocket. He knew that the conversation was over and he couldn't leave without some kind of evidence. If he was going to risk his life, he figured he should do it for something that was worthwhile.

"It's not paranoia. Don't you get it? It's impossible for that recording to be twenty years old and have my voice and my girlfriend's voice on it."

"Get out. I don't know what you're talking about, and I don't care."

Joaquin had no doubt that the bat would be used on him if he continued arguing, so he backed slowly toward the door, keeping his eyes on the angry archivist.

"Excuse me. I'm sorry. But this matter has really affected me. My *life* depends on finding this show."

"Of course it does. You probably received your orders from aliens who want to invade Earth too. Get the hell out of here."

Joaquin reached the door, and opened it carefully. He walked out into the sunlight, which was still bright even though it was nearly evening. Winkler loudly slammed the door behind him.

Joaquin had the proof that something strange was happening to reality in his pocket. However, he still hoped to find a rational explanation. Was it possible that Winkler had confused the tapes? But what about the newsbreak? How had that gotten there? Bleed-over from an earlier recording? Even Joaquin found that unlikely.

He climbed into his car and shut the door behind him. He leaned back and closed his eyes. He needed to shut out the world. He needed a moment when nothing strange was happening. He opened his eyes and night had fallen—a dark night. Joaquin closed his eyes again, this time in terror. When he opened them, the afternoon sunlight shone once more. He examined his reflection, his eyes, in the rearview mirror. In an almost childlike way, he considered covering his face again to see what would happen. He gazed at the palms of his hands for a few seconds, and touched them to his face. He closed his eyes, remaining like that for a moment. He opened his eyes, and again, the car was surrounded by blackness. He finally lost all composure. He fell apart. Up to now, he'd been confident that everything, somehow, would start to make sense. He thought that these strange events would eventually be reduced to a few curious anecdotes, forgotten along with many other unexplained, but relatively minor, occurrences.

chapter 44

ANOTHER BROADCAST

Joaquin stopped at the first motel he came across. A no-frills place without a name. The clientele appeared to be mainly seedy couples who slithered cautiously through the shadows from their cars to the rooms and back.

Joaquin was in no condition to look for anything more sophisticated; he just needed sleep and refuge from all of the bizarre things that were happening to him. At first, he'd wanted to go home. There was no reason to stay in Houston. His trip had been a fiasco. He considered calling Alondra, but what would he tell her? After what had happened that day, he didn't want to think about how their conversation would go. Still, he had an intense urge to dial her number, to hear a voice that would bring him back to normal and remind him of his everyday life. A voice that would make him feel like no matter what, he could always go back home again.

He didn't call.

Home seemed like such a vague destination. Almost an abstraction.

Since Prew's call, Joaquin hadn't rested for a moment: The muscles in his back and legs were giant knots. He fell back onto the bed without removing the polyester coverlet. He'd heard those stories about semen stains and bacteria on the quilts in motels, but right now he didn't care. Even Ebola seemed innocuous compared to the threat hanging over his head. Words floated through his mind like specters: psychosis; schizophrenia; manic depression; temporal-lobe epilepsy, Alzheimer's. There's something really wrong with me, he thought. There was no other explanation for what was happening: a neurological short circuit, a faulty connection, or a progressive, degenerative brain disease. The notion terrified him, but the alternative was even worse. He considered the stories he listened to every day about grotesque accidents, sensational crimes, and inexplicable apparitions. Worse than those horrors, he thought, was the absence of stories, the disappearance of memories, a silence of the imagination. Was he headed there? Headed into that abyss?

A crushing anxiety overcame him: a horrible sinking feeling, as if he and this lonely motel room were slipping into the asphyxiating depths of an abandoned mine shaft. The moment this thought popped into his head, a spasm, like an electric shock, ran from his back into his hands. He remained frozen, afraid that even the tiniest shift of his eyes would change his surroundings, and he would really find himself at the bottom of a mine shaft.

The telephone rang, breaking Joaquin's paralysis. He raised his head and looked over at it. He hoped it was Alondra, calling to find out when he was coming back, to ask him how everything was going, and to tell him that everything would be okay. But everything wasn't okay.

It hadn't been okay for a long, long time.

He tentatively reached for the phone, as if there were snakes, ready to strike, hidden in the mattress, and picked up the receiver, glancing at the caller ID in hopes that the small screen would offer him some assurance.

Instead, the digital readout only made him uneasy. It just displayed a single name: *Joaquin.*

"I'm probably not the best person to be calling me right now," he said to himself.

He considered letting the voice mail pick it up. Confronting a recording would be less intimidating than answering the phone and exposing himself to who knows what. For some reason, though, he did answer.

"Hello."

"Hello, Joaquin. On vacation?" said the strange voice that had become familiar to him.

There was no one Joaquin wanted to hear from less than this individual, the mysterious crank responsible for everything that was happening to him.

"Who are you? What do you want?"

"Why not let me ask the questions: who are you . . . now?"

"The same guy I've always been."

"The same guy who was hosting a radio show two decades ago?"

Joaquin remained silent. How did the caller know about the tapes?

"You know that's not what's going on here. Your world is falling apart."

"You're the one behind all this weird stuff. How'd you get my phone?" Suddenly a twisted theory clicked into place and he blurted out, "You killed the shaman!" He shook his head, amazed this hadn't occurred to him before. It made perfect sense.

"That's a very serious charge, especially coming from the man who beat up the deceased just before he was murdered."

"Are you following me?"

"Can you even be sure he's really dead?"

Just then, there was a knock on the door. Joaquin jumped up, dropping the receiver. For a moment he was disoriented. The room seemed huge. What was wrong with his eyes? He couldn't see the door, the window, the television. He stood up, recovered the telephone, found the door, and shouted:

"Who is it?"

"Sir, you left your credit card at the front desk."

Joaquin opened up his wallet, tensely looking through it for his card. It wasn't possible that he had forgotten it. He never lost things like credit cards or cell phones. He gripped the receiver tightly in his right hand as he let the cards and money slip through the fingers of his left. He scanned the floor, looking at all that plastic and green paper arrayed like a broken fan. It wasn't there. Frightened of what he would find, he opened the door to reveal a bellboy holding the card in his hand. When he looked up, he saw J. Cortez, the shaman, staring him straight in the eye. The faded bellboy uniform barely fit him. The pants were too short, and the jacket was stretched tightly around his belly.

The receiver hung loosely from his hand, but Joaquin could still hear the laughter booming on the other end.

"You! What are you doing here?" Joaquin asked, trying to shake his head free of its confusion.

"You ought to be more careful. It's dangerous to leave these lying around," Cortez said, handing him the card.

"What happened to your wounds? To Barry?" Joaquin blurted out, even though he knew it was useless to expect answers.

"Everything's fine. As for Barry, I'm afraid he's still wandering around. Poor lad." There was a gleam in his eye as he said it.

"What's going on?"

"What do you mean?" Cortez asked, cocking his head.

The voice on the telephone chimed in: "Give the poor man a tip and stop bothering him with stupid questions."

Joaquin took a long look at J. Cortez or Cuahtémoc, or whoever this man who'd been dead a few days ago really was. The man smiled, holding his right hand palm up in what seemed like a mocking gesture. Joaquin picked a bill up off the floor and dropped it in the outstretched hand. His smile widening into a grin, the pseudo-shaman-bellboy-pastor left.

"What was that all about?" Joaquin said into the receiver.

"I wanted you to see the kind of quality service your motel offers."

"I'm hanging up now."

"And honesty, let's not forget that. Honesty."

"Good-bye."

"You won't hang up. You're too curious about what's happening to you."

"At this point, I don't know if I want to understand anything. You can keep my phone."

"Thanks. I will. Considering all the stuff of mine you've kept, it's the least you can do."

"What the fuck are you talking about?"

"You know exactly what I'm talking about. Your career as an impostor."

"What are you saying?"

"I want you to ask yourself a question. Is this what you survived for?"

"I don't understand."

But Joaquin knew, deep down he had known from the start who was on the other end of the line; now he no longer doubted it. He was talking to a dead man, someone he'd seen on a slab in the morgue. The voice was his, the cynicism, the black humor. But where was the generosity, the friendship? Only deep resentment remained.

"You understand only too well. With you, someone's always got to die: your parents, Gabriel, Cortez, whoever. Soon it will be Alondra's turn, and after that, who knows? Anyone who gets too close. For you, no sacrifice is good enough. And all for what?"

"The only one who's gonna die is you, you son of a bitch."

"What made you become this complacent, arrogant coward who has to hide behind a microphone to relate to the world, Joaquin? This scaredy-cat who abandoned music out of fear?"

"I don't have to give you any explanations. I don't even have to talk to you."

"You're wrong. You owe me that much, and more." The voice was like an explosion, like a roar emerging from the receiver and spreading in all directions, filling the entire room, bouncing off every surface. It seemed to delineate the shapes in the room like the signals of a ghostly sonar. Joaquin turned around slowly. He knew he was no longer alone. When he saw Gabriel, he dropped the phone and fell back heavily onto the bed.

"What are you doing here?" he said.

"That's my question: What are *you* doing here?" answered Gabriel. His voice was colored with anger.

"What kind of question is that?" Joaquin wanted to say Gabriel's name, but he couldn't form the syllables. After years of hosting a radio show, he had never felt so verbally impotent.

"You know exactly what I mean. You've wasted your life."

"Even if that were true, why should you give a fuck?"

"Because I trusted you. I trusted you desperately, hoping you would do what I couldn't."

"Is that what this is all about? You're frustrated that I haven't done what you wanted to do with your life?" Little by little, Joaquin found himself recovering from his shock at being confronted by a ghost.

"What we both wanted to do."

"How do you figure that?"

"After I was gone, you should have continued on the path. Instead, you abandoned everything that you were passionate about, that gave your life meaning. How long were you planning on wasting your life this way?"

Joaquin couldn't find the words to defend himself; his eloquence had truly evaporated, his arguments ripped to shreds before they even left his mouth. He felt vertigo and an acute pain in his temple.

"You're really interested in the existence of those who are no longer with us? I'll tell you all about it. Come on, let's go for a drive. I'm guessing you're not too busy." His sarcastic tone was eerily familiar.

Gabriel left the room and Joaquin followed him to the door without protest, resigned to his fate, whatever it might be.

"Let's take your car. I want to go back to the city we grew up in."

Thoughts danced through Joaquin's head: Any minute he will vanish. I'll wake up cold, sweaty, and alone. He recalled what Alondra had told him about lucid dreams and the techniques he used to know. You could tell if you were in a dream, the theory went, by looking at your right hand. Okay, he told himself. Look at your right hand.

Slowly, he felt his arm lifting. His fingertips tingled. Then his right hand came into view palm up.

Now what? he wondered.

In dreams, you can never turn out the lights, he recalled Alondra saying.

He flipped the light switch off. The light stayed on. Joaquin flipped the switch on and off several times. The room remained intensely lit. He smiled. Gabriel stepped back in and caught him playing with the lights.

"If it makes you feel better to think that this is just a dream, that's fine. But let's go."

"If it isn't a dream, how do you explain this?" Joaquin said, flipping the switch once more.

The lights went out.

"Don't forget that in dreams, nothing is permanent. Everything is in flux; solids are liquids, their identities interchangeable," Gabriel said, walking toward the parking lot.

Then, in an instant, they were in the car. *In dreams, everything is in flux.*

"Where are we going?" Joaquin asked as he started the car.

"Just drive."

As they pulled out of the parking lot, Joaquin asked the question that had plagued him since Gabriel's reappearance.

"How'd you come back?"

"You brought me back. I was on the other side of what some of us like to call the *fourth wall*."

"Isn't that a theatrical term?"

"Yes. Imagine we're separated by a pane of glass. You're on one side, we're on the other."

"So you're always watching us through the glass."

"Not really. It's different on the other side. I spent a long time not even knowing what I was. I just felt a need. A need to find something. A need to settle scores. On this side, we aren't aware of the boundaries that you feel. We feel you all the time, even when we don't know what that means, but only a few of us can interact with your side. Only the special ones. And I'm one of the special ones. I searched you out and found you, the only way I knew how. Through sound. Through radio. Oh, and a little light show you may remember. I've had the privilege of listening to you and your callers blather on about your fantasies regarding our universe. I cannot imagine what they did in our world before the invention of radio. Marconi, we love you."

"You listen to the radio?"

"It's incredible how nothing changes around here," Gabriel said.

Joaquin was about to reply that he thought exactly the opposite, when he realized where they were. He was driving on the same highway where, decades before, he and Gabriel had met in their fatal, and fateful, head-on collision.

"We're here," Joaquin muttered.

"We're always here."

Joaquin pulled the car to a stop on the shoulder of the highway. They climbed out of the car, thick waves of traffic speeding past them. Somehow it shifted to midday. The sun beat down, bright, clear, anonymous. This time, he accepted the change easily, watching the flow of traffic, enjoying the dance of sunlight on metal. "Have you seen them?" he asked. He knew Gabriel would understand he meant their parents.

"They're still here. Perhaps the biggest difference between us is how we remember, how we experience our memories. Memory is something that resides in a dark corner of the mind; it's invoked in different ways to catch glimpses of the past. Random images from your life are engraved in your mind, but over time, those traces keep changing, they are modified, distorted. For you, memories are internal, they're personal, they're fragile. They whirl about your mind like dust devils, forming one moment, disappearing the next. It's different here. Memories are all around us, as radiant or sordid as the day they were made, and always accessible. And real. Very, very real. You keep them locked in a dark drawer, we—the special ones of the other side—can visit them daily."

Listening to Gabriel, he remembered Gabriel's mania for Polaroids, for constantly creating instant memories that would authenticate his experiences.

"Why did you bring me here?" The exposition on memory was clearly a preamble to something more.

Then he saw the gray van approaching. He wanted to close his eyes, escape, wake up from this strange dream, but he couldn't look away. The van lost control, rolled, and skidded across the asphalt. The black Volvo crossed over into oncoming traffic and met the green Ford head on. They collided in an explosion of metal, heat, and sound. For a moment a penumbra of light surrounded them. Fragments of the car flew through the air. He saw everything: the sparks, the flames, the blood, the metal. Saw it all. Saw the death of his parents. His father decapitated, his head spinning across the hood. His mother impaled by a ghastly shard of metal. He wanted to look away. But he couldn't. He heard a concert of percussive sound, as if every noise were reaching him on its own channel. He could focus on one aspect, or every aspect at the same time. It was an unprecedented aural experience. Then he remembered that voice: *You should really listen.*

"I'm gonna fuck your old lady. I wanted to let you know so we can avoid all the unpleasantness, like the last time we shared a girlfriend. You remember that little redhead I screwed in the backseat while we were waiting for you?"

"What are you saying? What the hell are you talking about?" Joaquin said. He could still see the crash, but he saw something else at the same time. It was Luca, the redhead in question, sitting on Gabriel with her skirt raised and her underwear around her ankles.

At the time, Joaquin had tried to act cool, like he didn't care. But when he heard her moaning, saw her moving up and down over Gabriel, he broke out in a cold sweat and shook with rage. He'd really dug Luca and couldn't believe Gabriel had betrayed him. He didn't say a single word, though. He just got in the front seat and drove. As the car lurched over a pothole, he heard them coming. She with a high-pitched squeal, Gabriel with a guttural grunt. No one mentioned it afterward, but the rest of the evening Luca and Gabriel would smile at each other like accomplices in some forgotten crime. Joaquin had slept with one of Gabriel's ex-girlfriends a few days before, someone Gabriel had said he didn't care about anymore. He understood that this was his revenge. But it ended like so many other things. After a bottle of Scotch and a joint, they talked it over, gave each other a hug, and all was forgiven. Or so Joaquin had thought.

Joaquin watched the Walkman, his Walkman, fly out of the car and hit the pavement, cracking and breaking before it was crushed to bits by a Toyota. Traffic came to a halt. Several drivers got out and stood in the road, staring at the burning remains of the collision. A bloody shoe lay near Gabriel's feet.

"Come on. Let's see what was left of us," he said.

Joaquin followed helplessly. He walked among the other onlookers, but unlike them, he stared coldly at the victims like someone contemplating a diorama; he seemed to be analyzing the parts, trying to read meaning into the scene, deciphering the motives behind it. He started when he saw himself, thrown to the ground, covered with abrasions, his chest bare and eyes open, a strange grimace on his face. No, not quite a grimace. Something else. Almost a smile. He never imagined that he'd been found in that condition. It was no wonder people had preferred to avoid visiting him; his eyes looked dead, but his mouth looked happy.

"They found us here, like that, because we were destined for something big, something important," said Gabriel.

"Important for whom?" Joaquin finally choked out. He had to struggle to breathe.

"Important for us—important for everyone. Important for anyone who believes that music and art transcend a radio program about ghosts."

"Not important to me."

"You're lying. You aspired to something more than entertaining insomniacs and scaring little old ladies. I wasn't the only one who wanted to do something great with my life."

Sirens blaring, the paramedics and police cars arrived.

A woman in a colorful striped sweater ran by screaming, "Shit, shit! My skin's burning, my skin's burning! Come quick, Roger, it burns!"

A gray-haired man with a limp, probably Roger, followed her in silence.

"I've always wanted to know what the fuck was wrong with that broad," said Gabriel.

"Anyways," said Joaquin after a moment, "it's too late for you to do anything important."

"Think so?"

"I want to go back to my hotel. I can't stand being here another second."

"Good luck. I should warn you that the geography here is a little weird; capricious, if you will."

"What's that you said about Alondra a while ago?" Joaquin said, remembering the crude comment.

"That I'm going to fuck her."

"You're an asshole. I never thought being dead could do that to people."

"You think I'm an asshole? You can't imagine how disappointed *I* am. I thought you'd become something. Something really special."

"So why visit me now?"

"It was that radio confession that made me realize there's no hope for you—that I'd become the justification for your descent into mediocrity."

"I'm leaving."

Gabriel was silent. He didn't seem to mind being left behind. Joaquin sensed that the conversation would continue.

Joaquin had often dreamed of Gabriel's return. He wanted it, prayed for it even: ghost, human, monster. It didn't matter. He wanted Gabriel back. He'd seen the return in his mind. Played it out a hundred different ways. But it had never been like this. He never expected Gabriel to be so furious with him. He would never have thought Gabriel could become his enemy. He got into the car. It was night again; the wrecked automobiles and the chaos surrounding them had disappeared. As he pulled away, he tried to orient himself. There were no signs. He drove blindly into the night. Soon the pavement had disappeared, but he kept going, bumping through the desert. He checked his cell phone. No reception.

He turned on the radio, searching the dial for a broadcast. Nothing. Only static until . . . something . . . voices, laughter. He recognized what it was almost immediately. Alondra was talking to a caller who had a story, but was scared they'd make fun of him.

"While our caller decides whether or not to tell us his story, let's go to a commercial break. This is *Ghost Radio*. We'll be right back."

chapter 45

CALL 2109, WEDNESDAY, 3:22 A.M.
DOLLHOUSE

On the line is Lindsay, calling in from Dighton, Rhode Island.

"Go on. What brings you here this time of night?"

"I just wanted to say that I really like your program. I tune in every night, from start to finish."

"Thank you, Lindsay. Do you work the night shift?"

"Maybe she's a vampire, like that guy who called a while ago and said he was going to come over here and suck our blood," Watt added.

"No, the problem is, I haven't been able to sleep for some time now."

"Hmm. Have you considered medication?"

"Yes, and I'm in therapy. I can't take pills, though. When I do fall asleep, I have terrible nightmares."

"Because of some traumatic experience, I would imagine?" Alondra said.

"Yes."

"But not sleeping for long periods of time is very dangerous. You'll wind up doing yourself more harm than you would by facing your nightmares."

"I know."

"Well, frankly, no one here is a doctor. Why don't you just tell us what's on your mind," Joaquin said.

For the past five years, I worked as a babysitter—just until I graduate. But I had to quit. I really like kids; I worked for a family with two-year-old twins, and absolutely adored them. When they turned four, their parents enrolled them in preschool and didn't need me anymore. I started looking for a new job and found a want ad from a woman who worked for a major advertising firm. She needed someone to help look after a seven-year-old girl; let's call her Angie. She hired me without asking for any references, and gave me a very generous salary. I was happy to accept. Angie was polite, but she seemed a little too quiet, almost painfully shy. After about a week, I started to worry. I suspected that her mother hadn't told me everything. Maybe Angie was suffering from some kind of condition or illness. I thought it could be mild autism or something like that, because she avoided physical contact, she would remain motionless for hours, and she rarely talked. If I let her, she would spend the whole day playing silently with a fabulous dollhouse, the only toy that interested her. Her mom was gone practically all day long. I'd see her sometimes in the morning, or when she came home at night, but most days Angie was alone when I got there and alone when I left. Her mother explained that this was why it was absolutely essential that I be punctual. Each week my pay was set out for me in an envelope on the dining-room table.

Every day I picked Angie up at eight, took her to Catholic school, and came back at three to get her. I'd spend the rest of the day with her until I left at seven. It was practically the perfect job; I could prepare for my classes, spend the morning in the library, and do my Internet research and homework while Angie was busy with her dollhouse. I tried to play with her a few times, but every time I came over, she would pull away, and if I tried to insist, she'd become alarmingly hostile.

I understood her obsession with the dollhouse. It fascinated me as well. It was a spectacular Victorian mansion of considerable size, furnished with incredible detail. It looked like an antique, but I couldn't be sure because I'd never seen it close up. One of the walls swung open to expose the interior, and the whole house could also open into two parts so Angie could play inside, withdrawn completely into her own tiny universe.

One night in February there was a snowstorm. I didn't feel one bit like going out into the snow, but it was almost time for me to leave. It occurred to me that I could wait until Angie's mother came back and ask her to give me a ride home. I'd never done it before, but under the circumstances, it seemed reasonable. But as soon as seven o'clock came around, Angie told me I had to go. I was surprised that she minded me staying. I explained that I'd only wait a little longer for her mother and showed her my shoes, which couldn't handle the blizzard coming down outside. She insisted, though, getting more and more upset. She'd run to the window and then back to me, repeating over and over again that it was letting up and I could go now. Her attitude freaked me out. I wanted to know what she was hiding, and maybe have a talk with her mother. It wasn't normal for a girl her age to want to be alone on a night like that.

After a while the electricity went out. Angie had been beside me, but she disappeared into the darkness. Outside, the streets were deserted. There was no sign of her mother. I didn't want to just leave her there, alone. I shouted out her name, but she didn't answer. After a few minutes, I was really worried, and I went to look for a flashlight or some candles. After feeling through every drawer in the house, I finally found a flashlight. As usual, Angie wasn't making any noise. I went to the room where the dollhouse was. I was sure she'd be there. I called out several times before going in, knowing how much it bothered her when I invaded her space. When she didn't answer, I went in. She was inside the dollhouse. I thought that she probably felt safe in there. I heard noises, like little voices, and I called to her again. There was no answer. Finally, I opened up the hinged wall and saw her kneeling down, playing with what looked like dolls. A red glow shone from inside the house. She looked up at me with a vacant expression. Then I saw what she had in her hands. They were body parts: torsos, arms, legs, heads that wriggled with life, like the severed tail of a lizard. I moved closer to get a better look and saw that the heads had faces, their mouths open, screaming for help in tiny, desperate voices. In her small hands, Angie held a partly assembled human figure with a woman's midsection and a bearded male face. It tried to escape, kicking its legs and swinging its only arm. I was trembling; I couldn't believe what I was seeing, so I battled my disgust and moved closer. A boy's head moaned when it saw me.

"What is that?" I asked her, terrified and dazed by the impossible scale of these things, and their horrible realism.

"They're my dolls. Wanna play?" she offered with a disagreeable grimace that seemed like an attempt at a smile. I shined the light directly on them, hoping it would reveal them to be ingenious electronic or mechanical toys, but I merely exposed the expressions of horror and pain on their faces, and the shimmer of saliva, tears, blood, and vomit pooling around them. Angie took an arm from a small pile and stuck it to the body she was holding by pressing them together. "Now you can play with me," she said. This shook me out of my trance. I jumped to my feet, imagining my own disassembled body writhing in that ghastly mound of body parts. She stood up, holding her doll, which was squirming in her hand and screaming with all its might. I ran to the door, afraid that it would be like a horror movie, that I wouldn't be able to open it. Thank God I could. I ran out into the snowstorm without a coat and I struggled blindly through the snow until I got home. Ever since that day, I always hear the cries of Angie's dolls. Her mother never called me again.

chapter 46

THE BACKYARD DESERT

One thing's for sure in this country: the highways, even the most remote ones, don't just melt away into the desert, Joaquin thought as the car bumped along the rutted scrubland. On the radio Alondra was subtly teasing a woman who thought she saw her father's ghost appear every night.

Joaquin couldn't pay attention. He needed to find the highway again, and he was totally disoriented. He should have just been able to retrace his route, but he suspected that things weren't going to work that way. This labyrinth wouldn't let him out. He made a U-turn and accelerated, craning his neck out of the driver's-side window. The moment he looked ahead again, he had to slam on the brakes. Standing a few feet in front of the car was Barry, the shaman's assistant: a trembling figure dressed in rags.

Joaquin stared from behind the glare of the headlights, unable to believe his eyes. He opened the car door and approached Barry slowly, not knowing whether to ask "What are you doing here?" or "What happened to you?" After what seemed like an eternity, he found himself standing in front of the young man. He didn't know what he had asked, or even if he had said anything at all.

"It's cold," said Barry dully.

"You need to bundle up," Joaquin answered, even though he had no blankets to offer.

"Where are we?"

"I don't know, I'm lost too. Do you recognize me?" asked Joaquin, suddenly realizing that Barry hadn't seemed surprised at meeting him in this strange place.

"I'm here because of you. Since you appeared in my life, everything has fallen apart," Barry said finally, raising his eyes from the ground.

"I don't understand."

"Why am I here? Let me go."

"I had nothing to do with this."

"I never recovered from that infection I picked up in Guerrero. You're an incubus from hell."

"Get into the car. In a few minutes, we'll be in a Starbucks drinking coffee."

"Let me go. If I'm dead, let me go."

"Hop in," Joaquin said. "I'll take you home. C'mon, it's cold out here."

Barry looked at the car as if it had just materialized.

"What makes you think we'll get anywhere in that thing? Look around you. Where are you going to go?"

"Climb aboard. If this car got me here, it'll get us out again."

"No, I can't go back. Look what I've got now."

He unzipped his pants and let them fall to the ground. He wasn't wearing any underwear. He stood before Joaquin, naked from the waist down. That, however, was less surprising than the fact that there was a face where his genitals should have been. Joaquin saw a large, aquiline nose with small, inexpressive, bestial eyes on either side. Below it, a lip-less mouth opened and closed over and over again, like a fish struggling to breathe. Joaquin felt the bile rising in his throat.

"What is that shit?" He gagged.

Then he saw another face on Barry's knee, more repulsive than the first. Its tiny mouth drooled and moaned.

"You tell me. What's happening to me? If the master were here, he would have protected me from you."

"Barry, Cortez is alive. I just saw him. He was working as a bellboy at a motel. I have nothing to do with what's happening to you."

"Go to hell."

"Let me take you to a hospital."

"What, you think they're going to prescribe an antibiotic and cure me of *this*?" He gestured at his extra faces.

"I don't know. Will you just get in the car?"

"Leave me alone. Please, just leave me alone."

He turned and walked back into the darkened desert, pulling up his pants as he went. Joaquin shouted after him but he didn't stop, and Joaquin watched helplessly as he disappeared into the blackness.

Joaquin saw flashes of himself in Barry—a broken, fragmented man, a walking cadaver.

No, he told himself, I'm not that! I won't become that.

He got back into the car and drove. The landscape became more treacherous with each passing second. He had the nasty feeling that each bump and divot would be the vehicle's last. Finally, he saw the lights of a house in the distance. Rocks and huge cactuses made driving impossible. Without a second thought, he stopped the car and walked, almost ran, toward it, hoping to find something or someone. An answer? Some respite? Even a battle. Hell, he thought, even something frightening and horrific would be better than being lost any longer, gradually transforming into what Barry had become.

Joaquin looked down at his joints, searched his skin for unfamiliar markings, touching his penis now and again just to make sure it was still there. By the time he reached the house, he was out of breath. It turned out that it wasn't a house, but a country store. The only thing barring entry was a battered screen door. He pulled it open and called out:

"Hello, is anyone there? Can I come in?"

No answer.

He repeated the question. Again, nothing. He entered cautiously and heard someone talking inside. He called out again as he stepped across the threshold. The floorboards squeaked, and there was a monotonous voice . . . chanting? When he got closer, he saw an old radio sitting on the table. It was tuned to a religious station. The voice was an evangelist sermonizing about glorytogod, and the salvation only achievable by accepting ourlordjesuschrist as youronlysavior.

"Do you accept him as your savior?" he asked, his words tinged with a slight Asian accent.

He recited prayers, threatened his listeners' souls with perdition, and then wrapped up the whole thing with an offer: "To be saved, call 1-900-SALVATN! To make a donation, dial 1-900-GODGOLD!" According to the announcement that followed, the pastor's name was Yoong-Go Chung. Unfortunately for Pastor Chung, thought Joaquin, there's no one but me around, no loyal followers to hear his message of redemption. Nothing more appropriate in this desert than a redeemer preaching in solitude.

He passed the radio and knocked at a closed door on the other side of the room. There was no answer. He twisted the doorknob. It turned. He crossed the threshold into the next room, then stopped short, flabbergasted. He was in the lobby of his motel. He quickly retreated back into the store. But now it wasn't a store. It was an office. He dashed toward the exit, went outside, and found himself in a parking lot with two huge garbage bins and a wall covered with graffiti. One of the tags read KILL KILL KILL THE POOR. His car rested in the exact spot where he'd left it. He went back to the lobby and walked up to the reception desk.

"Good evening, sir. Everything all right in your room?" asked the clerk enthusiastically.

"Yes, I believe everything's fine," Joaquin answered.

"You have a message, from a Miss . . . Algebra."

"Algebra?"

The front-desk clerk pulled out a slip of paper from under the desk.

"No, sorry, Al-on-dra. The person who left the message is named Alondra."

Joaquin took the piece of paper and headed toward his room.

chapter 47

RADIO SHAMAN

His room looked completely different from the way Joaquin remembered it. He tried to determine how much time had passed since Gabriel's call. Fifteen minutes at most. Maybe less. Even though it was likely he had gone no farther than the motel parking lot, he felt a curious, mute euphoria at having returned, at not having turned into something like Barry, at no longer being lost in the desert. He wanted to believe it had been a dream. In fact, he wanted to believe that about much of his life. Who wouldn't? Joaquin welcomed this pleasant thought. It eased his mind. But it changed nothing.

His life was still in chaos. Questions remained unanswered. And this moment of calm, like all of the others in the last few days, quickly evaporated.

What had happened? What was happening? Perhaps he'd wandered through an intermediate realm between dreams and wakefulness. An intermediate realm between dreams and wakefulness? What did that mean? Every puzzle turned into another puzzle. How much longer could he cope? Could he handle a life where reality possessed the transience of dreams? He was exhausted, but he had to call Alondra.

"Hi, I heard you called."

"Finally. I've been waiting to hear from you."

"How'd you know where I was?"

"Telepathy, long-distance vision, spy satellites. Or, more likely, from your message."

"My message."

"The text message you sent me."

"No . . . are you sure?"

"Of course I'm sure. I got the message from your cell phone a couple of hours ago."

"From my cell phone, but not the one I'm calling with. The other one. Right?"

"Yeah, the old one. Did you find it?"

"I found it."

Joaquin knew who'd given her the information, but he didn't want to explain it over the phone.

"I dialed both numbers lots of times, but no luck."

"Yeah. Where I was, there's practically no reception."

"Did you find what you were looking for?"

"What I was looking for?"

"Joaquin, are you awake? Are you listening to me?"

"Sure, sure, I'm just very tired."

"Okay, let's give it a rest, we'll talk tomorrow. It's late."

"No, don't hang up yet. I didn't find what I wanted . . ." Joaquin started to say, but just then he stuck his hand in his pocket and took out the tape he'd stolen from Winkler. It was the closest thing to evidence he had. "Actually, I did find something. I'm not too sure what good it will do me, but the trip wasn't a total washout."

"Well, that's good."

"I heard the program. Listening to your voice was the best thing that happened to me all day," he said, making an effort to sound affectionate.

"We weren't on the air today. It must have been a repeat. But I thought no one broadcast us Sundays. You know, religious shit. I'll check it out. When are you coming back?"

"On the first available flight."

"Fine."

He listened to her breathing. He sensed she wanted to say more.

Joaquin needed something more intimate than just good-bye. He wanted to tell her everything that had happened. He wanted to share what he'd seen and warn her about what might lie ahead. But what did lie ahead? He had no idea. The fact that they hadn't been broadcasting that day didn't even surprise him. Reality had become a puzzle whose pieces had deformed and didn't fit together anymore.

"See you soon."

"Yes. Tomorrow. Good-bye."

They hung up.

The dry farewell deepened Joaquin's somber mood. He was hurting and tired. He took off his clothes, turned on the television, and got into bed. He needed sleep, but anxiety got the better of him; he surfed channels, leaning back against the headrest. One channel featured Pastor Yoong-Go Chung, the televangelist who still intoned glorytogod and ourlordjesuschrist and youronlysavior. He flipped channels, and J. Cortez appeared on the screen. When he saw him, Joaquin leaped out of bed. Would this nightmare ever end? Cortez sat in a generic office chair; the only scenery was a cheap-looking backdrop decorated with Aztec, Mayan, and other pre-Hispanic symbols, all mixed together in no particular order. Under his face in red letters it said PASTOR CUAHTÉMOC ILLUICAMINA: 1-900-CHAMANI. He was in the middle of a sermon about the path of the Toltec warrior.

"Reality was just an illusion," he preached, "a collage of perceptions, emotions, and mirages."

Under other circumstances, Joaquin would have found this incoherent nonsense amusing. He would have dismissed Cortez as just another phony preacher, getting rich by exploiting insomniacs and lonely hearts—the depressed and the desperate.

But today he found it soothing.

He listened intently as the pastor continued:

"The fabric of reality is held in place by the tension that exists between the domains of the living and the dead. These two act as the poles of a universal dynamo, generating the energy that keeps the world in balance. Although they are separate, they can be traversed through portals, disruptions in the order of things caused by a variety of different factors, Joaquin."

What? Did the pastor just say his name?

"Factors such as people on their deathbeds, for example, highly morbid necrophiles, or those who have undergone near-death experiences."

Near-death experiences? Is that what incited all this?

"If there's one thing that the living and the dead do share, it's radio. The radio can be heard in the other dominion, just as it can in ours."

"They already explained that to me," Joaquin said sarcastically. The television was addressing him, why shouldn't he talk back?

"What they didn't explain to you," the TV shaman said, "is that under certain circumstances, radio stations themselves can also open up portals between the two dominions."

Joaquin didn't need him to draw a map. He knew what had happened that night at the radio station, or at least he thought he did. The signs were scattered everywhere. Even if he didn't quite get the mechanics of it, he knew he'd crossed a threshold that night. Crossed the thin veil into the other world.

"But in order to fully understand what happened," Cortez said without looking into the camera, as if he were reading, "you ought to go over to 123 Nyqvist Drive and pick up some souvenirs you lost along the way. You shouldn't have any trouble recognizing the place."

Joaquin knew what the man on TV was talking about. There was an old industrial building at that address where he and Gabriel had lived as squatters just before the incident at the radio station. He could never, ever forget such a peculiar address. After the accident, he never went back. What for? It was practically impossible there'd be anything left. Even if the other squatters hadn't stolen everything, the building probably had legal tenants by now.

"And, if you want to continue on the path of the Toltec warrior, call now and make a donation to the Temple of Christian and Toltec Redemption. Come on, Joaquin, don't be a cheap bastard. Make the call."

Joaquin stood up. It was late, but he had to go see what awaited him at 123 Nyqvist Drive. He dressed quickly, gathered his belongings, and left the room. He needed sleep, but he would get no rest until he solved this puzzle.

No rest at all.

Old memories and unknown images bounced around in his head at dizzying speeds as he walked toward the parking lot. He drove like someone possessed, arriving at his destination without being aware of the trip. The two-story ocher-brick building with black bars looked just as he remembered, unchanged in more than twenty years.

He knocked on the door, not knowing what he'd say if someone answered. Was that even likely? At this time of night? Who'd take the risk? They might find a crazy man standing on their porch. Tonight they *would* find a crazy man standing on their porch.

Then he remembered how Gabriel picked the lock when they'd absentmindedly left their key somewhere. He climbed down from the porch and surveyed the ground. He needed a piece of wire, thin but sturdy. He looked around. Nothing. He walked over to the sidewalk, the gutter.

There he found it. A thin piece of copper wire: just the right thickness. Just the right density. Had it been placed here just for him?

Then he grabbed a rock, and headed back to the door. He slid the wire into the keyhole, and banged on it with a rock. He struggled a little trying to twist the knob, but on the third try the door gave and swung open. Before he could step inside, a frying pan crashed against the doorframe, missing his face by inches.

A woman was screaming, and Joaquin saw a man charge the door, trying to slam it shut. Joaquin took the blow and pushed the door as hard as he could, throwing it wide open and sending the man, a short, stocky guy with blond dreadlocks, rolling on the ground. The woman, still screaming, threw a kitchen knife at Joaquin, which hit him on the arm—fortunately with the handle end, not the blade.

"Easy! I don't want to hurt you," Joaquin yelled.

"Kill him, Dash. Kill him!" the woman screamed.

Actually, Dash could barely get up off the floor.

"Out of my house!" he yelled, not too convincingly.

Joaquin picked the knife up off the floor, brandishing it.

"Easy, I'm not going to do anything to you. I just want to ask you something."

The woman threw everything within reach at him. He evaded the onslaught with varying degrees of success, until finally he leaned down and pressed the point of the knife blade against Dash's neck.

"Stop it, or I'll cut Dash's fucking head off!"

The woman froze. Dash moaned something along the lines of, "No, please, don't."

"I didn't come here to hurt anybody, I'm just looking for my stuff. I lived here a long time ago, and I left everything behind."

He looked around the living room, pointing out different items:

"Those bookcases, that table, those paintings, the graffiti on that wall, they were all mine. All I want are some souvenirs, things that wouldn't have any value to you."

What exactly was he looking for? He had no idea.

When he saw that he had their full attention, he lowered the knife and helped Dash to his feet.

"I'll be out of here soon. Please, just let me look for my stuff."

"Yeah, it's him, Lizzy," Dash said to the woman.

"I already recognized him," she answered.

"What are you talking about?" asked Joaquin. Were they fans of *Ghost Radio*?

"There's a box of photos and crap. We kept it in case someone came around looking for it. You're in most of the photos. I recognized you right away. Well, right after I realized you weren't a murdering psychopath."

"That's what I want."

"Let me go get it," Lizzy said.

"Sorry for barging in like this. But I just really needed that stuff back."

"We thought you were from the city. They've come by a few times to try and evict us."

The woman presented him with a shoe box crammed full of photos, papers, envelopes, and various other objects.

It wouldn't be long before daybreak.

Joaquin took out a fistful of old, fading Polaroids. Gabriel's memories, the testimonies to his experiences and adventures, were being inexorably erased. Among the dusty papers was an envelope that looked recent. He took it out of the box. It was addressed to him; he recognized Gabriel's handwriting.

"That's the only thing that's new," Dash said.

"Yeah, your friend brought it a few days ago."

"What friend?"

"That guy," he said, pointing out one of the photos that Gabriel had taken of himself.

"What did he do?"

"I found him sitting outside on the sidewalk. He told me the same thing as you, that he'd lived here and left a lot of stuff behind. I thought he'd want it all back, so I told him that when we got here the place was empty. But he starting listing all the shit we'd inherited from you guys. Then he reassured me there was nothing to worry about, that I could keep it. But he asked me to give you this envelope, along with everything else in that box, whenever you showed up."

Joaquin took Gabriel's latest appearance in stride. His capacity for surprise had vanished. Under the curious gaze of Dash and Lizzy, he emptied the contents of the envelope out onto the table.

He smiled at the items arrayed before him. A blast from the past: photos, diagrams, and notes, all relating to Gabriel's last day on earth. He gazed for a time at the floor plan of the radio station, remembering the day Gabriel first showed it to him. His eyes wide and clear, speaking of becoming pirate-radio legends.

But then his smile faded. One item on the table didn't make sense. A photo. He picked it up slowly, his fingers trembling, and an eerie chill coursing through his body.

No, he told himself, this is impossible. It just can't be.

His hands were paralyzed. The photo slipped from his fingers and fell to the floor. Sweat beaded on his forehead and his knees buckled. He grasped a chair to keep from falling.

In the photo, Joaquin and Gabriel stood arm in arm, smiling. And on Joaquin's right slouched a very serious-looking Alondra.

chapter 48

CALL 1288, MONDAY, 2:13 A.M.
LUCY'S APPLE

"What's your name?" asked Joaquin.

"Nell."

"And where are you calling from, Nell?"

"San Francisco."

"Well, let's hear your story."

"I heard this story from a couple of ladies talking at a bus stop and I told it to my friends from school. It kind of became an obsession with some of the girls. So people used to say that I was the one who started the whole thing."

"Started what?"

The story I heard was that you could find out who you're going to end up marrying by eating a green apple with a long stem in front of a mirror at midnight. I don't know how many of my friends tried it, because they would never admit it if they did. The most important thing was that no matter what happens, you can't turn around. Anyways, one night I was with my cousin Lucy. As always, we were obsessing about boys. "Boy crazy," my mom calls it.

Lucy really, really wanted to know who she was going to marry. She was really hung up on it. You know, whether she'd find the right guy, if anyone would ever love her, and all that stuff. Even if she would have a fancy wedding. She hardly ever talked about anything else. She got a green apple and waited till midnight, when her mom and dad and brothers were asleep, then she went into the bathroom with it. She stood in front of the mirror, thought real hard about who she was gonna marry, and started eating. She chewed on the apple for a long time till she finished it off, never taking her eyes off the mirror. She told me that she was beginning to see a guy in the mirror, when she felt something behind her, like a shuffling or something. She'd locked the door, so she knew no one could have come in. Now, like I said, there's one big rule for this game: You must never turn away from the mirror and look behind you, no matter what. If you turn around, the man you were supposed to marry will die.

You'll live out your life alone. A spinster. An old maid. Lucy was terrified of that. But she couldn't stop herself. The sound was scary. And it wasn't going away. She turned. What she saw . . . she said it was like a dark figure, like an "out-of-focus person" or something. It freaked her out.

She screamed, and when her parents broke down the door, they found her all by herself. She told them she'd been sitting on the toilet, dozed off, and had a nightmare. She didn't sleep for the rest of the night. When she got to school the next day, there was a lot of commotion. All of the kids were whispering to each other. And all the teachers were totally serious. She asked what was going on, and her best friend told her that one of the boys in class 4D, Mark Spencer, had dropped dead the night before. Out of the blue. He wasn't sick or anything. They found him in his bed, dead, with his eyes wide open, staring at the ceiling. The doctors couldn't figure out what killed him. When his parents came to clean out his locker, they found a picture of Lucy. It turned out he had a crush on her, and he was still trying to work up the courage to ask her out.

chapter 49

MEMORIES OF COLETT

The moment I saw the photograph, my mind was flooded with memories of the girl we met that day in the desert.

I remembered Colett.

I remembered entering the radio station with her.

I remembered the mastiff almost biting off my nose.

I remembered my horror of the dogs eating Gabriel while the rescue workers tried to resuscitate me.

Gabriel's photo released a hemorrhage of visions, memories, and conflicting feelings. Forgotten for so long. But the images looked real. They looked familiar. More than that, they felt real. They felt like the truth. And not much had in the last few days.

They awoke in me something that had lain dormant for years, like breaking a spell, like waking up after a century of sleep. I was altered, changed, transformed. Nothing would ever be the same again.

But this photo of Colett wasn't a photo of Colett. It was Alondra.

Under different circumstances, in another time, another world, I would have dismissed it as a fake. Just Photoshop nonsense. But I was beyond reason and logic. This was certainty. I had to accept it.

I couldn't move. The walls breathed, audibly and hypnotically, like a giant cat purring itself to sleep.

The past surrounded me: objects intimate and familiar. A sofa retaining the shape of my body, shelves that once held my favorite books, tables with rings from long-forgotten cups of coffee and glasses of tequila. Under my shock and fear rested another feeling: A feeling of beckoning.

The past seemed a blink away; I could relax into it, fall back and let the decades evaporate.

Oh, how I wanted to do this. Just let the present slip away. Forget my life, my relationships, my job. Forget the Internet, cell phones, DVDs, TiVo, *American Idol,* and the War on Terror. Forget all the pain and joy. Just let it all spiral off into the ether, chasing lost radio signals in the heavens. It felt so close, so possible.

But this sensation vanished when I noticed Dash and Lizzy watching me, mesmerized.

"Hey, I don't wanna be rude. But you've got your box now, and we're exhausted."

"Yeah, I gotta go," I said. "I'm flying home in the morning."

But I still couldn't move.

My desire to return to the past melted away, disappeared, the inexplicable urgency transformed into doubt. Since the chat I'd had on the air with the man who'd reminded me of Gabriel, I had wavered between fear and curiosity, between skepticism and the desire to experience for myself what dozens of people confessed to me on the show every day. Before, of course, I believed ghosts only existed in people's imaginations. This made them no less real. But it dissociated them from haunted mansions, prisons, dark alleys, or any kind of physical space. I knew that Gabriel, or his ghost, or whatever had appeared to me, had always existed in my head, a kind of superego always watching over my shoulder, judging my every decision, my every weakness. Talking to him was just another way of engaging in an internal dialogue. Another way of thinking.

All of that I could almost accept. Almost.

But this Colett/Alondra photo was different.

Could Alondra and Colett really be the same person? I remembered the first time I met Alondra at that party in Mexico City; I replayed, in my mind, the natural way she approached me, talked to me about that ridiculous zombie comic, how we went out to eat and took the first faltering steps toward love. I tried to determine if anything about that night offered a sign. If any of her words or gestures revealed the clue, allowing all of the pieces of the puzzle to fall into place.

My tattoo, she'd been quite intrigued by my tattoo. I rolled up my sleeve and looked at it, hoping it might offer me a message.

But it didn't. Maybe it couldn't.

Gabriel's voice echoed in my ears, speaking of memories living in the darkest corners of the mind.

For you, memories are internal, they're personal, they're fragile.

He was right. They were fragile. Fragile as rice paper.

Finally, I stumbled toward the door. All of this had left me punchy. When was the last time I ate? Slept?

"You all right, man?" said Dash.

"Yeah, I just need some rest."

When I stepped through the door, dawn was breaking.

Driving to the airport, I imagined confronting Alondra. What would I say? Would I accuse her of lying to me all these years? Would I yell that she was part of a conspiracy against me? Would I force her, by any means necessary, to confess the details of this cruel deception? Or maybe it would be better to get the truth out of her gently, by tricking her somehow. Perhaps I could try talking to her sincerely, explain what I'd discovered, show her the proof, and try to figure out from her reaction whether she was part of this bizarre comedy of errors or whether she was, like me, a victim of something inexplicable.

Then again, maybe the best option was to destroy the photograph, and convince myself that everything I'd experienced had been a sort of delirium brought on by exhaustion and stress. I liked that alternative. But I couldn't shake the knowledge that the point of this entire trip had been to get me to discover this picture. I felt almost as if my actions over the past few weeks had been meticulously programmed and narrated like some kind of show, as if I'd been obliviously following a script in which my every step, decision, and word had already been written down. I replayed everything in my head over and over as I drove, and no matter how many times I told myself I was just being an idiot, I always reached the same conclusion.

I couldn't pay attention to the road. I kept crossing the lane dividers, sometimes going too fast, sometimes too slow. My eyes kept going back to the box of photographs and souvenirs on the seat next to me. I really didn't want to look at the photo again, but I knew I had to. I had to be sure; I couldn't go on without confirming what I'd seen. Colett was clear in my mind, walking toward the station, sitting down at the console, eating tacos next to me, picking up the flower I'd drawn.

But there was nothing consistent about my memories; the characters shifted, the locations differed, the words changed, never repeating the same way twice. My erratic driving didn't improve over the course of the trip. Other drivers swerved to avoid me, or honked in anger. Finally, the airport appeared on the horizon like an oasis.

As I approached I passed the café I'd seen when I first arrived in Houston. It was just past dawn, but there was still a small crowd gathered around a radio, listening intently. No one moved; the whole thing was like a tableau. This time, I slowed down and rolled down my window. I only needed to hear a few words; it was tuned to *Ghost Radio*. I rolled up my window as fast as I could, accelerating toward the airport and my flight home.

Hordes of people crowded the terminal, mostly businessmen, dragging small suitcases while talking on cell phones or thumbing BlackBerrys. I got a seat on the next flight. I had almost an hour to kill, but I really wanted to kill the voice that wouldn't stop chattering in my head. I bought a small suitcase to hold my box of recovered memories. I was tempted to deep-six the whole thing, to throw it in the trash, or just leave the package at the gate. But I couldn't help imagining the bomb squad, enveloped in their clumsy, cushioned space suits and surrounded by a gaggle of dogs and robots, paralyzing the entire airport while they destroyed the suitcase of souvenirs and reviewed the security tapes in search of the terrorist who'd left it there.

It made no sense to try to get any rest; every time I started to relax, my internal monologue exploded with conjectures and proposals, denunciations and accusations. My head was spinning. I entered the only café open, sat down at the bar, and ordered some orange juice.

While I waited for the server—a good-looking young woman with dark hair, maybe Hispanic—I pulled out my cell phone and dialed Watt's number. I didn't feel up to talking to Alondra quite yet, but I wanted to make sure nothing had happened to her in the last few hours, that the mere existence of the photo in my suitcase hadn't somehow vaporized her, changed her into J. Cortez or Dash or who-knows-what.

"Hello?"

He sounded muffled. I'd forgotten it was so early in the morning.

"Watt, it's me."

"Who?"

My heart clenched. Was this another strange waking dream, one in which I didn't exist?

"It's me. Joaquin."

"Oh, Joaquin. Hi." He yawned. "What's going on? Alondra said you were out of town."

"Sorry to bother you so early, Watt. Just wondered if you talked to her since last night."

"To Alondra? You guys have a fight or something?"

"No, I just had a bad feeling."

His voice got a little edgier. He was obviously irritated. "You're calling me before seven on my day off because of a bad feeling? Are you losing it, Joaquin? No, I haven't had a chance to talk to her. I'm sure she's fine. Did I mention it's before seven?"

"All right, all right, I'm sorry."

He would get over it; in the long term, he had a high tolerance for my eccentricities. I was more worried about myself at the moment. Suddenly a thought struck me.

"Hey, Watt, you know about radio waves, right? I was talking to"— I paused for a moment, unsure how to proceed—"someone. I was talking to someone I ran into here, and he had a theory about our broadcasts. That somehow they could reach beyond our world, into, well, I know it sounds crazy, but into the spirit world. The afterlife."

He perked up a bit at this, sounding more alert, if no less grumpy.

"There's still a lot we don't know about electromagnetism, Joaquin."

Gradually, I'd been realizing how strange it was, hearing Watt's voice from hundreds of miles away. Almost as if Watt himself were being distilled into the very waves we were discussing and sent through the air, through the ether, through space, through time. It wasn't such an absurd concept, but it hit me with the force of a jackhammer. The air around me, I realized suddenly, was full of voices. Every person who was on the phone in the airport. Every TV newscaster, every traffic report, every security guard with a walkie-talkie. What were these waves taking from us? I sat in front of a mike, sending my voice out across the country five hours a day—what were they taking from *me*?

"When you're talking about waves that don't need air or water as a medium, signals that can move through empty space, signals of pure energy, well, who knows where they can go? If we wait long enough, four or five years, aliens in the next star system could be listening to *Ghost Radio*. Hell, knowing our show, some of them might even be callers."

I couldn't help but smile, although I still felt queasy.

"You're right about that. Look, I'm sorry I bothered you. I'll be back in a few hours. Do me a favor and check up on Alondra when you get a chance."

"Sure. Just don't think too hard about this stuff, Joaquin. Who cares where our signal goes? We're worried about you."

He hung up.

The waitress came back with my juice; I tried for a while to start up a conversation with her, but she seemed too overworked and tired to even feign interest. I could tell my small talk annoyed her, but I couldn't stop. I felt like I'd just done speed and been rendered indifferent to my surroundings. It was obvious that this minimum-wage employee didn't need this, as she satisfied the demands of a half-dozen executives ordering coffee, sandwiches, croissants, and yogurts without detaching themselves from their cell phones.

I started talking about the inane security measures that only complicated travel and didn't make anyone safer, pointing out, like a cliché machine, the incompetence of the baggage checkers. No one paid any attention to my ranting. The server turned on a radio behind the counter and cranked up the volume. The words died in my mouth as I recognized the voices. It was *Ghost Radio*.

"That's me," I told the waitress when she passed.

"Who?" she asked, pushing her hair from her face with the back of her hand.

"The guy on that show, *Ghost Radio*."

The woman remained expressionless.

"The program you're listening to. I work there."

"Oh yeah? And what do you do?" the employee asked, with fatigued curiosity.

"I'm Joaquin—I'm the host."

"I've never heard that name and I've been listening for years," she said, and moved off.

It might have been a way to demonstrate her indifference, or to put an arrogant patron in his place—no doubt she'd run into loads of them—or maybe she was telling the truth. I listened to the voices on the radio, but I could only identify Alondra. There was a male voice that could have been mine, but I couldn't hear it clearly. When the young woman passed by again, I insisted:

"You're telling me you don't know Joaquin, from *Ghost Radio*? Really?"

"What do you want me to say? Okay, fine. I know Joaquin from *Ghost Radio*," she answered irritably.

She brushed the hair out of her eyes with the back of her hand again and went off to serve more decaf and plastic-wrapped food. Eventually, she returned to the counter. I couldn't contain myself.

"Excuse me, but it's just that I'm Joaquin. That's me. I'm the guy who created the show."

"You mean Gabriel," the woman said, staring straight at me. "Gabriel is the host of *Ghost Radio*. He's called Gabriel, not Joaquin."

The floor seemed to fall out from under me.

The waitress moved off to feed more hungry, sleepy executives. As she stepped away, I recognized the voice on the radio—it was mine. I *was* sure. She was talking nonsense. It was a program from a few months ago; a night when a caller claimed he'd trapped *chupacabras*. Watt had laughed so hard, he pulled a muscle in his abdomen. I really wanted to debate with the waitress, tell her she was wrong, that there was no Gabriel on the show, and that if she had access to my nightmares, she should do me a favor and go fuck herself. But she'd already disappeared behind a door marked EMPLOYEES ONLY.

I paid my check, picked up my suitcase, took a few steps toward the exit, then stopped. I turned and walked back to the counter. I strained to listen to radio over the din of the restaurant. I wanted to hear Alondra's voice once more. To my surprise, though, it was a local morning show. The host, Howard Stern–style, suggested to a young porn actress that she'd "be more comfortable naked." Guffaws greeted the comment. A red-haired waitress wearing glasses stopped in front of me and asked if I needed anything.

"No; nothing, thanks, I'm leaving. But someone just changed the station. Can you put it back to where it was before?"

"No one's changed that station in years," she said. "Look." She pointed at the radio's tuning dial, which was missing.

"But a second ago it was playing *Ghost Radio*!" I cried. "The young lady who waited on me even said she knew the program real well."

"*Ghost Radio?* That's on at night, very late."

"Yes, I know, but the other waitress, the dark-haired one, told me . . ."

I went behind the counter and opened the "Employees Only" door, revealing a tiny pantry.

"Miss!" I called.

A hand firmly grasped my shoulder and pulled me out. It was the redhead, furious.

"Sir, what are you looking for back there? No customers allowed! I'm gonna call security."

"Sorry," I said quickly. "I just wanted to ask your coworker something, the young lady who waited on me."

"There's no one in there—and I don't have any coworker. I'm the only one who could possibly have waited on you, because I'm the only one here. Please get out of there; can't you see I don't have time for this?"

"She was a young woman with dark hair . . ." I repeated dumbly.

"Just me," she said, with an aggressive stare, and pushed me toward the exit.

The executives had stopped their telephone conversations, stopped biting into their donuts and bagels, dropped their briefcases and PDAs. They stared at me distastefully, as if I'd embarrassed the entire traveling community by demanding anything other than food from the waitress. I tried to ignore their looks and discreetly remove myself from their field of vision, but I felt their stares following me as I exited the restaurant. The boarding call for my flight came over the loudspeaker. I forced myself to ignore that the voice sounded like Gabriel.

As I took my seat, I had a clear recollection of Colett jumping the station fence in her boots, concentrating on the console, drinking, eating, smiling, and brushing back her hair with the back of her hand.

chapter 50

A SECURITY HAZARD

Joaquin's return trip was not especially comfortable.

The episode at the airport café had left him too keyed up to sleep. He wondered if he'd every sleep again. If he'd ever think a rational thought again. If he'd ever . . . oh God, the list was endless. Even the prospect of going home provided no comfort. What would happen when he got there? What day would it be? What week? What month? What year? The thoughts terrified him. As his flight prepared for takeoff, he felt his sanity slipping away.

He fought to maintain it, fought to make sense of things. Maybe he could find a rational, even scientific, explanation for all that had happened to him. But where? How?

He gripped the armrests; he was losing the battle to make sense of this. He was in some kind of a time warp, a temporal crossroads where different stages of his life intersected, future, past, and present all within reach, all mixed together. Quantum physics suggested things like this. Didn't it? No hypothesis seemed any more believable, or even any more real, than the next. He regretted not knowing more about the intellectual labyrinths and logical contradictions involved in time travel and parallel dimensions, but he thought nothing was going to make him feel better at this point.

Never before had he experienced such intense vertigo; as the plane taxied toward the runway he felt like he was entering an operating room, steeling himself for a brutal surgery. But as he heard the routine announcements that no computers or CD players could be used during takeoff, and to switch off cell phones for the remainder of the flight, Joaquin realized that he was in a kind of isolation capsule, a space free of radio signals. If Gabriel could be believed, radio waves were audible beyond the world of the living, but they couldn't reach this airplane. Up in the sky, he was safe from *Ghost Radio,* safe from his counterpart, safe from the demons in his brain that were demolishing common sense. But he'd have to land eventually, and confront the public and their calls, confront the visions and apparitions. Maybe he should resign from the program. Maybe that would rid him of ghosts, hypothetical time travel, and this endless state of waking somnambulism. Even more important, perhaps it would dispel the pall of confusion that now surrounded the only part of his life he wasn't willing to give up: Alondra.

He repositioned himself in his seat and tried to go to sleep. He felt a hand on his shoulder.

"Mind letting me through? That's my seat."

Joaquin jumped, startled; he'd thought the airplane door had already closed. He pulled back his legs, rubbed his eyes, and let the stranger pass. But looking up, he realized it wasn't a stranger. It was Gabriel.

"What a coincidence. This great big plane, and here we are seated right next to each other."

He grinned from ear to ear, showing Joaquin his boarding pass as he eased into the window seat.

"I didn't think *you* needed one of those to be able to fly," said Joaquin.

"I didn't want to miss the chance for us to chat again. We have so much to talk about."

"What do you want from me?"

"Not much, my friend. You don't have a lot to offer anymore. Actually, I'm the one who's giving *you* things, like those souvenirs in your luggage. Happy days, huh?"

He smiled again. Menace gleamed in his eyes.

"Let's not talk, okay? I need some sleep."

He pulled a magazine from the pocket in front of his seat and casually flipped through the pages.

"I just thought you might have some questions," he said offhandedly.

I remained silent.

"Like about Alondra."

"What about Alondra?" I asked, unable to remain silent.

"I said 'Colett.' You do seem to get those names confused, don't you?"

"You said 'Alondra.' I heard it clearly."

"Want me to roll back time, and show you what I said."

He shook the magazine and the photo of Colett fell out.

He picked it up and considered it.

"Hmm . . . how did this get here?"

I stared at him, my eyes narrowing with anger.

"Do you want it back?" he said, offering it to me.

I grabbed for it, but he snatched it away. Then he turned it over and looked at the back.

"That's odd, I thought this was a photo of Alondra. Look what it says."

I looked at the back of the photo; written in black marker was the name Colett.

"It says 'Colett,'" I said blandly.

"No, it doesn't. Look at it again."

I looked at the back again, and watched as the letters rearranged themselves, until they spelled a different word. The word: *Toltec*.

"What is that supposed to mean?" I said handing the photo back to him. "Are you trying to tell me Colett is a Toltec?"

"Colett? Who's that?"

He showed me the back of the photograph again. Now it said "Alondra."

"Do you really want to live this way, blind, always vulnerable to a past you can't even remember—a past still crouching in the shadows, ready to jump out and bite you on the ass?"

"I can take anything you can dish out. Always could."

"You can be taken. I'll give you that."

Cute. But Joaquin refused to let it get to him. Then a thought seemed to cross his mind. A rich, juicy thought. And, for the first time in hours, he smiled.

"Okay, I have some questions for you."

"Uh-huh," Gabriel said, his eyes returning to the magazine.

"You said that on the other side, you couldn't hear us, couldn't hear anything, right?"

Gabriel nodded without looking up.

"How are we talking?"

"It says here that Lindsay Lohan is open to nude scenes if it's 'integral to the plot.' Surprising, huh?"

"Did you hear me?"

"Not surprising that she'd do a nude scene, but that she knows the word 'integral,'" Gabriel said, chuckling to himself.

"I asked you a question."

"I know. I heard you."

"And?"

"Haven't you figured it out yet?"

Joaquin took a deep breath.

"I should never have given it to you?"

"Given me what?"

"*Ghost Radio.*"

"You didn't give me *Ghost Radio*. I created it. I created it without you."

"Created it? You don't even know what it is."

"It's a radio show."

"No, Joaquin, it's not a radio show. It never was. It's a machine."

chapter 51

A GHOST IN THE MACHINE

Joaquin woke suddenly. He looked around. Gabriel was gone.

Joaquin's attention was diverted momentarily by one of the flight attendants passing in the aisle.

"Is this seat occupied?" he said.

"No, sir, everyone is on board and the door is locked. You're in luck—you'll be able to stretch out and rest."

"Did you see someone here just now?"

"No. Just you."

"Excuse me," Joaquin said, and stood up.

"Sir, we're about to take off. You have to remain seated."

"It's an emergency."

Joaquin started quickly down the aisle, looking at all the passengers. He knew he wouldn't find Gabriel, but he was alert for anything suspicious, some kind of clue. Part of him still stubbornly refused to rule out the notion that this was all someone's idea of a practical joke. He knew it was impossible for anyone to take a joke this far, but he couldn't, or wouldn't, discard the idea.

The flight attendant followed him nervously.

"Sir, I need you to take your seat."

Joaquin ignored her and continued his brisk pace, searching the faces of the surprised passengers, some of whom had already seen him humiliated and ejected from the café for his strange behavior; he recognized their scared, yet judgmental expressions. He didn't care. He reached the back of the plane and, one by one, opened the doors to all the bathrooms, hoping to reveal the impostor masquerading as Gabriel. A second flight attendant joined the chase.

"Sir, if you won't sit down, we're going to have to postpone takeoff," she said, with deliberate loudness so people would hear her and pressure him as well.

"Sit down already, godammit!" one passenger said.

"Get him off the plane. He's nuts," added an old man wearing a visor.

Joaquin reached the kitchenette, where two more flight attendants told him in unison to return to his seat. He took a quick look around then went back up the aisle, coming face-to-face with his pursuers.

"I'm going, I'm going," he said, pushing them out of his way.

However, instead of returning to his seat, he kept walking toward the front of the plane, checking all the passengers. As he reached the first-class curtain, an arm shot around his neck and squeezed, cutting off his breathing. He felt the barrel of a gun pressing into his temple.

"Don't move, you son of a bitch! U.S. marshal!" the man howled in his ear.

Sky marshal, just my luck, Joaquin thought. Another one of those things that only happens in movies.

He heard shouting, then a swelling ocean of voices. He tried to break free, but the chokehold had him completely paralyzed. Every time he tried to breathe, the marshal's arm applied more pressure.

He knew what this was: a sleeper hold. New York cops had abandoned it back in the eighties. Too many people died.

He relaxed, hoping the marshal would loosen his hold. He didn't want to become another statistic.

It didn't work. He still couldn't get enough air. His vision blurred.

The voices of the flight attendants, asking passengers to return to their seats, echoed in his head. The passengers seemed reluctant, voicing concerns. Several times Joaquin distinctly heard the word "bomb." The pilot's voice came over the intercom, announcing that someone behaving suspiciously had been detained.

"There's no cause for alarm," he said, "but we're going to have to go back to the gate."

The passengers weren't calming down. Joaquin heard voices rising, demanding to be allowed off the plane. Several people turned to gape at him. He saw the distrust in their eyes. Did they mistake him for an Arab? It happened with Hispanics sometimes.

"Please, let me go," he finally choked out. "I'm not a terrorist. I'm just looking for someone."

"Tell it to the FBI."

Joaquin heard the door of the plane open. Several agents came down the aisle, handcuffed him, and escorted him off the plane to a small room with a table and two chairs. As soon as they sat him down, he tried to describe what had happened as calmly as possible. But even he realized his explanation sounded totally insane.

"I was just looking for someone who I think might be blackmailing me. He was on board the plane, but I got distracted and he disappeared."

"Are you sure? What's this person's name? What is your relationship? What are his motives?"

Every explanation sounded more ridiculous than the last, and his fatigue didn't help. It wasn't going to be easy to get out of this. It seemed to be a foregone conclusion that he'd spend the night in jail.

He watched his captors search his suitcase. They examined Gabriel's photos and scrutinized the other souvenirs.

"What is all this?"

"My life . . . in pictures," Joaquin said, forcing a grin.

The FBI agents weren't amused.

The fact that this was his only luggage made him look even more suspicious. Joaquin explained that it had all been a mistake, that he was really embarrassed, and that he only wanted to go back home. He swore he wouldn't ever behave like that again. The officials listened like robots, repeating the same questions over and over again.

"Do you have any ties with terrorist organizations? Do you have any intentions to commit criminal acts against U.S. citizens?"

And so on.

One of them got a phone call and left the room to talk in private. Joaquin and the other agent sat quietly until he returned.

"Well, his story checks out. We're going to put him on the next flight. Please. Just relax."

Joaquin couldn't believe his ears. How could they forgive him for disturbing a flight that way? How could they ignore the fact that he'd behaved like a lunatic and forced a U.S. marshal to reveal his identity? His actions had cost them thousands, tens of thousands, maybe even hundreds of thousands of dollars. But he wouldn't contradict the only friendly words he'd heard all day, or during his whole trip, in fact. So he thanked his interrogators as they removed the cuffs.

"If this ever happens again, I'm afraid we're going to have to press charges."

The agents escorted him to the gate. One of them offered him a Xanax to "take the edge off." He accepted the pill, just in case, and put it in his shirt pocket. An option if things went pear-shaped again.

Joaquin waited quietly in the departure lounge, the agents on either side of him. In a little over an hour, the flight began boarding. Finally, his head was filled only with silence. One of the agents gave him a cold goodbye and sent him onto the plane with a single, ominous warning.

"If this happens again, I promise you I will *personally* fuck you up."

"You'll never see me again," said Joaquin. He hoped it was true.

He found his seat on the new plane. He'd heard lots of stories about people whose unusual behavior on flights had landed them in Kafkaesque situations, held as prisoners for months, years, simply because they'd had a panic attack or acted suspicious. He had behaved like an imbecile, and if they had wanted to, he felt sure they could have sent him all the way to Guantánamo. He plopped down with relief and buckled his belt, feeling surprisingly refreshed, as if he'd taken a shower after a good night's sleep. Then the telephone mounted in the back of the seat in front of him rang. The madness wasn't over.

He pushed the button to dislodge it and held the receiver to his ear.

"I'll just wish you bon voyage this time."

It sounded like Gabriel.

Joaquin hung up.

He looked around; the airplane was identical to the one before. This was nothing unusual. All 767s look alike. But he recognized the faces of the people from the café, and some from the previous flight. They regarded him coolly, without hostility, without curiosity. They had the weary, anxious look of travelers and nothing more. The flight attendants were equally blasé. One of them stopped next to him and smiled.

Risking even more trouble, he said, "I'd like to apologize."

"For what, sir?"

"For the way I behaved before."

"I'm sorry, but I don't know what you're talking about."

"My mistake. I thought you were someone else," he said quickly.

The attendant walked off with a puzzled frown on her face and went to see to other passengers who had just boarded. It had been another dream. Joaquin laughed, remembering Gabriel's words:

You really don't understand dreams.

He touched his shirt pocket. The Xanax was still there. He looked at it for a moment, then swallowed it without water.

chapter 52

WHEN THE PLANE LANDED,
JOAQUIN WAS ASLEEP

A flight attendant straightened her skirt, leaned over, and spoke to Joaquin:

"Sir, we've landed."

All the other passengers had deplaned. She tried again.

"Sir, you have to wake up. We've landed."

Nothing.

Perhaps he was dead, she thought. It wouldn't be the first time. The idea worried her. She knew what that involved. Police. Paramedics. The endless paperwork. She shook him.

"Wake up! Sir, get up!"

The other flight attendants joined her, concerned looks on their faces.

"He's not responding? Should we call medical services?" one of her colleagues asked.

"I had a bad feeling about this one from the moment he boarded," she remarked, and then yelled again: "Hey, wake up!"

"Is he breathing?"

One of them put her hand under his nose.

Finally, Joaquin opened his eyes.

The drug had had a wonderful effect; he felt rested and ready to face whatever lay ahead. He looked around, slightly dazed. Three flight attendants were considering him with concern. It amused him.

There was a wonderful absence of unexplained apparitions and demented hallucinations. His dreams didn't seem to be spreading into his waking life. A good thing.

He fingered the back of the seat in front of him, then his own seat, then his improvised luggage. Its normalcy washed over him in waves of pleasure. He stretched out, grinning even though he knew it was quite possible that his problems were far from over. Joaquin jumped up, grabbed his bag, and got off the plane as fast as he could. A voice in his head told him that he'd reached a turning point. His car was waiting in the parking lot. The familiar smell of the leather seats and the way his hands felt on the wheel were comfortingly familiar. He sped all the way home. Cars advanced down roads, drivers talked on their phones, kids fought in backseats. The sun was bright in the sky. It all made him giddy. So giddy that he almost missed his exit.

He couldn't deny what he'd experienced during his trip. Every strange situation, every encounter, every blow and threat still weighed on him like millstones. If that wasn't reality, then nothing was.

In retrospect, much of the past few days seemed to have come straight from a horror movie, a B movie. Over the years, he'd seen dozens, hundreds, perhaps thousands of horror films, and it felt like he had the lead role in a fusion of all the different stories, a potpourri of scenes and clichés. As if his memory were playing a disjointed compilation of the film archives that he carried around in his head. The appearances and disappearances, the identity games, the leaps through time and space could all be tied to specific movie moments—not just horror movies, but all the films he'd seen.

Joaquin had pondered the horror of a nonlinear life, a life in limbo. Death was the absence of narrative, and nothing reflected this better than the perversion of personal anecdotes into plotlines borrowed from popular entertainment.

Perhaps he could still turn back the machinery of chaos, the forces that deconstructed reality, by rewriting his story, whatever that might be.

Joaquin was thinking all this over as he reached his building, the pleasant, overprotected chrysalis where he hoped to find Alondra. Alondra, the person he most wanted to see and whom he most feared. Everything seemed to hinge on her now. If his reality shifted with her, it was all over. There'd be no going back to an ordinary existence.

On the other hand, if she remained the same person, how would he explain the photo? Just an uncanny resemblance? A coincidence? Would his chaotic, feverish trip to Houston become an interesting story to tell on his program? Too much to hope for, he thought.

He locked the car and headed for the apartment.

For answers.

chapter 53

THE CONFRONTATION

Joaquin entered the apartment, moving carefully as if the hardwood floor might suddenly drop out from under him. He gripped the small suitcase tightly in his hand, afraid it would either disappear or pop open, the photos spilling out infecting everything like a virus. Alondra came out of the bedroom and threw her arms around his neck, something she didn't do very often. Neither of them spoke. She held him against her. He felt the tense muscles in her back relaxing. They kissed, forcefully and with pleasure, tinged with desperation. It was several minutes before they could articulate any words. They looked into each other's eyes, feeling each other carefully with their fingertips, as if each were something fragile that could fall apart at a single touch. It was as if Alondra knew what was happening to Joaquin. He didn't have to tell her what had happened or what he was thinking; it was as if she understood the depths of his doubts and fears.

However, something about it frightened him. Was she really Colett? Was she a Toltec pulling him away from the fantastic truth to the crude mechanisms of the everyday? Was she the linchpin, holding him to this reality? Joaquin knew he couldn't answer these questions. He wondered if he could confront her with them. Demand that she answer him. But he was unsure. He had to describe everything as best he could, then ask her, or beg her, to give the mystery some meaning. To confirm his perceptions.

Alondra's welcomes were always affectionate. But this was much more intense. Joaquin had the impression that something was askew. This woman, who never lost her cool, was on the verge of hysteria. He didn't know how to begin, and an emptiness in his chest kept him from exhaling.

"Everything's going to be all right," Alondra said, breaking the prolonged silence.

Her words weren't comforting. They were a declaration. A soldier's challenge. But, as her words hung in the air, the phrase became a question.

"What happened?" she asked him.

"So many things happened, things I don't understand."

"I kept feeling as though you wouldn't come back, that something broke, something we can't fix."

These words took him by surprise.

"Well, I am back. I'm not really sure about what's going on, or at least what's going on with me, but I know there must be some way to stop it, to set things in reverse."

"Explain it to me. I'm ready to listen."

"I feel like reality is collapsing around me. Like the past, present, and future are all tangled up into a kind of Möbius strip." He didn't even mention the most disturbing phenomena, like Gabriel's appearance or his strange trip through the desert, but being back home made him realize how ridiculous it would sound.

"That doesn't make sense."

"I know, but something is definitely going on with my perceptions. Maybe with yours too."

He opened up the suitcase and fingered the photo of Colett, then stopped. Fear crept over him. Could he really show her this photo? What would happen? At that moment anything was possible: the implosion of the universe, Alondra's disappearance, a rift in the space-time continuum.

"What do you have in there?" Alondra asked.

"Old, unwanted memories. Nothing important."

"Let me see."

"Later."

"No, I want to see it now, if we're searching for signs and clues."

"I'd prefer to leave it alone for the moment."

"Why? What's in there?"

"Photos and souvenirs. But here's another interesting piece of the puzzle," he said, remembering the tape.

He took it out of his pocket.

"An audiotape?"

"Yes. A recording of *Ghost Radio*, but dated 1983."

"Okay . . ."

"This has to be the broadcast I listened to with Gabriel when we were in the hospital, the one I told you influenced me to create our show."

"I didn't know it had the same name. You copied it?"

"I didn't remember that was the name, I'd forgotten what it was called."

"And why is that tape from an old radio program so important now?"

"Because we're on this program that was allegedly recorded twenty years ago."

"Twenty years . . . ?"

Joaquin described his visit to Winkler's archives.

"I lost my head, and with it the chance to take this any further. The guy was kind of creepy, no doubt about it, but he had no reason to con me, and he couldn't be so careless as to have randomly misclassified dozens of the exact recordings I was interested in."

Alondra insisted that there were plenty of ways to explain it. This kind of thing happened all the time with archives. She gave him some examples of poorly classified documents, even in libraries with the best reputations in the world. Joaquin listened patiently.

Then he told her about the newsbreak.

That set her reeling. She gripped the top of chair, and took a series of deep breaths.

"Something strange *is* going on, but you know we have the tendency to get carried away by our imagination. We overanalyze to the point that we confuse and complicate things."

"Gabriel has appeared to me several times. I've seen and talked to him just like I'm talking to you now. It's like I keep tuning in to his station on the spiritual airwaves. Unless I'm completely psychotic, I can't think of any other possible explanation."

"Dreams?"

"That's what he says. But if they're dreams . . . well, they're a world beyond anything I've ever encountered."

"What does he want?"

"I don't know. He says I've wasted my life, that it isn't fair I survived and he didn't."

Joaquin didn't want to go into any greater detail; it felt weird talking about it.

"You mean Gabriel wants to hurt you somehow?"

"I'm not sure. I don't know."

"But you talked to him. It wasn't clear to you what he's looking for?"

"No. Although he did express some interest in you."

"What are you saying? Is this a joke?"

"No."

"I've fulfilled every Goth girl's dream: a suitor from beyond the grave."

"There's more," Joaquin said, now that Alondra seemed to be open to his tale. "I want you to see this photo."

Joaquin took out the picture of himself standing next to Alondra-Colett an hour or two before Gabriel had died.

"Many years ago, on a pivotal night, I met this young woman who looks a lot like you."

He hesitated, and then showed it to her. She was smiling again now. Whatever had worried or scared her during Joaquin's absence was apparently starting to fade away. She took the photograph, but as she looked at it her expression changed; her face seemed to crumble and her eyes filled with tears.

"The resemblance is astonishing, isn't it?"

Alondra didn't answer. She remained frozen, as if she couldn't hear him. She seemed to be gasping for breath. Joaquin jumped up to his feet and reached for her. She was much paler than usual, her pulse was weak, and her eyes rolled back. Joaquin said her name and gently shook her. The Polaroid fell from her hands. He fell to his knees in front of her and picked it up off the floor. It showed, with unusual clarity for such an old photo, Alondra-Colett lying on the floor of the radio station with her eyes rolled back. She looked dead.

But she wasn't dressed as a Goth. She was dressed in ancient Meso-american garb. The clothes of a Toltec priestess.

Joaquin laid Alondra down on the sofa, and tried to think. It seemed as if her life was slipping away with each passing second; no wonder, if he'd confronted her with proof of her own death. He dialed 911, and then saw Gabriel standing beside the living-room window.

"Don't waste your time," he said. "The paramedics and doctors can't do anything for her now."

"What did you do, you son of a bitch?" Joaquin yelled, slamming down the telephone. He approached the specter threateningly.

"I didn't do anything. You still don't get it."

"Leave her alone! Do whatever you want to me, but leave her alone."

"It's not like that, Joaquin. You've got to understand. I don't have any power over Alondra, or over you, or over anyone. I can put together little shows; perform tricks that take advantage of your gullibility. I can show you interesting, tragic, morbid things. But I don't pull the strings around here. Now, when Alondra gets to my world, I can't make any guarantees."

"What's happening to her? She collapsed when she saw the photo you gave me. You set me up!"

"You saw the photo I gave you. She saw something else."

"What is the photo of, then?"

"In certain cases, the observer affects the phenomenon merely by her presence."

"What?"

"You know, it's an observer effect, like Schrödinger's experiment with the cat; the cat isn't alive or dead until someone sees it. Or, to put it in terms you'll understand, a radio signal doesn't exist until someone hears it."

"Alondra's dying, and you're spouting physics bullshit?"

"I've become very interested in science. It's fascinating."

"What do I have to do? I'll do anything to save her."

"I'm telling you, it doesn't work that way. This isn't a Wes Craven movie. I can't affect those who are on the other side."

"You're lying. You blasted my way out of the hospital. If that isn't intervening in the world of the living, then what is?"

Gabriel laughed. "It wasn't like that."

"Who did it, then?"

"That was in your hands, just as this is in your hands."

Joaquin went back to Alondra. She felt cold. He looked for Gabriel, but he'd disappeared. He thought about Gabriel's parting words. In my hands, he repeated to himself as he picked up Alondra and held her in his arms. He dialed Watt's number. "Watt, I need you here right now, come to my apartment. It's Alondra; she's real bad, hurry up. Use the key I left you."

Joaquin hung up before Watt could ask for an explanation or even say anything. Time was precious. He couldn't waste a second. Once more, he considered calling 911, but an internal voice told him there wasn't any point, that only he could save her. Just then, the shaman's apartment came to his mind, and he thought of the strange similarity between the chaos in there and the design of the pseudo-religious punk altar, baptized by the Mexican media as "narco-satanic," that he and Gabriel had installed at the radio station. Finally, the strange sensation he'd had in the shaman's apartment made sense. He grabbed the car keys and took off running.

He drove like a madman, ignoring the other cars, going up on the sidewalks and down one-way streets. The possibility of having an accident couldn't have been further from his mind. In just a few minutes, he reached the street where the temple-apartment of the pastor, Cuahté-moc, J. Cortez, could be found. He wasn't sure how he'd found it, but he knew, almost by magnetic attraction, that it was where he had to go. He parked hastily, jumped out of the car, and ran into the building. The stairs seemed endless. He knocked on the door, first hesitantly, then harder, desperately. No one came to open it, but he could hear voices inside. He tried the knob and it was unlocked. The apartment was just as he remembered it, except there was no trace of J. Cortez's body. The radio was on; it was a discussion, and someone was furiously screaming insults. Joaquin examined the apparent disorder. He studied the objects with a growing feeling of certainty. They were the same objects that Gabriel had used to build his altar. But he couldn't remember the arrangement.

Ghost Radio *isn't a show. It never was. It's a machine.*

Gabriel's words echoed in his head. A machine that had triggered all that had happened in the last eighteen years.

But how could he build it? How could he make it work?

And as these questions coursed through his brain, a CD player across the room turned on, and "Kill the Poor" by the Dead Kennedys blared from the speakers.

As he stood there, listening to the lyrics, he realized the song could be viewed as a rallying cry of the Toltecs. Kill the poor with empire, kill them with a false sense of nobility, kill them in their quest for technology. Their quest for the machine.

He rushed over to the CD player, found the jewel case, pulled out the lyric sheet, and stared at the lyrics. These lyrics somehow provided the clue:

> *Efficiency and progress is ours once more*
> *Now that we have the Neutron bomb*
> *It's nice and quick and clean and gets things done*
> *Away with excess enemy*
> *But no less value to property*
> *No sense in war but perfect sense at home:*

The sun beams down on a brand new day
No more welfare tax to pay
Unsightly slums gone up in flashing light
Jobless millions whisked away
At last we have more room to play
All systems go to kill the poor tonight

Gonna
Kill kill kill kill kill the poor: Tonight

Behold the sparkle of champagne
The crime rate's gone
Feel free again
O life's a dream with you, Miss Lily White
Jane Fonda on the screen today
Convinced the liberals it's okay
So let's get dressed and dance away the night

While they:
Kill kill kill kill kill the poor: Tonight

He stared at the words for a long time. But he couldn't figure it out. He paced about the apartment, screaming at the insanity of it all. He looked at the lyrics again. Looked at them long and hard. And then he saw it. The first letters in the first two stanzas. He pulled back his arm and looked at his tattoo. Yes, they were the same, and the pattern of his tattoo provided the arrangement.

But what object went with what letter?

He studied the first line ("Efficiency and Progress is ours once more"), scanning the room for anything that matched it. As he searched, searing images of Gabriel's altar danced through his mind. Then he saw it, peeking out from under a book.

A newspaper with the headline: EFFICIENCY AND PROGRESS KEY TO

INTERMEDIA'S SUCCESS. He grabbed the yellowing newspaper and placed it on the floor.

On to the second line: "Now that we have the Neutron bomb."

"Bomb, bomb," he mumbled to himself as he studied the objects surrounding him.

Ah, there we go, he thought, grabbing a toy rocket and placing it below the newspaper. The two objects began to glow. Tendrils of light stretched between them, stitching them together. He was on the right track.

The next line: "It's nice and clean and gets things done."

That's an easy one. He snatched one of the Kwik Kleen bottles and placed it below the rocket.

Outside, lightning flashed. But it wasn't ordinary lightning. It had a distinct reddish cast.

The fourth line: "Away with excess enemy."

Hmm . . . excess enemy . . . excess enemy. This one really puzzled Joaquin. He struggled with it:

What does excess mean? A glut. A surplus. Too much. Something you already have enough of. An extra enemy. An extra nemesis. One opponent too many.

He rubbed his brow.

A flash of crimson lightning filled the room.

He grabbed an alphabet block from a box of them sitting on the table. He tossed it up and down as he continued puzzling through the bewildering line. He walked over to the window, placed the block on the sill, and looked outside.

Bathed in sporadic explosions of bloodred lightning was a world in flux. A strange rain seemed to wash away the very fabric of reality. Signs on buildings morphed into other signs, streets rerouted themselves.

A family was rushing down the street with newspapers shielding their heads from the rain. A truck zoomed by, splashing them with water. When it passed, the family was gone. Only the father remained. Dejected and alone, he trudged down the street, oblivious to the downpour.

A hard wind hit him and with it came a different family. Where the other wife had been brunette, this one was blond. And the father's two sons were now replaced with three daughters.

Joaquin shook his head, barely able to process the odd scene. The last twenty-four hours had been rife with the bizarre, but these sights boosted it to a whole new level. He felt unhinged but exhilarated.

He'd passed from the world he knew to a land of boundless and frightening possibilities.

He considered the alphabet block that rested on the window sill. Its brightly painted *E* looked up at him, like the eyes of a child. It calmed and centered him. Abruptly, the building, possibly the whole world, shook. Joaquin was thrown across the room. He slammed into the table, knocking the blocks to the floor. He barely kept his balance. One of the blocks caught his eye. It was an *E*. He glanced back at the windowsill, the other *E* still perched there. It gave him an idea. He dropped to his knees, and found two other duplicated letters: An *N* and an *M*. The last line was a trick. It wasn't "excess enemies." It was "excess *N*, *M*, *E*s."

He grabbed the blocks and placed them under the Kwik Kleen bottle.

On to the next line: "But no less value in property."

Another easy one, he thought as he grabbed the brochure of a realty firm and placed it under the alphabet blocks. Now the final line of the first stanza: "No sense in war but perfect sense at home."

"Home," he whispered to himself as he grabbed a toy house and placed it below the brochure.

The entire line of objects glowed with a beautiful sky blue light. The first stanza was complete.

On to the second stanza: "The sun beams down a bright new day."

He scanned the objects and quickly saw the one he needed. A replica of an Aztec sun stone: that strange mixture of calendar and mythic tableau that honored the sun god Tonatiuh. He picked it up and placed it on the floor.

The building shook again, and lightning flashed through the window, disappeared into the floor. Joaquin reeled, trying to understand what was happening.

The floor beneath him was splitting apart. Vast shafts of crimson light shot up from the cracks. Slowly, the cracks expanded. Joaquin was forced to retreat to a corner of the room as the entire floor disappeared, replaced by a blinding light.

He closed his eyes to blot out the glow. But it seeped through his eyelids, searing his retinas, searing his brain. He screamed in pain, and then the wall behind him gave way and he fell and fell and fell.

After several seconds, the light dissipated and he cautiously opened his eyes. Beneath him, there was a jungle. An ancient, verdant landscape stretching as far as the eye could see. And then, as it drew closer, he made out a city among the riot of vegetation. A city of pyramids and ziggurats and grand stone plazas. A Mesoamerican city. A Toltec city.

He made out greater details as the city rushed up to greet him. He saw a vast crowd moving toward one of the central plazas where a large object glowed with pale blue light. As Joaquin came to within a hundred feet of the ground, his descent slowed, and he touched down gently at the edge of the plaza.

He pushed through the crowd, making his way toward the center and the blue light. Finally he reached the center. And through the blue light he saw brightly costumed figures constructing a great machine. They fitted together gleaming metal objects while the crowd cheered.

And then he noticed something odd. Although he could still make out the Toltec priests and their mechanical contraption, layered over this image was an image of him and Gabriel constructing their altar in that damp radio studio so many years ago. And even fainter was the arrangement of glowing objects on the floor in the room he had just left.

Suddenly he was back in the room. He rapidly finished the construction. An old coin ("No more welfare tax to pay"); a flashlight ("Unsightly slums gone up in flashing light"); a wire whisk ("Jobless millions whisked away"); a postcard of children playing ("At last we have more room to play"); and the CD itself ("All systems go to kill the poor tonight").

The entire room was enveloped in light and he felt himself slipping away.

Watt sat beside Alondra, who was rubbing her eyes and smiling, like she'd just woken up. Joaquin walked over to them, but when he was within a few inches he stopped, unable to go on. He couldn't touch Alondra. He couldn't hear them, and it was obvious they couldn't see him. They were separated by something that looked like a shop window or the glass walls in the snake house at the zoo. Joaquin stood still, taking it all in. Everything was completely normal, except for one fact: He'd crossed over to the other side.

chapter 54

THE OTHER SIDE

Confused and disoriented, Joaquin wandered into the complex labyrinth of ever-changing hallways and corridors that winds around and behind the world of the living. He looked for an exit, a gate out of this strangely familiar, yet completely unknown world. He had the sensation that he was looking into a waterless aquarium where those who have passed on can see what the world is doing, in which they can spy on moments public and private, but silenced, muted. And just as Gabriel had told him, Joaquin became aware of a cacophony of radio signals. It was only necessary to move slightly in order to tune in to one broadcast and disconnect from another. Resigning himself to this strange semisolitude, to inhabit this confined, transitional space forever, was not easy. Joaquin, who had given up everything else, was at least left with the consolation that he'd always be able to hear Alondra's voice through the disembodied transmissions of *Ghost Radio*.

Finally, after having captivated the radio audience and the recording studio for what seemed like an eternity, the voice on the phone fell silent. The host interrupted the dead air.

"Gabriel, I gotta tell you, your story has put us all in a trance. Thank you. Unfortunately, that's all the time we have. So, my friends, we leave you with this tale still ringing in your ears, about a radio host who becomes an energy vampire, and who breaks the cycle of death by trading his being for a woman's life. To all you insomniacs out there, and to all of you who just woke up and are only now tuning in, we'd like to say thanks for listening. Join us again tomorrow, from midnight until five A.M., and please stay tuned for the early-morning news.

"Have a nice day."

chapter 55

AFTER THE SHOW

Alondra shut off her microphone and leaned back in her chair, shooting Watt a tired smile. Somewhere else in the building, the early news team had picked up the broadcast reins, beaming information to the busy CEOs, short-order cooks, and housewives whose lives ran on a normal schedule. It was an experience she and Watt shared every morning, but that made no difference; it was always a tremendous, unburdening joy, that of a Sherpa who finally lays down his load after scaling a cliff, a packhorse released to graze while the master pitches his tent for the night. Even on those nights when the stories left them with a lingering sense of dread, those last few minutes when they shut off the equipment gave them a palpable sense of relief.

Hosting a program solo was tiring, that was for sure. Thank God Watt really knew his stuff. Alondra found herself wondering for the thousandth time where he'd honed his skills; he had mixed the voices of dozens of callers a night, making them sound like they were sitting in the studio with her, and he was a master.

"Quite a night, wouldn't you say?" she said.

"One of our better ones, yeah."

"I would never have imagined that a DJ could be the subject of one of our tales." She laughed a little, half to herself. "Maybe I need to pay more attention to what goes on around me. I might be in the middle of a ghost story and not even know it."

Watt gave her a sly, sidelong glance, the way he sometimes did when he was in a good mood. "Well, you better close your bedroom door tight, if that woman who called earlier was telling the truth. Her 'thigh-caressing demon' might come after you."

She gave a chuckle that was indulgent, if a little uncomfortable, and collected her things. As she was heading out the door she turned.

"What did you say?"

Watt was bent almost double, checking the wires under the mixing board, and hit his head as he sat up. "Huh? When?"

"I thought you just said something."

"No. Can't say that I did."

She looked at him strangely, her skin prickling. What she thought she had heard was a man's voice, intoning as if from far away the words "In a dark corner of your mind, remember me." It didn't sound like Watt. She had the strangest sensation that she had forgotten something; it was on the tip of her tongue, if only she could find the words.

Watt stared back at her. She could tell that he had sensed something too. For a few moments they each turned inward, searching for something unknown, perhaps unknowable.

"You okay?" she said finally.

"Yeah. Déjà vu."

She nodded slowly, agreeing with no one in particular, her hand still on the doorknob. "I'll see you tonight."

He winked. "The devil himself couldn't keep me away."

Lost in thought, Alondra closed the door behind her and moved down the hall as if it were a river and she were swimming, slow but determined, against the current.

< < < *acknowledgments* > > >

I'm deeply grateful to Naief Yehya and David Rutsala: without you two, this book would have never been possible. Same goes to my brother and partner in crime, Everardo Valerio Gout, who keeps me from turning to the dark side of the force.

Gracias!

Thanks to James Patterson the wizard, for his wonderful mind, and Steve Bowen, with whom I'm learning so much. Thanks to all my partners and artists at Curious Pictures who have graciously given me a playroom to create. Thanks to my editor, Rene Alegría, whose insightful contributions, patience, and trust got me here. Thank you, Jesse Norton, the Fates Crew, Klaus Lyngeled, Mark Corotan, and Jon Girin: our images are a huge part of the story. Thanks to Wim Stocks for loving the waves.

Special thanks to my friends, real and imaginary, whose work has inspired me, such as Michael DiJiacomo, Avi and Ari Arad, Adam Sadler, Eric Dubowsky, Duncan Sheik, JT Petty, Amy Kaufman, Danny DeVito, Lenny Beckerman, Jon Levin, Susan Holden, Michael Costanza, Eli Gesner, Carmen Boullosa, Laura Knight, Skip Williamson, Gary Lucchesi and Tom Rosenberg (for believing), also to Richard Matheson, Francisco Jose De Goya, Tom Friedman, La Mano Peluda, Mikhail Bulgakov, Gregory Crewdson, Vija Celmins, and Joseph Beuys.